THE BOYS and their BABY

Stonewall Inn Editions

Michael Denneny, General Editor

LARRY WOLFF

THE BOYS
and their
BABY

St. Martin's Press
New York

This is a work of fiction. All names, characters, and incidents, except for certain incidental references, are products of the author's imagination and do not refer to or portray any actual persons.

Owing to limitations of space, acknowledgments of permission to reprint previously published material can be found on page 263.

THE BOYS AND THEIR BABY. Copyright © 1988 by Larry Wolff. All rights reserved. Printed in the United States of America. No part of this book may be used or reproduced in any manner whatsoever without written permission except in the case of brief quotations embodied in critical articles or reviews. For information, address St. Martin's Press, 175 Fifth Avenue, New York, N.Y. 10010.

Library of Congress Cataloging-in-Publication Data

Wolff, Larry.
    The boys and their baby.
    First published by Knopf, 1988.
  I. Title.
PS3573.0534B69 1989   813'.54   88-35934
ISBN 0-312-02878-4

First published in the United States by Alfred A. Knopf, Inc.

For Perri Klass

AMANDA: And India, the burning Ghars, or Ghats, or whatever they are, and the Taj Mahal. How was the Taj Mahal?

ELYOT (*looking at her*): Unbelievable, a sort of dream.

AMANDA: That was the moonlight, I expect; you must have seen it in the moonlight.

ELYOT (*never taking his eyes off her face*): Yes, moonlight is cruelly deceptive.

AMANDA: And it didn't look like a biscuit box did it? I've always felt that it might.

ELYOT (*quietly*): Darling, darling, I love you so.

AMANDA: And I do hope you met a sacred Elephant. They're lint white I believe, and very, very sweet.

ELYOT: I've never loved anyone else for an instant.

Noel Coward,
Private Lives

THE BOYS and their BABY

CHAPTER ONE

WELCOME TO SAN FRANCISCO

*T*he building is pink, bright pink. Adam sets down his two heavy suitcases and nervously presses the buzzer for apartment three. Almost immediately there is a long, firm buzz in reply, plenty of time for Adam to wedge his foot in the door and maneuver his suitcases into the lobby. The lobby is mirrored on both sides so that Adam, looking first to the right and then to the left, sees himself flanked by two tired-looking images, both of them lifting up luggage for the very last effort of the journey. He walks up the central staircase, and his head brushes against a low-hanging chandelier of dusty-rose glass that tinkles just above his ears. Huck is waiting on the first floor at the open door of apartment three, grinning, holding the baby, who is also grinning, and Huck says, "Welcome to San Francisco."

Since the baby is on his right arm, Huck is holding out his left hand; Adam drops a suitcase and automatically extends his right. The handshake is awkward, their hands twisted to meet each other, left to right, and Adam finds the moment generally awkward: meeting Huck like this with the baby, in fact crossing the country to move in with him and the baby, after not having seen him for more than ten years.

"And this is Christopher," Huck is saying, stepping forward and lifting his arm to bring the baby face to face with Adam. Christopher looks straight at Adam from six inches away, his hands holding tight to his father's shoulder; the eyes are silver-blue, exactly Huck's eyes. In the silent moment that follows, Adam feels as if he has never in his life been confronted with a baby so intimately and so intensely. "Come on in, follow us," says Huck.

Adam follows, tired with jet lag, not taking much in. In fact, the one thing he manages to focus on is the face of the baby, still staring at him from over Huck's shoulder, examining him with a frankness that Adam finds almost intimidating. Adam tries a tired smile, but, when that fails to engage, allows himself a few seconds of reciprocal staring scrutiny as they enter the apartment. Christopher's face is very small alongside the back of Huck's head, and Adam observes the tiny individual features—the miniature nose and lips, the staring silver-blue eyes. From within his jet lag Adam finds this smallness alarming, even alien; it is true he has never looked at a baby so closely before.

"How old is Christopher?" asks Adam.

"Eleven months," says Huck, turning with the baby. Huck is still boyishly handsome, although he, like Adam, is no longer a boy. "You're eleven months, baby love. Do you know what that means? It means you're almost one." He taps one long finger on the baby's tiny nose, and the baby grabs the finger triumphantly. "Adam, you're moving in just in time to help start planning Christopher's first birthday party. It's going to be the gala event of the San Francisco season." If Christopher seems alien, Huck is tremendously familiar, even after all these years, even in this mixed patter of conversation with Adam and the baby. "There's Christopher's room, and that one next to it is mine, and this room here is yours." Huck kicks open the door, then stands aside for Adam to enter. "Bathroom's over there, if you want a shower now after the plane flight. Then come talk to us."

Adam is left alone in his new room. From the hallway he hears Huck's voice receding, singing dabadabadaba, and then Christopher trying to sing the same sound. Adam strips off his clothes and wonders why he feels so lucky to have arrived in time for Christopher's birthday party.

A shower, in fact, is exactly what Adam needs. He started out in Boston early that morning, waited two hours to change planes in New York, got a nonsmoking seat that was unfortunately just on the edge of the smoking section, sat on the plane through an interminable stop in Kansas City, and finally arrived in San Francisco, where his two suitcases were the last to be unloaded from the plane. The shower feels wonderful, and he soaps himself over and over to wash away the smells and irritations of the flight. As he begins to feel clean, he puts the plane behind him and lets his mind wander on to the new city, new apartment, new everything for which he wants to be clean.

Like the façade of the building, the tiles of the bathroom are pink. There is also a poster of a pink Disney elephant over an item of bathroom furniture the likes of which Adam has never seen before, but which must somehow be connected to babies and diapers. In the shower Adam breathes deeply; the remembered unpleasant odors of his journey are giving way to a powerful and unfamiliar smell that Adam tentatively identifies as that of diapering. But there is also in the air something much more familiar, something of college, the freshman dormitory, that particular room. Adam never thought of that room as having a characteristic smell, but now he recalls it vividly, and the hot water of the shower seems to cascade against his body with the force of nostalgia.

It was a tiny bedroom, and they slept in bunk beds, Huck on top, Adam below. On the wall opposite was a much larger than life-size poster of the head and shoulders of George McGovern; that was fall semester, 1972. Adam closes his eyes, lets the shower run right over his head, and he can see Huck poking his face down from the top bunk, the same grin then as now, and suggesting lights out.

On the other side of their dormitory suite, beyond the living room, was a second little bedroom that belonged to Huck and Adam's other roommate that semester, Slimy Sam, so slimy that he was actually for Nixon, whom he faintly resembled. Adam and Huck were happy to let Slimy Sam have the second bedroom all to himself.

Only a few weeks ago Adam had run into Slimy Sam, now a corporate lawyer visiting Boston on corporate business. Adam was polite, just as he had been back in college, even letting Slimy Sam insist that they share a cab to Park Street (though Adam could really only afford public transportation), even paying up when Slimy Sam casually divided the fare with an error in his own favor. Adam had always treated Slimy Sam with caution. It was Huck who had baited him, called him a fascist and a shithead—not that Slimy Sam ever seemed to mind particularly. And, in fact, Slimy Sam seemed to have forgotten any unpleasantness in the past: Well, Adam, he said, you say you've got a job in San Francisco, well, somebody told me our old roommate is out there now. That same night Adam called directory assistance for San Francisco and got Huck's telephone number. Adam hadn't seen him since that fall semester of freshman year, when Huck had been working in the McGovern campaign eighty hours a week. After November he had been too depressed to study, had flunked all his courses, had dropped out of college, and had simply disappeared from Adam's life. The upper bunk remained empty for the whole spring semester. So, when Adam dialed the number, he wasn't even certain that Huck would remember who he was.

"Hello." The voice was immediately recognizable.

"Hello, Huck?" Did he still use the nickname?

"That's me."

"Huck, this is Adam."

Pause. Then all at once, "Sonofabitch, I can't believe it; it's been a million years." There were peculiar gurgling noises on the other end, and Huck said, "Fuck, the baby's trying to eat the telephone, hold on a second." There was another pause while Adam wondered if he had just heard what he thought he heard, and then Huck came back on. "Adam, are you in San Francisco?"

"No, I'm in Boston. But I just got a new job in San Francisco, and I'm going to be moving out there in a month. And today I bumped into Slimy Sam—"

"Christ! I'd almost forgotten about Slimy Sam—is he as slimy as ever?"

"Just as slimy. And he said somebody had told him you

were in San Francisco. So, since I don't know anyone else there at all, I thought maybe you could tell me something about looking for an apartment. Is it hard to find a place out there?"

"Are you rolling in money?"

"Um, no, not exactly."

"Then it's hard. An apartment in San Francisco is an extremely desirable item. Do you know the city?"

"I've never been there. I was interviewed for the job here in Boston."

"Well, as soon as you get to know San Francisco, I promise you'll understand why hot apartments here are so hot. And you know, Adam—" There was a pause during which Adam heard more of those odd gurglings. "Adam, old buddy, old roommate, Adam." Huck's voice was becoming thoughtful, even serious. "Adam, actually, I have an extra room in my apartment that I was thinking about renting out. If you're interested . . . I mean, if you think we could still get along with each other after all these years. And if it didn't work out you could find someplace else. But this way you'd at least have someplace to move into when you get here."

"Huck, you really mean it? You were really going to rent out that room?"

"Definitely. It's not an expensive apartment, but it's a little too expensive for me, three bedrooms. If you can pick up a third of the rent for one of the bedrooms, we can share the living room and kitchen and bathroom. Hell, we ought to be able to live together in a three-bedroom apartment if we could live together in bunk beds jammed into a room the size of an elevator."

"Would it really be okay?"

"Definitely. Listen, there is also this other roommate
. . . Adam, do you think you could live with a baby?"

"A baby?"

"Yup, the real thing, you know what I mean—two feet
tall, crawls around on his hands and knees, drinks milk from
a bottle."

"Whose baby?"

"*My* baby. Do you think I'd be living with somebody
else's baby?" This was said so forcefully that Adam couldn't
quite ask, Yours and who else's? doesn't the baby have a
mother? and where will she live? In fact, Huck's forcefulness
seemed calculated to deflect precisely those questions, and so
Adam didn't ask.

Now a month later, when Adam is clean and dry, putting on
clean jeans in his new bedroom, there remains a certain
mystery: the apartment, the old friend and roommate, the
baby with his father's silver-blue eyes, all ultimately mysterious and unexplained. Surely there must be a woman involved
in all this, thinks Adam; surely there must be some female
presence to make sense out of two men living together with
a little baby boy. And when Adam appears in the living room
at last, there is indeed a woman talking to Huck and holding
the baby in her lap.

"It's your life, it's your child, it's your apartment, you
can rent the room if you want to, you can live with anyone
you want to live with, you can sleep with anyone you want to
sleep with, and it doesn't make a damn bit of difference what
she would think, because you don't owe her anything anymore—" And that is as far as it has gotten, spoken softly but

with the greatest insistence, when Adam enters the room and the speaker stops dead. She turns from Huck to Adam, then starts again on what is obviously a completely different track, now full voice and friendly. "Adam," she says, as if she has known him for years, "go sit down right next to Huck on the love seat, and Christopher and I will decide whether you still look like freshman roommates."

Adam looks at this woman carefully, just to be sure that she isn't actually someone he knows, but there is no question that if he had ever known her, probably if he had even seen her before, he would not have forgotten her. Though she is sitting in an armchair, it is clear that she is very tall, and her long legs in shiny black pants are stretched out into the room, shiny black shoes pointed at Huck. She wears a man's white shirt over an almost flat chest. Her hair is white-blond, her eyes and nose quite large, and her lipstick is blood red. No, Adam would not have forgotten her.

"I'm Lucille," she says, a little impatiently, as if he really ought to have known. "Now go sit next to Huck so we can compare you to the photograph. Christopher, I'll take that now." She takes a photograph from his hands, and, when he starts to protest, lets him hold on to one corner.

"Dada!" says Christopher.

"Yes," says Lucille, "that's Dada and Adam, back when they were little boys like you. God, I think it's such a scream that you two were freshmen at Yale together."

Adam catches just a glimpse of the photograph as he crosses the room to sit next to Huck on the rose-pink love seat, but a glimpse is enough to remind him of what photograph this must be.

"Good shower?" says Huck.

"Great shower," says Adam, and Huck seems pleased, as if Adam has declared himself content with the whole new arrangement.

Lucille is looking thoughtfully from them to the picture and back again. "Adam has changed more," she announces. "It's not just the beard he has now, but also you get a feeling for the transformation from adolescent to adult—trimmer, more attractive, more confident—like between then and now there's been some woman who took you in hand and helped you stop being a little boy. Is that right?"

Adam nods, solemnly. The woman who took him in hand five years ago is now far away, back in Boston. Has she really left such a mark on him that anyone can see it at a glance? For Adam there is something disorienting about knowing that to the world he is more and more irrevocably a man, an adult. At the same time, when he tries to remember what it felt like to be a boy, a college student, he can no longer imagine that either.

"Now, Huck," Lucille continues, obviously enjoying her own analysis, "you have not been transformed, you're still spiritually an adolescent, but—this is strange—you seem to have gotten older than Adam has. I mean, Adam has really changed, while you've just aged; you know, older skin on the same face. I would say that back in your Ivy League days you were both cute enough, but most people would have thought Huck was cuter. Nowadays I think a lot of people would think Adam has drawn even. I myself reserve judgment."

Adam steals a glance at Huck beside him and thinks that Lucille is wrong, Huck is still far better looking. His face is handsomely rectangular: the silver-blue eyes regular and candid, blond hair combed back off the high forehead, strong lines descending diagonally to the ends of long, even lips. It is true, his skin seems too old, too lined, considering that the spirit of the face remains so young, but actually it doesn't look as rough as it looked earlier, when he stood at the door holding the baby cheek to cheek.

"Now this is hard to tell from a black-and-white photograph," says Lucille, "but I think Huck has gotten blonder—is that possible?"

"Of course," says Huck, "after all these years in the California sun."

"Nothing to do with bleach?" suggests Lucille.

Huck laughs. "Adam will be our guinea pig. He's darker now than I ever was, and I predict that after one year in California he will be as blond as you are."

"Ha!" She runs a hand over her own extreme blondness. *"This* is not something Mother Nature could do for you, not even in California." She looks back at the photograph. "I want you to put your arms around each other's shoulders, just like in the photograph." She holds it up for them to see across the room. "I want to see if you'll still make a cute pair of roommates now that you're out of your teens."

Adam feels Huck's arm come down across his shoulder, and even though the scene is being stage-directed by Lucille, Adam finds the touch of Huck's arm strangely moving after all these years. He weaves his own arm under Huck's, then up over the shoulder so they are linked. "Wonderful," says Lucille, and then Christopher, who has been sitting quietly in Lucille's lap, suddenly begins to whimper. And from the way he is looking at the sofa, even Adam, with his absolute ignorance of babies, can see what he is whimpering about. Adam feels abashed, draws back his arm, but Huck is obviously amused and leaves his on Adam's shoulder. Lucille exclaims, "Little jealous one—isn't my lap good enough?" But Christopher continues to whimper at the sight of his father linked to someone else, so Lucille stands up with him (she *is* tall, maybe six feet), takes two giant strides across the room, and places him between Huck and Adam, half in one lap, half in the other. Instantly the whimpering ceases, and the baby is all triumphant smiles.

"We have to have a picture of the new roommates," announces Lucille, "of all three of you. Huck, where's your camera?"

"Desk in the bedroom, top drawer on the left, out of Christopher's reach."

Lucille, Adam thinks, seems quite at home about the whole apartment as she goes off to Huck's bedroom. "Jealous baby," coos Huck, "are you happy now, my love?" But Christopher, having gotten where he wanted to go, is not interested in talking to his father. He is much too busy trying to bite the buttons off Huck's shirt. He has teeth, Adam notices, uncertain when babies get teeth. "Do you remember when she took those pictures?" says Huck, one hand still resting on Adam's shoulder, the other holding the photograph.

Adam does remember, but before he has time to answer, Lucille is back with the camera. "Who was *she*?" she asks.

"There was this girl in our freshman class," says Huck, "Sally something-or-other. She was taking a photography course, and she wanted to do a project about roommates, and so she did all these studies of the two of us."

"Which one of you was she in love with?" inquires Lucille.

"Both of us, naturally," says Huck. But it was Huck she

was in love with, Adam recalls. "Good picture of the two of us sitting on the top bunk. I had the top, didn't I?"

"Of course you did," says Lucille, as if she too had been there. "You're obviously the type for the top bunk."

"There were other photographs too," Huck continues, "lots of them. I remember one with me on top and you on bottom, right? And wasn't there one of the two of us standing in front of my big poster of George McGovern, looking like the future of the young American left?" A little bitterness there still, Adam notices.

Adam remembers all these pictures very well, because spring semester, after Huck had dropped out, they were awarded a college prize and were displayed at the Commons. And he also remembers how wistful it made him feel to see those photographs of the two of them publicly posted as if to convey the quintessence of the freshman roommate spirit, and to know that the bunk was now empty and Huck was gone. Adam reaches out to take the picture from Huck, looks at it carefully. The two boys holding each other in the photograph certainly appear to be good friends. How could they ever have lost track of each other?

"Ready for the picture?" says Lucille. "Smile, Christopher. Hey, Christopher, leave those buttons alone for a second and look at me." As Christopher turns to the camera, Adam puts his arm back around Huck, and Lucille snaps the picture with a flash.

In the living room with Huck and Lucille and Christopher, Adam is suddenly overcome with tiredness, ready to collapse. He was up at five that morning to go to the airport in Boston, and now, early evening in San Francisco (but three hours later for Adam, Boston time), he barely has the energy to stand up and excuse himself before going off to his room.

The room is empty, except for his suitcases and a mattress on the floor in one corner, made up with a sheet, a pillow, a blanket. Without even taking off his jeans Adam drops on top of the blanket. In the few seconds before he falls asleep his consciousness is attacked by a sense of mysteries unfathomed, questions unasked: about Huck's life, about Huck's baby, about how Lucille fits in.

When he falls asleep it is still light outside, and when he wakes up it is dark, the middle of the night. He wakes up from a nightmare in which he was screaming and screaming. At first he doesn't know where he is; then he remembers, San Francisco, Huck's apartment. And then he realizes that even though he is awake the screaming from his nightmare has not stopped. The baby is screaming, terrifying screams. Frantically, Adam gets up from the mattress on the floor (still dressed), and in the dark gropes his way toward the door, guided only by a vague memory of where the door must be. He hears footsteps in the hall, and by the time he finds his door and opens it, the screams are subsiding.

The door to the adjoining room is open, and with the light from the hall Adam can see Huck, naked (he always slept nude, Adam remembers), standing alongside the crib, pressing Christopher in pale pajamas against his own bare chest. Christopher is silent now, and Adam hears only the very soft sound of Huck singing something indistinct, just above the baby's head. Huck looks up and nods at Adam, who interprets the gesture as a sort of dismissal—go back to bed—and he does.

He lies on the mattress on the floor, looking up into the darkness, wondering if this is what it means to live with a baby: screaming in the middle of the night. He remembers Huck with Christopher, both grinning, waiting for him this afternoon at the door of apartment three. Then he thinks of Huck soothing the baby back to sleep, a sort of solemn exorcism. Adam is again reminded of how little he knows about Huck's life.

The door opens, then closes. Someone has come into his room. Adam feels his heart beating, frightened, though he knows it must be Huck. The sound of bare feet approaching the mattress. Adam's eyes have adjusted to the darkness, and he can just make out the tall silhouette.

"Adam," Huck whispers.

"I'm awake," Adam whispers in reply.

Huck sits down at the foot of the mattress, pulls his knees up to his chest and clasps his arms around them. "I'm sorry, Adam. I'm really sorry he woke you like that when you were so dead tired."

"It's okay." Adam senses that Huck is seriously upset, wishes he could somehow soothe Huck the way Huck soothed the baby. But there is nothing Adam can imagine himself doing except saying it's all okay.

"He's gone back to sleep now. It doesn't happen every night, but sometimes he has nightmares or gets scared or something. Maybe he's tense tonight because there's someone new in the apartment—but he's fine as soon as he sees that I'm there. Adam, is it really okay? You're not lying here thinking about moving out, are you?"

"No, Huck, it's really okay."

"If you want to, Adam, we could try switching his room

and mine, so that I'm next to you and he's a little further down the hall. But I think you'd hear him anyway if he started screaming, and also . . ."

"Huck?"

"Also this way, with his room between our rooms, it gives the two of us a little more privacy. What do you think?"

Adam doesn't know what he thinks, doesn't know enough about Huck's life to understand the significance of privacy, doesn't have a life of his own yet in San Francisco to be private about, doesn't know quite what privacy is going to mean between two people who slept in bunk beds from Labor Day to Christmas so many years ago. Anyway, all he can do is reassure Huck that it's okay, whatever it is, it's okay.

CHAPTER TWO

THE PACIFIC

Adam—I am going to work and leaving you to sleep since you obviously need it. Why don't you spend the day exploring San Francisco and then meet me and Christopher at five at the day-care center at the corner of Vallejo and Octavia? We can go shopping together—I invited Lucille to dinner tonight to celebrate your first day in San Francisco. Try not to acquire too many new vices before dinner, and think about what we should cook. Sorry about last night.

Huck

The note is waiting for Adam on the kitchen table when he finally wakes up at half past ten. Alongside the note Huck has left a set of keys and a folding map of San Francisco. Though his eyes are still blinking from the kitchen sunlight, though he has not yet brushed his teeth to get rid of the nasty taste of jet-lag sleep, Adam cannot resist unfolding the map right away. He knows almost nothing about San Francisco and spends a few minutes identifying the most distinctive features of the map: the strong diagonal of Market Street, the narrow rectangle of Golden Gate Park (green on the map), stretching from the Pacific Ocean to Haight-Ashbury, the big Presidio Military Reservation (gray on the map) coming to a point at the Golden Gate Bridge. And there is also a penned red arrow, which Huck has labeled "Home Sweet Home" and which presumably points to the little pink apartment building on Hyde Street. Adam examines the grid of streets around the arrow and discovers that Home Sweet Home is in the neighborhood called Russian Hill.

He rereads Huck's note, then goes to brush his teeth. So Huck has gone to work—what work?—and Christopher is spending the day in a day-care center. Until this moment the idea of day care has been a purely abstract concept for Adam. He strips off the clothes he spent the night in, the clean jeans he put on yesterday when he arrived, now uncomfortably scratchy. Suddenly Adam remembers the middle of the night—Huck and the baby—that's what the apology in the note is referring to, and Adam had forgotten completely. Even now, as he tries to remember—the cries of the baby, Huck singing him back to sleep, Huck in Adam's room, Adam reassuring Huck that it was okay—none of it seems quite real after the intervening hours of sleep. Adam takes a shower, puts on his third and last pair of clean jeans, and sets off to explore the city, just as Huck suggested.

The sun in San Francisco is not like the sun in Boston. Adam looks up happily at the pink building, then walks toward the corner. August in Boston is unpleasantly hot and humid—Adam can remember what it felt like just the day before yesterday. But here there are wonderful cool breezes that seem almost to be part of the sunlight. Adam stands at the corner and looks up the hill. Russian Hill, it seems, really is a hill, and a steep one. Then he almost loses his balance as he turns and looks down, way down over the city that is unrolling before him, like a splendid carpet, from the point at which his sneakers touch the corner sidewalk. As he lifts his gaze the city rolls further into the distance on one side, and down to the bay on the other. And there in the sunlight, not so far—Adam feels as though he could almost reach his hand across the valley of the city and take hold of it—there is the Golden Gate Bridge, not golden at all but shining red.

Two possibilities present themselves to Adam's imagination. First is the possibility of somehow crossing that valley and reaching the bridge. But, once having reached it, he would certainly feel compelled to cross it, and crossing the bridge seems somehow metaphorically wrong for today. It is clear from the map that crossing would take him out of San Francisco and that, Adam feels, would also be wrong—to leave the city on his very first day. So Adam decides instead upon the second possibility, and consults his map to find the bus route that will take him across the city to the Pacific Ocean. He has never seen it before, and the Pacific Ocean, after all, is not likely to tempt him to an immediate crossing.

Adam rides the bus to the last stop, then gets out alongside a city highway. In front of him is the ocean, which does, in fact, just as the map suggests, come right up to the edge of the city. This surprises Adam, and pleases him. He walks down toward the beach and finds that it is almost empty; that too is a surprise. The sun that was shining so brightly on Russian Hill must have undergone a transformation somewhere along the bus route, for here there are clouds and even fog, which gives the ocean an ominous character. Before Adam is a sign to warn him that swimming in the ocean is very dangerous here; the undercurrents are deadly. Waves crash fifty feet from where he stands, and as he looks out to sea he thinks of how big this ocean is, how it goes on and on, twice as far as he has already come from Boston. A way out from shore there is the head of someone swimming, oblivious of the posted dangers.

Adam takes off his sneakers, then stuffs his socks inside them and walks toward the waves. As he passes by the only people on this stretch of beach, he sees that they are two men, fully dressed, not young, lying on the sand kissing. They do not even seem to notice Adam, and what he finds most remarkable about the scene is how little of an impression it seems to make on him, as if this were pretty much what he expected to find at the edge of the Pacific Ocean. He knows, of course, that this is a part of what San Francisco is famous for, but he has barely thought about it; homosexuality, like day care, has never been much more than an abstract concept to him.

The two lovers behind him and the vastness of the ocean before him (with one single crazy or courageous swimmer), Adam steps onto wet sand and, a moment later, feels the surf of the Pacific swirling around his ankles.

Adam Berg didn't just go to college at Yale; he actually grew up in New Haven, not a particularly attractive town in which to grow up. Adam's father was a German physicist who (since *his* father was Jewish) decided to get out of Germany in 1935 after the promulgation of the Nuremberg Laws. He ended up teaching at Yale, and when he was almost fifty he finally married. Adam's mother was the daughter of a fellow émigré physicist, French and Catholic, who fled after the fall of France in 1940 and also ended up at Yale. Adam's mother was almost thirty years younger than his father. They were married just after her graduation from Bryn Mawr in 1950, and she was accepted as a graduate student in English at Yale. Adam was born in 1954. Two years later his father had a heart attack and died. To Adam he has always been a photographic image, an unknown ancestral figure with heavy eyebrows and a very full antique mustache. Since, as a boy, Adam could not remember his father, he developed a variety of brilliant and heroic fantasies to fit the patriarchal image. As a man, Adam finds that he can no longer remember clearly even his former fantasies.

Adam's mother, on the other hand, was such a presence in his life—and remains such a prominent figure in his reflections and speculations, not fantasies—that her actual image eludes him when he tries to bring it to mind. When Adam was young he found his mother beautifully mysterious and hopelessly foreign, not quite connected to the world around her, almost odd in her reactions and relations even to her son. He always supposed that being an adult would mean understanding her at last, yet still he puzzles over her.

The woman in Boston who took Adam in hand five years ago told him sometimes—and with increasing frequency as their relationship gradually collapsed—that he thought about his mother too much, that his mother seemed to be the most important person in his life. Adam, though he knew that such observations were intended to cast unspecified aspersions (which Suzanne occasionally made specific) on his independence and maturity, found himself wrestling with the fact that as a man he continued to regard his mother with the same fascination that he felt as a boy. He had always suspected that his bewildered love was not exactly what a boy should feel, and he has been told explicitly (by Suzanne) that it is still less appropriate for a man. And yet the one painful thought inside him as he stands barefoot in the surf, looking out at the Pacific Ocean, is that his back is turned to New Haven, and his mother is very far away.

When Adam was a child he knew other children whose mothers had jobs; his own mother, however, was so constantly at home in their apartment that he almost never thought of her as a woman with a career, let alone a vocation. Only in retrospect did he realize that throughout his childhood his mother was slowly completing her graduate course work, then writing a doctoral dissertation. They lived on the patched-together but quite adequate income from his father's life insurance, some help from his mother's parents, small graduate-student stipends, and occasional teaching assistantships.

Simone Berg, born in Rouen, always spoke French with her parents, even after they had all been living in New Haven for twenty years. In the late fifties she was reading the new and untranslated works of Roland Barthes and Claude Lévi-Strauss, and thinking through structural analyses of Melville and Hawthorne. Really she didn't have that much to do with her professors and fellow graduate students, who, from what little they understood of her work, regarded her as academically eccentric. She was quiet and private, with European standards of courtesy, so that professors found her pleasingly respectful and graduate students unthreatening. She spent most of her time with her son and her parents, and she didn't discuss her work with them either. Then she finished her dissertation, two chapters were published in journals of criticism just at the moment when Americans were starting to recognize the revolutionary significance of structuralist criticism, and after ten years as the most obscure graduate student in the department she was appointed assistant professor of English at Yale. The year before Adam enrolled as a freshman, his mother was promoted to full professor and granted tenure. It was, ironically, around that time that her structuralist approach was beginning to seem old-fashioned in the light of French post-structuralist theoretical developments that she was reluctant to embrace.

When Adam lived on campus with Huck, Simone Berg, a distinguished scholar of international reputation, still made dinner for her son twice a week. Once he even brought Huck along, but the evening was not a success since Huck could think of nothing but the McGovern campaign that fall, and Adam's mother never had any interest whatsoever in politics. Huck couldn't even try to persuade her to vote, since she remained a French citizen. Adam heard students say that his mother was brilliant, but he himself never took any of her courses, even though he ended up majoring in English; he concentrated strictly on English literature, while her courses were either on American literature or on literary theory.

Adam's new job in San Francisco is teaching English at a private high school. When he had first moved to Boston, fresh out of college, he had worked as a prep-school English teacher, and that's what he'd been doing in Boston most recently too. In the intervening years, however, he had experienced some professional ambivalence, perplexed by his own satisfaction at discussing Shakespeare and Dickens with adolescent boys and girls, suspicious of his inclination to pursue what was, after all, his mother's career on a much less exalted level. He gave it up, and, on an impulse that he can no longer explain, trained to become a telephone repairman. At the time, he was living in a house in Cambridge with four other men; the five of them played basketball as a team on Sundays, and also constituted an informal but dedicated woodwind quintet. Adam was greatly valued for his easy jump shot, rather less so for his merely conscientious approach to the oboe, and he was generally liked as a housemate. Two of the men were carpenters, one was an assistant professor of linguistics at M.I.T., and another supported himself by selling recreational drugs to Harvard undergraduates.

For Adam the one exhilarating thing about being a telephone repairman was climbing telephone poles. He proved to be naturally sure-footed, and he loved the heights and the aerial views. Inside repair work, however, was not so interesting, and Adam was hopelessly bad at threading wires through tiny holes in walls. Often he would carefully check the wires outside on the poles even when he knew there was nothing wrong with them, just to avoid getting down to the inside job. He wore on his hips a broad sling, a sort of belt on which his repair tools hung, and his girlfriend at the time—who worked in a jewelry boutique—got a special charge from undoing the sling and removing it from his hips.

One day, on the job, Adam was sent to repair the phone of someone who turned out to be a graduate student in American literature at Harvard. Adam noticed his mother's book on a shelf, commented on it, and Suzanne was immensely intrigued to discover that the telephone repairman was the son of Simone Berg. Adam called Suzanne the following week (obviously he had her phone number), and six months later they moved into a small apartment together on Beacon Hill in Boston. Suzanne was not interested in the erotic possibilities of Adam's tool belt, and—with her encouragement—he began to look for a way out of the phone company, back to discussing Shakespeare and Dickens with high school students. The housemates in Cambridge replaced Adam with a dental student who played the oboe like a dream but couldn't put a ball in a basket to save his life. So Adam still occasionally played basketball with them, long enough to learn that his former girlfriend from the jewelry boutique was now happily involved with the assistant professor of linguistics.

When Adam moved in with Suzanne he was more in love with her than he had ever been with anyone else; when he moved out five years later they were barely capable of being polite to each other. In retrospect Adam thinks of the first meeting between Suzanne and his mother as somehow a fateful turning point. Not that they didn't get along—they had a tremendous discussion of Hawthorne and Melville and Barthes and Foucault, which Adam found pretty dull. But Adam was made uncomfortable by watching Suzanne discuss literary criticism with his mother, and perhaps Suzanne was made uncomfortable by the fact that Adam said nothing. Until that evening—it was a dinner at Simone Berg's house in New Haven—Adam was looking for a moment to raise the subject of marriage with Suzanne, but afterward he let it slide. After that, also, he began to feel as though he were being called upon to explain himself to Suzanne: explain that he really liked teaching high school students, that he really didn't want to go to graduate school, that he really had no interest in academic scholarship—he would rather climb telephone poles. He did, however, have a definite taste and preference in literature, English not American, and one of the things he found attractive about the new job in San Francisco was that it involved teaching only English literature; someone else was already teaching the American literature courses. Another attractive thing about the San Francisco job was that it came up at a time when he knew his relationship with Suzanne was being wrecked by mutual antagonism. And, finally, Adam was ready to move across the country in vague reaction to his mother's finally remarrying after all these years. She recently married a man who, as far as Adam is concerned, is not nearly good enough for her: Harvey, her ophthalmologist. Simone has promised to come visit Adam in San Francisco when he is settled, and he already knows that he wants to bring her right here to look out at the Pacific Ocean with him.

At five o'clock Adam is waiting at the corner of Vallejo and Octavia. At ten past five Huck steps out of a gate half a block down Vallejo, and pulls a stroller out behind him; Christopher holds a bottle of milk in both hands and drinks intently as he is strolled. Huck is wearing a charcoal-gray suit, a white shirt, a dark red tie; somehow none of it looks properly sober on him, as if he were dressing up—just as when he was eighteen at Yale and used to put on a jacket and tie to go across Connecticut campaigning for McGovern. Adam remembers Lucille's remark that Huck has not been transformed, has not become an adult. And is that supposed to mean that no woman has taken Huck in hand, as Suzanne took Adam? Yet there must have been a woman in his life, because, after all, there is Christopher.

A woman comes out of the gate behind Christopher's

stroller, and she too then pulls out a stroller of her own. She and Huck walk toward Adam, both in dark suits, both with identical silver-and-gray, metal-and-plastic strollers, elaborate modern constructions, both with babies. They chat with each other, until Huck catches sight of Adam at the corner and waves, then pokes at Christopher, trying to get him to wave at Adam too—but Christopher has eyes only for his bottle. The other baby waves.

"Adam, this is Deborah," says Huck. "And this little beauty is Sasha." Sasha is wearing green corduroy overalls, and Adam feels very stupid because he cannot tell whether Sasha is a boy or a girl. He does not ask. Instead he nods at Deborah and says hello to Sasha, who says hi. So Adam says hi, and Sasha says hi again, and Huck says hi, and Sasha says it again, and Deborah says hi, and Christopher continues to drink his bottle. Deborah leaves them at the corner, strolling Sasha along Octavia. When they are well out of hearing, Christopher suddenly hurls his bottle down onto the sidewalk, smiles grandly, and calls out over his shoulder, Bye-bye.

"Christopher and Sasha are soulmates," Huck is explaining, "because they have the same stroller. It's the new model, very fancy."

"It looks like a spaceship," says Adam.

"Exactly. And all the other babies in the day-care center have the older model, the blue one that only looks like a stroller, and their parents are envious and insecure because they're afraid their babies may not be as classy as our babies."

"I'm sorry I'm so stupid, but . . . is Sasha a boy or a girl?"

"A little girl, Christopher's girlfriend, the woman in his life."

"The woman in his life?" repeats Adam, thinking that this might be an opening, that now he can ask—

But Huck doesn't give him a chance. "Don't feel stupid about it," he is saying. "All the babies wear overalls, so you can't tell whether they're boys or girls unless you're actually diapering them. We parents all wear the same clothes too, you know—Deborah's suits are probably more expensive than mine, but in her line of work it's expected."

"What does she do?" Another promising opening.

"She's a corporate lawyer, like everyone else now-adays."

"I'm not a corporate lawyer," says Adam. And then, "Are you?"

"Me? Are you kidding? I'm a politico. Work for the mayor."

"What do you do for the mayor?"

"I help out, you know, political troubleshooter, issues consultant, one-man public-opinion poll, wardrobe advice, sort of a jack-of-all-trades. I live to serve the mayor."

"And does he appreciate you?"

"Adam, old buddy, the mayor of San Francisco, like little Sasha, is a girl. And her suits are even more expensive than Deborah's. And she is the greatest politician in America, and she will one day be President." The tone of these last sentences takes Adam back to October, 1972. He remembers what a miserable wreck Huck was after the election, when he was flunking out of Yale, and he thinks how strange it is to hear him talking this way about a politician now. "What about you, Adam? What profession is it that preserves you in such perfect ignorance of the great names in American municipal politics?"

"I'm a high school English teacher."

"Sonofabitch, corrupting America's youth!"

Adam laughs, grateful to Huck for not immediately making some comment about Adam's mother, the distinguished professor of American literature. Christopher hears Adam laugh, and twists his head around from his seat in the stroller to find out what is so funny.

At the little market at the foot of Russian Hill, Huck admits that he is a terrible cook and appeals to Adam for help in deciding on a menu for their dinner with Lucille. Suzanne, in the course of taking Adam in hand, taught him to cook three dishes: quiche (which he does not like), chicken in wine (he never told Suzanne how pathetically it compared to his mother's coq au vin), and spaghetti with tomato sauce. Adam suggests spaghetti to Huck, who is immediately enthusiastic, especially because Christopher loves spaghetti. Adam collects the pasta, canned tomatoes, chopped meat, and an onion. Huck tells him not to worry too much about ingredients since with Lucille you never know what you're going to end up eating. What do you mean? asks Adam, already nervous about cooking dinner on his first day in the new apartment. But Huck has disappeared down the freezer aisle, coming back with two containers of chocolate Häagen-Dazs ice cream, one of which he immediately opens and starts feeding to Christopher on his finger. Eventually the three of them climb Russian Hill with a bag of groceries and two huge cardboard boxes full of paper diapers.

The first thing they do when they get home is go straight to the bathroom and lay out Christopher on the diapering table. Huck starts unsnapping Christopher's little denim overalls, telling Adam that he doesn't have to stick around and watch if he'd rather not. Adam insists that he would like to help (though Huck is obviously perfectly self-sufficient in this respect), and Adam is fascinated (although, at the same time, perhaps a little repelled) by the whole process. He has never seen a baby diapered before. And he has never even imagined a baby being diapered by a man in a charcoal suit, white shirt, and dark red tie. What's most extraordinary is how casual Huck is about it (talking nonsense to Christopher the whole time), how he takes it for granted, as if he has done it a thousand times—and it occurs to Adam that he probably has. Christopher indulgently allows himself to be diapered, occasionally catching Adam's eye and gurgling to remind him that he is privileged to be present.

While Huck is still expertly fastening the adhesives of the clean paper diaper, there are three knocks on the door and Adam leaves the bathroom to answer. It is, after all, his apartment too now. At the door are two young men, both with tidy mustaches, both in bright-colored running shorts and track shirts: the tall and fair one in purple shorts and a green shirt, the short and dark one in bright orange shorts and a red shirt. Purple-and-green is carrying a record album with the title *Anyone Can Whistle.* "Is Huck around?" he asks hesitantly.

"Yes," says Adam, "he's diapering the baby." Adam feels a little silly saying this. "I'm Adam. I've just moved in with Huck. And Christopher." He feels a little silly saying that too.

Purple-and-green and orange-and-red both examine Adam with interest. "I'm Tommy," says purple-and-green. "And this is Timmy. We live right upstairs."

Huck appears with Christopher. "Tommy and Timmy!" Huck exclaims, as if he thinks the conjunction of their names is the funniest joke he knows, and they smile as if they think so too. "I take it you've met Adam now, my new roommate, also my old roommate—a very complicated relationship."

"Just bringing back your record album," says Tommy, offering *Anyone Can Whistle.* "I love it."

"Love it," says Timmy. Tommy speaks with exaggerated enthusiasm, and when Timmy repeats the last words there is a hint of parody of Tommy's exaggeration.

"Just going running," says Tommy, backing away from the door.

"Everyone in California goes running," explains Huck to Adam. "I used to go running myself before Christopher. Now I guess I just have to resign myself to getting fat." He pats the bottom of his tie over his stomach, which is, as far as Adam can see, perfectly flat.

"Why don't you go running now?" Adam hears himself suggesting. "I'll take care of Christopher." What am I saying? he wonders. Do I have any idea how to take care of Christopher?

"Yeah, come running with us, Huck," says Tommy, stepping toward the door again. "We're just running down to the marina and back again. It'll only be a half hour."

"Only a half hour," echoes Timmy.

"You really don't mind babysitting?" says Huck, and Adam, who hadn't thought of the word *babysitting* until Huck said it, and who has never done it before, can see that Huck really wants to go.

"Not at all," says Adam. "What are roommates for?"

Two minutes later Huck is wearing a white tee shirt and an unspectacular pair of faded blue shorts that say YALE along the hem. He leaves Christopher in Adam's arms, kissing Christopher on the nose, then jogs downstairs with the brilliantly colored Tommy and Timmy.

Adam wonders if he is holding the baby right, and when Christopher begins to squirm, Adam puts him down immediately. This seems to be just what Christopher wants, and he crawls into the living room, with Adam walking behind him. What if something should go wrong? What if Christopher should hurt himself? What if some city maniac gets into the building? Adam runs back to the door to check that it is locked, then returns to the living room, where Christopher has pulled himself up so that he is standing in front of Huck's bookcase, holding on to the second shelf with one hand. With the other hand he is removing books from the bottom shelf one by one and tossing them onto the floor: *The Making of the President 1960*, *The Making of the President 1964*, *The Making of the President 1968*, and so on. Soon the shelf is empty, and Christopher reaches up to the next level. He is intent on what he is doing, apparently enjoying himself, and Adam only hopes that the supply of books will last until Huck returns.

When Christopher says baba, Adam thinks at first that he is talking to himself. Only when the baby interrupts his pillaging of the bookcase to turn to Adam and repeat the sound very insistently does Adam realize that Christopher is talking to him. But what is he saying? Baba! says Christopher a third time, shrieking now and pointing at the bottle of milk that Huck has left out on the table. Desperately relieved to have understood, Adam rushes to obey and brings the bottle over to the baby. Christopher sucks at it for a second, then throws it to the floor and turns his attention back to emptying the bookcase.

CHAPTER THREE

ANYONE
CAN WHISTLE

"Let me see what you've bought," says Lucille. She has arrived before the return of the runners, swooped Christopher up in her arms, and gone off to the kitchen, leaving Adam to put the books back on the shelves. "Is this everything?" she calls from the kitchen. "This little treasure trove in the brown bag?"

"We got two big boxes of paper diapers," Adam says, apologetically, jokingly. "They're in the bathroom."

"Yum, yum," says Lucille. "Take two paper diapers, remove adhesives, mince and sauté in butter, add herbs—the perfect base for every spaghetti sauce. Christopher, let go of that onion, it's all we've got." Adam hears a soft thud as the onion hits the floor.

He stands back, admires the neat bookcase, then goes into the kitchen and picks up the onion. Lucille has the baby on her arm and is writing out a list at the counter. Fresh basil, she is muttering, hot sausage. Capers, almonds, and chili peppers. She is dressed as she was yesterday: the black pants and man's white shirt, with the addition this evening of a shiny red bow tie that matches her lipstick. "Just making a little list," she says to Adam. "Is there a bottle of cold wine in the refrigerator?"

"I don't know," says Adam. He goes to the refrigerator, opens it, and finds that there is. On the refrigerator is a large photograph of a handsome woman who looks a little like Adam's mother.

"California wine," observes Lucille. "Drinking California wine in California is almost too Californian for me, but this is going to be your new home so you might as well immerse yourself in the complete experience. I'll have a glass."

Adam finds two glasses in the cupboard, fills them, and Lucille announces a toast. "Welcome to San Francisco, Adam, for as long as it lasts." She offers a sip of wine to Christopher, who immediately grabs hold of the glass and tries to wrest it away from her. She wins. Christopher is cheerful about losing, and looks up and smiles at Adam from Lucille's arm; he had not smiled at Adam once, in fact hardly looked at Adam, during the twenty minutes that they were alone together in the apartment.

"Isn't it going to last?" says Adam.

"Of course not, there's going to be an earthquake, the city is going to fall into the sea, everyone is going to die—if AIDS doesn't kill us all first. Somebody must have told you about earthquakes before you moved out here?"

"Well, I suppose San Francisco is famous for earthquakes, but I never really thought about it." He thinks of himself standing at the edge of the Pacific this morning, and tries to imagine the city falling into the ocean; he cannot imagine it. He starts over again: he is standing in the surf, the sea is calm, and then suddenly the earth shakes and there appears a giant tidal wave roaring toward him, overwhelming the scream of the lone swimmer. "You know, it's scary," he says aloud.

"Damn right it's scary," says Lucille, "unless you're crazy. But we all just go on living here, singing our songs, dancing our dances, never really thinking about it. You'll see. Maybe you'll think about it seriously two or three times, and then you'll just make jokes about it—the way I usually do, the way Huck does. And here's Huck bringing up a baby in this deathtrap, talk about crazy."

"Has he actually considered leaving San Francisco because of the baby?"

"Not Huck. You know, he has this philosophy for bringing-up-baby. Christopher, your father has a philosophy for bringing you up. Huck has decided that when you have a baby you have to try to live, as much as possible, the way you would live if you didn't have a baby—except that there's always a baby to think about so there are built-in contradictions. Huck says that way you don't resent the baby for changing your life, and you don't turn into a completely false person with your baby, who otherwise never knows you the way you really are but only the way you are with a baby. Do you follow?"

Adam nods. "It sort of makes sense, doesn't it? And it fits the way Huck is with the baby—at least from what little I've seen—so I suppose he's living up to his philosophy."

"Yes, but on the other hand the philosophy was invented to fit the way he is. I can respect it myself, but you also have to remember that it works as a justification for complete selfishness, for living however he wants to, like in

a city that is going to be destroyed by an earthquake someday."

"You don't think he'll decide to leave?" Adam asks. He
is slightly alarmed at the thought—for what would living in
San Francisco be like for him if Huck weren't here?

"No," says Lucille, quite definite. "Huck is too infatuated."

"Infatuated?"

"With San Francisco."

"Oh."

"And with *her.*" Lucille points a long painted red fin-
gernail at the photograph of the handsome woman on the
refrigerator.

"Who is she?"

"Who is she? That, my dear, is the mayor of San Francisco, your roommate's grand crush, the cause that gives
meaning to his life. Huck thinks that if there is an earthquake
she will just stand at the edge of the crater that will open up
in front of City Hall, that she will elegantly remove one of her
extremely expensive high-heeled pumps, that she will drop it
into the crater, and the earth will close up and the city will
be saved. Naturally, the other pump of the pair will be en-
shrined in the Academy of Sciences in Golden Gate Park,
where the adoring masses will gather to worship it and wonder at which shoestore the pair was originally purchased."

Adam is laughing, and Lucille obviously enjoys having
amused him. Christopher seems to think he is in on the joke.

"Huck says she's going to be President of the United
States," says Adam, leading Lucille on. "Then she'd go to
Washington and Huck would go too, right? And you too,

Christopher." Adam is a little surprised to find himself talking so easily to the baby.

"Ha! She will become President on the day that I become the first flat-chested Miss America. Aside from the fact that she could never be nominated or elected, neither she nor Huck is biologically capable of breathing outside the San Francisco city limits. After all these years here they have developed very specialized gills."

They hear the door open in the hall, and then Huck calling, "Christopher, where's my baby?" Huck, sweaty, appears in the kitchen, grabs the baby from Lucille, and presses him against his wet tee shirt. He leans over the baby and kisses Lucille on her supremely blond head. "Have you and Christopher been okay?" he asks Adam.

"Fine," says Adam. "Christopher took all your books off the shelves in the living room, and I put them all back again. We're a terrific team."

"Thanks for taking care of him. It was great to go running, first time in months and months. I've invited Tommy and Timmy to have dinner with us too. They're upstairs taking showers. I can run out and get another package of spaghetti, and we can make the sauce do for five."

"The sauce is going to need a lot of help in any case," says Lucille, "and I'm glad you've decided to go out for more spaghetti, because there are a few other things I want you to get for dinner." She passes Huck the list she has made, about twenty items.

He looks it over and says with mock querulousness, "How am I going to recognize the fresh basil?"

Lucille is firm. "You're going to show the grocer your

list, and tell him your mommy sent you to the store, and ask him please will he help you find everything so mommy won't be angry. Now scram, we're hungry, and we can't start cooking until you get back."

"Yes, mommy," says Huck, handing Christopher to Adam, and trotting back out the door.

The spaghetti sauce, for Adam, is a revelation. While they are cooking (he and Huck are put to work peeling cloves of garlic, chopping hot peppers, slicing eggplant, opening a half dozen cans and jars), Adam tries to keep track of everything Lucille is putting in the pot. Partly he wants to learn whatever there is to be learned from watching her; partly he is nervous about not quite knowing what it is he will end up eating, since everything is being thrown together so promiscuously. He asks questions: "What are those?" "Capers." "What are capers?" "Try one."

Tommy and Timmy appear soon after the cooking has begun; they have dressed for dinner, matching navy-blue blazers that seem to be humorously intended, polka-dot ties. They sit at the little kitchen table and chat with the three cooks, and soon Adam completely loses track of what is going into the sauce. The only really stupid thing he does is to ignore Lucille's very explicit instructions to cut the little green hot peppers under cold running water. The peppers looked so innocuous, and he hadn't quite understood what she meant by cutting them under water, and so now, as everyone is about to start eating, his fingers are burning. Under the table he presses them hard against his jeans, as if to put out the fire; then he gives up, lifts his right hand to his fork, and, with some trepidation, takes a first bite. The spaghetti sauce is the most exciting thing he has ever eaten.

There is no dining room in the apartment, so they are eating at a big round table in the living room. Five chairs and a high chair just fit, and Huck is taking food from his own plate and feeding it to Christopher. Since the sauce is powerfully seasoned, and, by Adam's standards, rather strange, he is a little shocked to see the baby wolfing it down. Christopher takes a tiny fistful from Huck's fork, sucks up the spaghetti, then greedily licks the sauce from his hands.

The living room is simply furnished: the table, the bookcase, an armchair, the rose-pink love seat right under a big window with a view up Russian Hill. There are two framed pictures on the wall. One is a museum exhibit poster of a famous Edward Hopper painting, "Nighthawks." The other is a real painting, and though it is more or less abstract, Adam thinks he recognizes a seascape. The sea is frightening, wild with thick swirls of green paint, and there is a pink spot in the foreground, which, Adam suddenly thinks, could be a person, perhaps a swimmer. Again Adam imagines himself at the edge of the ocean: the earth shakes, the sea is rolling toward him.

"Tell us about your new show!" Tommy is saying to Lucille. "We're dying to hear all about it!"

"We're dying," Timmy echoes, ironically.

"Well," says Lucille, "I suppose I can't let you die."

"Tell us, tell us," chorus Tommy and Timmy, and Adam finds himself joining in even though he really has no idea what they're talking about. Any revelations are welcome to him.

"Gershwin," announces Lucille dramatically. "One

wonderful Gershwin song after another, what do you think of that, boys?"

"Wonderful!" says Tommy.

"Wonderful," says Timmy, mimicking Tommy.

Gershwin, thinks Adam. He cares about music, especially classical music, truly classical: Bach, Handel, Haydn, Mozart. The tone of the oboe, the magic of the double reed, is also something he cares about, and years back, when he lived with the woodwind players, he practiced for hours to achieve a musical line that would not dishonor his more talented housemates. As for Gershwin, Adam might recognize *Rhapsody in Blue*, but he can't think of a single Gershwin song, let alone one wonderful song after another. "Wait, what are you all talking about?" he finally asks. "What kind of a show is this?"

"It's Lucille's show," explains Huck. "A sort of cabaret, this time with Gershwin songs. Lucille is a star—she's famous in San Francisco."

"Only in certain circles," says Lucille. "My fame is profoundly limited."

"When do you open?" asks Timmy.

"Beginning of October. A little late for an opening, I know, but I have no intention of trying to compete with opening night at the opera and that fat Pavarotti. None of my fans are *that* loyal."

"We are!" says Tommy, but Timmy doesn't chime in, and Adam supposes that he may be more loyal to the opera.

"Thank you, Tommy," says Lucille. "I know you won't be disappointed. We're already rehearsing like crazy."

Tommy says, "Are you going to have those two cute little guys singing behind you, the ones who were in your Rodgers

and Hart show? I just loved them." Timmy raises his eyebrows.

"They just loved each other," says Lucille. "I had to get
rid of them. They were constantly getting into these little
lovers' quarrels just before the show, because they were nervous, and then during the show they'd relax and want to make
up, and so they'd start singing the back-up lyrics to each other
instead of to the audience. Once during 'Small Hotel' it was
so obvious that the audience started tittering, and I almost
smacked them both. I really couldn't do another show with
them; this time it's just me and the pianist."

Huck takes Christopher into his lap and sings to him,
swaying, "There's a small hotel with a wishing well; I wish
that we were there together." Tommy and Timmy exchange
a glance of fond recognition. Adam does not know this song.
He's not sure he would recognize any songs by Rodgers and
Hart. He's familiar with the famous Rodgers and Hammer-
stein musicals, but they are not really to his taste.

"Huck sweetie," says Lucille, "you can sing in the
shower all you like, but if I were you I would try not to sing
to the child." Adam remembers Huck singing to Christopher
last night, in the middle of the night. Lucille dips the end of
her napkin into her water glass and leans over to wipe the
spaghetti sauce from Christopher's face, meanwhile continu-
ing to lecture Huck. "It's not just that you can't carry a
tune—it's more like you don't know what a tune is, and you'll
ruin his pitch long before he reaches the age of consent."

Lucille turns her attention back to Tommy. "What I
really loved, though, about having Freddy and Maximilian in
my show was the symmetry—they looked like twins. That's
hard to come by. I mean, think how wrong it would look if

you and Timmy were singing behind me. Even in matching blazers and polka dots there's no point in combining tall blonds with short brunettes. Back-up singers are supposed to match, like bowling pins or something."

"Otherwise they distract attention from the star," whispers Huck to Christopher, loud enough for everyone to hear.

"Right," says Lucille.

"What about me and Huck," suggests Tommy. "Do we match?"

"Let me see you side by side," says Lucille.

Everyone has finished eating, and they have also put away two bottles of California wine. Lucille takes Christopher into her lap and lets him drink out of her wine glass, while Huck and Tommy, both tall and blond, both a little drunk, are directed through certain simple dance steps. Lucille even allows them to sing a few bars from "Small Hotel," first carefully covering Christopher's ears to protect him from his father's faulty pitch. If they are going to be in her act, Lucille insists, either Huck will have to grow a mustache or Tommy will have to shave his off; this ultimatum provokes a mock deadlock as both men refuse to give way. So Lucille calls on the short dark ones, Timmy and Adam, to audition, and Timmy agrees in principle to acquire a false brown beard to match Adam's, though Lucille isn't sure she wants any beards at all in her act.

Adam has never been silly quite like this before, and he is a little surprised that he can be this way at all. There was none of this lightheartedness in his earnest love for Suzanne or hers for him, no comparable silliness in their domestic rituals. Adam wonders if he is going forward or backward, but if this is regression it must go very far back. This moment bears no relation to basketball humor, or getting stoned in college, and even as a child Adam was not often silly with his dignified mother. Yet here he is, playing along with the boys, with the men, even singing when Lucille demands a few bars of "Small Hotel" once again—by now he knows the opening lines. And he and Timmy get high marks; Christopher is allowed to listen. Tommy comments on Timmy's success that at least something has come out of all that time at the opera. Timmy expresses doubt that Puccini has particularly influenced his rendition of "Small Hotel." Adam, with his narrowly classical taste, barely knows Puccini any better than he knows Rodgers and Hart.

"Shall I tell them?" says Tommy to Timmy mysteriously.

"No," says Timmy.

"Tell us, tell us," cry Huck and Lucille and Adam, all a little drunk, and even Christopher is saying something.

"No," says Timmy.

But Tommy ignores him. "We were listening to Ella Fitzgerald singing 'Small Hotel' the first time we ever kissed each other," says Tommy, his voice full of somewhat intoxicated sentiment.

"How romantic," says Huck.

"Lucky Ella," says Lucille.

Am I shocked? Adam asks himself, but he isn't at all, not even really surprised.

"We met at a bar on Polk Street," says Tommy. "It was three years ago last month, and we liked each other right away, but then, instead of suggesting that we go home together, Timmy invited me out on a date, invited me to go to the opera with him later that week. I had never been to the opera before, and I had never been asked out on a date before, so I thought the whole thing was extremely romantic."

"Which didn't stop him from going home with someone else after I left the bar," Timmy remarks.

"Well, did you expect me to go home alone?"

"I went home alone."

"Timmy doesn't believe in picking people up in bars and going to bed with them," Tommy explains. "So he used to meet them in bars, invite them somewhere else, and *then* go to bed with them. That way he didn't feel like such a slut. I always thought it sounded like ultimately the same thing except with one extra step in the middle."

"It was not the same thing," says Timmy, emphatically. "It's hard not being a slut in this world, but I tried."

Am I shocked? Adam asks himself again, just checking. But he really isn't.

"So we went to the opera," Tommy continues, "and I thought he would probably try to hold my hand, or try to make out or feel me up or something, but of course I didn't know Timmy and I didn't know anything about people who go to the opera, and Timmy devoted his complete and undivided attention to Montserrat Caballé, and I felt totally neglected. Anyway, it was an endless performance, but when it was finally over, we came back to my place, right upstairs, and I put on an Ella Fitzgerald record, and halfway through 'Small Hotel' I kissed him. And the rest is history."

"History," echoes Timmy.

Just then there is a knock on the door.

Huck goes to answer, and comes back with a very young man wearing a broad cowboy hat and pointed cowboy boots. He is emaciated, and the prominent bones of his face—the hard cheekbones, the unnaturally narrow nose, the sharp chin—give him a startling appearance. He is extremely pale, and the pallor seems somehow connected to his reserve as he follows Huck into the roomful of company. Huck introduces him as Wayne, and Wayne takes off his hat.

Tommy and Timmy greet him as if they know him; Wayne responds with a very good-natured smile that suggests he has no idea who they are. Lucille says nothing, but Adam guesses from her face that she knows Wayne and is not at all happy to see him here. Adam himself is won over by that first smile at Tommy and Timmy, but then, when it is turned on him, he begins to feel uncomfortable; there is something alarming about the combination of this young man's good nature (he is very young, no older than twenty) and his emaciated pallor. Only Christopher seems really comfortable with the newcomer. He climbs down from Lucille's lap and crawls over to Wayne, pulls himself up against Wayne's boots and grabs the cowboy hat from his hand. Wayne squats down, smiles at the baby with the same detached good nature, and then absently begins to stroke the baby's head, as if he were a pet.

There is no room for another chair at the table, and Huck breaks the silence by suggesting that they leave the dining corner and sit on the love seat, the armchair, the floor. Lucille naturally ends up in the armchair, and no one disputes Tommy and Timmy for the love seat. This leaves Adam, Huck, and Wayne on the hardwood floor with Christopher. Adam sits cross-legged, very aware of Wayne sitting next to him but a little behind. Directly in front of Adam is the wild seascape with the human spot. Out of the corner of his eye he is aware of Wayne taking out a cigarette, lighting a match.

Then Lucille leans forward from the armchair and says, almost without expression, "Don't smoke in here, not with the baby." Next to Adam the match goes out, and he has a sense (though he doesn't turn to look) that Wayne is hurt.

Tommy rescues the party by starting to tell Huck effusively how much he loved the record *Anyone Can Whistle,* Timmy chiming in to mimic Tommy's effusions. Huck tells them that Lucille gave him the record. Then Lucille tells them all that she was in a little San Francisco production of the show quite a few years ago, and she knew it would be perfect for Huck. Tommy wants to know if Lucille was Mayor Cora or Nurse Apple, and Lucille says that unfortunately then she was much too young to be Mayor Cora, and Tommy says that anyway Nurse Apple sings the title song and that's his favorite. Adam wonders what on earth they are talking about.

"Perfect for Huck," suggests Timmy, "because everyone knows about Huck and lady mayors, right?"

"And not just that," says Lucille, "but also—"

"Don't tell them!" Huck interrupts, laughing. "It's too embarrassing."

"Huck can't whistle."

"I'm so embarrassed!" exclaims Huck.

"You can't whistle!" chorus Tommy and Timmy, and Adam also thinks it is remarkable. Huck seems like just the sort of person who ought to whistle.

"He is one of the most truly and deeply unmusical people I have ever known," Lucille is saying.

"Your most truly and deeply unmusical fan," Huck reminds her.

Adam is aware of Wayne at his elbow, absolutely silent,

still petting the baby. The conversation has pretty much regained its full spirit now, as if Wayne weren't even there. He seems to represent some sort of problem that they have all overcome, for the moment, and Adam can't quite bring himself to turn his head and look.

To distract himself Adam asks what *Anyone Can Whistle* is all about, and Tommy begins to tell him in a very confused way. It is an old Sondheim musical with a corrupt lady mayor, and a false miracle in which water comes out of a rock, and a chorus of crazy people called cookies who escape from a lunatic asylum called the cookie jar, and a nurse who doesn't know how to whistle, and a madman who tries to teach her. Tommy's narrative collapses, and first he, and then everyone else (except Wayne), begs and begs Lucille to sing the title song. When they have begged enough, she graciously consents.

She turns out the lights, finds the spot in front of the window where there is a glimmering from a streetlight, and sings unaccompanied. The dim light shows the white of her shirt and the white-blond of her hair, and her red lipstick seems to glow.

> *Anyone can whistle, that's what they say, easy.*
> *Anyone can whistle, any old day, easy.*
> *It's all so simple:*
> *Relax, let go, let fly!*
> *So someone tell me why can't I?*

Christopher has crossed the room, and is now sitting on the crack of the love seat between Tommy and Timmy; he remains miraculously still and silent while Lucille sings.

I can dance a tango, I can read Greek, easy.
I can slay a dragon any old week, easy.

Adam is enchanted, slain.

When Christopher finally falls asleep in Huck's lap, Tommy and Timmy take that as a sign that it is time to go home, upstairs. Tommy can't stop telling Lucille, ever more extravagantly, how wonderfully she sings, how wonderfully she cooks. Adam remembers that the evening started out as a dinner that he and Huck were going to cook for Lucille. As Tommy and Timmy leave, Adam notices a nod from Huck to Wayne, and Wayne too rises to go, puts on his hat. He looks around at no one in particular, says goodbye, and he is gone.

Huck puts Christopher in his crib, and Lucille then sends Huck to bed since he must work tomorrow morning; she and Adam can sleep late, so they will do the dishes. Adam washes, while Lucille, who seems to know where everything goes, straightens the kitchen.

"Who is Wayne?" asks Adam, when they are alone.

"A friend of Huck's." She speaks from behind him, and he hears over the noise of the running water. Her tone is flat.

"You don't like him," Adam ventures.

"He's a dumb Okie," says Lucille.

"An Okie?"

"Yeah, a messed-up little boy from Oklahoma who ran away to the big city."

For a moment Adam, though he has been living in Boston, though he must be ten years older than Wayne, nevertheless finds himself identifying with the little boy in the big city. But he knows that isn't really the point, knows that Lucille is evading his question. "You weren't happy to see him here tonight," says Adam.

"He wasn't invited."

This insistence on the formality of invitation sounds so arbitrary, so much more false even than the slur on Oklahoma, that Adam resigns himself to the fact that Lucille is not going to tell him why she doesn't like Wayne. "He has a strange face," says Adam. And then, obstinately, "But I like him." Adam remembers that detached good nature, remembers how the boy took off his cowboy hat entering the room.

"I think he's attractive," says Lucille. "But I don't like him."

Adam changes the subject so abruptly that he surprises himself. "Who is Christopher's mother?"

"Not me," says Lucille, as if that was what Adam was hinting.

"Yes, but who?" He has stopped doing the dishes, turned off the water; he faces Lucille, and she, reluctantly, stands still to answer him.

"Does it really matter?"

"Who his mother is? I think so. Is it such an unnatural question to ask?"

"If it's so natural why don't you ask Huck?"

What can Adam say? "All right, I will, tomorrow."

And Lucille, facing him across the kitchen, says, "No, don't do that. You know it's not something he wants to talk about; that's why you haven't asked him. Christopher's mother is a pathetic, disturbed creature with whom Huck had a pathetic affair almost two years ago, and one of the pathetic things about her was the way she managed to get pregnant when she wasn't fit to be pregnant and, God knows, couldn't possibly take care of a baby."

"Where is she now?" asks Adam.

"In the cookie jar." She points over Adam's shoulder, and he turns, half expecting to see someone behind him, but there is just a large and beautiful blue ceramic jar with the inscription COOKIES. It takes Adam a minute to remember Tommy's confused retelling of *Anyone Can Whistle.* "Oh, that kind of cookie jar."

"And I hope she stays there, because she is one sick cookie, and Huck is going to really suffer if she comes back here for him and the baby. Really suffer. Sad but true, the only way he can go about living his life with Christopher is if they keep the lid on that cookie jar."

"Where is the, um, hospital?"

"Los Angeles, that's where her mother lives, but as soon as someone lifts the lid, she'll be back in San Francisco."

"And what will happen if she does come back to San Francisco?"

Lucille shrugs. "I don't want to think about that yet." As if it is something that she will have to deal with somehow, eventually. Adam is struck by the way Huck's life seems to be entrusted to Lucille's care; he does not know if she has assumed this trust, or if Huck has made it over to her.

"Am I living in her room?" he asks Lucille, though he has already guessed the answer.

"It's Huck's room," says Lucille fiercely. "It's his name on the lease, and he pays the rent." She relents a little. "And now it's your room because he's renting it to you." And a little more. "Yes, she used that room."

"Didn't they sleep together in the same room?"

"Sometimes, sometimes not. But she used to work in that room."

"Work?"

"Paint. She was good, in a sick way."

Lucille beckons him to follow her into the living room, and right away he knows what she is going to show him. She just points, and he walks toward it: the seascape with the pink spot. Up close it is just swirls of paint, but the pink spot, he clearly sees, is the color of flesh. Down in the corner, scratched into the thick paint, is the name Miriam, in childish block letters. Just a first name, also like a child's painting.

Adam sits down on the love seat, and Lucille comes and sits beside him. He is suddenly aware again of the burning in his fingers from the hot peppers. "What are you going to wear to the opening of my Gershwin show?" asks Lucille, lightly. They have finished discussing Christopher's mother, it seems.

"I don't know. I haven't thought about it."

"Think about it," says Lucille.

But Adam really can't think about it now, can't begin to plan or even imagine the details of his life in San Francisco. He can't even think ahead two weeks to the new teaching job he is about to begin after Labor Day. Instead he allows his mind to hover very vaguely around two unrelated anticipations. The first is the possibility of a visit from his mother, and the second is Christopher's birthday in October. Adam thinks of Christopher and Huck sleeping in their bedrooms, Huck who cannot whistle even though he seems like just the sort of person who would be whistling all the time.

"The song you sang before," Adam begins. He wants to tell Lucille how much her voice moved him, how he almost fell in love with her while she was singing: white-blond hair, glowing red lipstick, anyone can whistle. But he doesn't get to finish his sentence, never even decides what he is going to say, because Lucille leans over and kisses him.

CHAPTER FOUR

OLD WORLD, NEW WORLD

Dear Suzanne,

All evening I have been thinking that I would write to you, but I have not been able to get up the courage to begin. I puttered around my room instead, and finally fully unpacked the suitcases I brought out to California with me, into my closet and a little wooden dresser I found at a junk sale a few days ago. So thanks to you I am unpacked, and then I thought I really ought to write at least to thank you for that. There are more important things that I mean to thank you for, but let me see if I can work my way up to them. Anyway I am lying on my stomach on my mattress on the floor (I found a little dresser, but not, so far, a little desk). I am writing, and wondering what you will think when you see a letter from me in our mailbox (your mailbox now, I'm sorry). Whether you'll answer. I know I could telephone from San Francisco, but right now I am still enjoying the notion that I've traveled a very, very long way, and it would be deflating for me just to press ten buttons and be talking to you in Boston. And, besides, I can't imagine how we would talk. I mean, could we really just chat after such a momentous separation? Or would we end up being ponderous, or mournful, or furious—and then somehow start fighting the way we kept doing during that last month?—hell, during the last year. In a way the most natural thing, and the easiest thing, would have been just not to write to you. And then we would just lose touch with each other completely. The end, new life. But that scares me: the idea that whatever happened between us over the last five years, however we draw the balance, could be forgotten or suppressed, as if there had never been anything there at all. I'd feel like I'd lost a part of my life. At my age, it doesn't seem to me that my life, my past, has so many parts and pieces to it that I can really afford to lose hold of the important ones—not absolutely.

What can I tell you about my new life? Remember, I told you that when I called Huck and he suggested that I come live with him, he asked if I thought I could live with a baby. Well, sure enough, there is a baby. And of all the big and little things that make my new life new and strange, living with a baby is the newest and strangest. His name is Christopher, and he is almost one.

My great achievements for this first week in San Francisco are: (1) learning about shopping in my neighborhood, Russian Hill, which is actually on a hill (San Francisco, after all), so shopping involves certain calculations about how many bags you'll be carrying from one altitude to another and whether gravity will be working for or against you; and (2) learning a little about bus routes so that I can leave Russian Hill and get back to it again, though actually the most convenient public transportation to and from my apartment is the famous San Francisco cable cars, crammed full of tourists, except that I am not a tourist (but I get a silly thrill from the cable cars just as if I were); and (3) learning to diaper Christopher.

The first time I saw Huck diaper Christopher, I thought I would never, never be able to do it, and at the same time I was definitely curious to know whether I *could* do it, as a sort of ultimate test of my masculinity or humanity or something—like climbing telephone poles. And so the next evening when I was in my room wondering if I would ever unpack my suitcases, I heard Huck exclaim, "Look who's all wet!" (I know that must sound like a strange exclamation, but that is the tone Huck takes, and I've even started talking like that myself to Christopher.) Anyway, I rushed out of my room and met them in the bathroom at the diapering table (if you can imagine such a thing), and asked Huck if I could try. And he watched me and sort of talked me through. ("Now, Adam, always one hand on the baby or he'll roll over and fall on the floor; when you change the baby you have to use all six hands.") You simply cannot imagine how ridiculously proud of myself I was. I have been puffed up about it ever since (see how I bore you with my boasting), and have several times repeated the exploit.

Christopher's mother is mysteriously absent (she is, I am told, in a mental hospital in Los Angeles), and I have this odd feeling that I am somehow filling her place in the apartment, or rather that Christopher thinks that is what I am doing. Yesterday I was in my room, reading, with the door open, and I suddenly knew I was being watched, and when I looked up there was Christopher on all fours at the threshold peering in. And he was watching me so seriously, so intensely, that he didn't even seem to notice that I'd looked up at him and called out his name.

I feel as though he likes me, but half reluctantly, and I find myself desperately eager for him to accept me as, well, as a roommate perhaps—but I do sometimes feel like a sort of stepparent who must court a naturally suspicious stepchild. And when I hear myself saying things like "Look who's all wet!" I become aware that unconsciously I must be studying Huck to learn the secret of winning over Christopher. Is all this about the baby very boring for you? You were so definite about not wanting children. I respected that, respected the fact that you had an opinion at all, since I had no real opinion on the subject. I don't think I ever even thought about babies seriously until last week.

I am having an affair. Or at least I think I am having an affair. Her name is Lucille, and she is a cabaret singer, and we have gone to bed together twice. Is this a touchy thing for me to tell you, seeing as we have just separated after being lovers for five years? I think it's okay, especially since it was your telling me that you were sleeping with your Professor Klingenstein that partly provoked our separation. Anyway, I am not telling you about Lucille to be spiteful or to get even; I'm telling you because I'm not sure who else I can tell. Actually, after all our years together in Boston I don't feel like I'm leaving behind any other really close friends. That's sort of what I mean by too few parts and pieces. I'm not sure when I last visited my old house in Cambridge—or which of the guys are still there, or what we used to talk about anyway. And here in San Francisco my only friend is Huck. Back in college we were really friends—though I'm not sure what exactly that meant to either of us then. I don't think we talked to each other seriously about sex, and I don't know exactly how we are going to be friends now, and what things we'll talk about and what will be private. Anyway, he's not the right person to confide in now, because he is closer to Lucille than he is to me, and, besides, I do not know exactly how things stand between the two of them.

What surprises me about sleeping with Lucille (also what excites me, what scares me a little, what makes me feel compelled to write about it to someone) is the completely passive role I am cast in. One night she kissed me. I know that is not supposed to be a big deal, but, frankly, no woman had ever done that before, kissed me first; I suppose I have led a rather traditional love life. And with Lucille the kiss was just the beginning. In bed also (on my mattress on the floor) I was completely passive. She told me exactly what to do, how to lie, where to touch her, harder or softer, and, when she was ready, she climbed on top of me and made love to me—until I came, which she also seemed to control. And I was carried away by it while it was happening, even though I knew that afterward I would feel embarrassed. And I did. Also as if I didn't really know myself or the world—which is how San Francisco in general makes me feel. Like I don't understand how old I am—or maybe how young I am. Is it okay, my writing to you about all this?

In a week or so I will start my new teaching job (I know, you don't approve, you want to know when am I going to get a Ph.D. and start taking literature seriously, like you, like my mother), and then I will really be established in San Francisco. Right now my life here has the air of a vacation, as if I might just fly back to Boston next week, and back to you. It is a little frightening to catch myself thinking that way.

Maybe also frightening not to know yet what exactly this new life is going to make out of me. I feel like a child; I constantly find myself identifying with Christopher. But I am aware that other people see me as an adult, and Lucille says I probably owe that to a woman in my past. I suppose she's right, and, of course, the woman is you, and I am grateful to you for having helped me to find at least the semblance of maturity.

With love,

Adam

Dear Maman,

I am writing instead of telephoning because last night I wrote a letter to Suzanne, and the act of writing left me feeling very good about myself and about my "new life," as I glibly refer to it after a week in San Francisco. There, I know I am revealing myself as a sort of case study in contemporary literary theory, but the fact is that writing about my new life really did make me feel more like I was actually living it. And the anticipation of receiving a letter here, addressed to me, makes me feel like it is, in fact, my address. I don't know if Suzanne will answer me, considering that we separated forever last week, and not very graciously. But I know you're a fine correspondent, always ready to write a ten-page letter to any brave young scholar in New Zealand explaining why his article on *Moby Dick* fails to come to terms with Melville's fundamental structural binary opposition between whale and non-whale, whatever that can possibly mean. I know you never said anything like that about *Moby Dick* (and I've never even read *Moby Dick*), but before I left Boston I went with

Suzanne to one last Harvard Comparative Literature function, and I heard Professor Oswald Klingenstein holding forth about whale and non-whale. I thought it sounded supremely structuralist. Anyway, you will write to me, won't you?

I am sending you a copy of a photograph of me and Huck and Huck's baby, Christopher, taken the evening that I arrived in San Francisco. Looking at it now, I can't get over the way we already look like a little family, even though that evening was the first time I'd seen Huck in years, and I'm not sure I'd ever really been that close to a baby before. You certainly can't tell from the picture; you can't even tell that I was suffering from terrible jet lag and was about to collapse. But photography anticipated life, and by now we really are a sort of little family, a strange family I guess, two old college roommates and a baby. Last night I wrote to Suzanne at length about the thrill of learning to diaper, so I will spare you the details. Anyway, you must know the details, since you've had a baby of your own. I suppose you used cloth diapers and safety pins, which Huck says are very difficult to diaper with; we use disposable paper diapers with sticky tapes.

Do you remember Huck? Do you remember the time he came to dinner and tried to convince you to vote for McGovern, and you had to tell him you were a French citizen and couldn't vote in this country? I hope you are indulgent enough to have forgiven him by now for scolding you then, because I want you to like him. He and I are friends again, just as if all those years hadn't passed between then and now—though it's strange, our friendship feels very much the way it felt back then, as if we are now just superannuated freshman roommates; there are things we don't talk about at all, or at least not so far. I am awestruck by the way he moves through life with this baby, and I love watching the two of them together. Sometimes I think of you, just because you also raised a child by yourself—though I always took that completely for granted, whereas Huck's doing it seems utterly phenomenal. Christopher is not yet one; we will have a birthday party for him in October. Papa was still alive when I was that age—I'm not sure why I keep reminding myself of that. Christopher's mother is alive, but she is not here and she is not sane; that is one of the things that Huck and I do not talk about. There is a sort of scary sense here that if she should someday appear it will be somehow disastrous. There is a picture she painted hanging in the living room, signed with just her first name, Miriam.

Christopher, you can see in the photograph, looks like Huck; if there could be a tall, handsome, blond, blue-eyed one-year-old, that would be Christopher. The person who took the picture, by the way, is a friend of Huck's who is now my friend too. She lives around the corner from us and is a sort of San Francisco celebrity, a cabaret singer. Her name is Lucille, just Lucille. Huck told me that she professionally uses just the one name for her shows, but she seems to have eliminated her last name from her private life as well. I asked her last week what it was, and she asked me if it really mattered.

My first day in San Francisco, Huck and I made dinner with Lucille, and invited our upstairs neighbors, Tommy and Timmy. Tommy is a federal civil servant who has something to do with administering school-lunch programs. He talks in exclamations, and if he were a character in fiction you would probably try to analyze him by studying the punctuation marks in his speech. Timmy works scooping ice cream, and he lives to go to the opera; I don't know if he is susceptible to serious literary criticism. When they were here for dinner, the conversation was mostly about songs I'd never heard of, like one called "Small Hotel" and another called "Anyone Can Whistle." I felt sort of culturally inadequate, or maybe just displaced, and I write to you in the sincere conviction that you also will never have heard of these songs. And your cultural credentials, of course, are irreproachable. Yesterday I took out my oboe for the first time in San Francisco, and played the Haydn sonata over and over in my room, until I was getting it almost right (I am so badly out of practice), and that somewhat restored my cultural confidence.

Tommy and Timmy are lovers, which is, in San Francisco, apparently something taken so for granted that you don't even mention it. I mention it to you just because I am too new here to let it pass without mentioning it to someone. I have this feeling that in my past life there were simply no homosexuals at all, but in San Francisco every time I go out I see men together who are couples. Do you think that in the photograph Huck and I look like a couple? That bothered me at first, but I suppose that with the baby in the picture no one would think we were gay. When I cover the baby with my thumb I still feel a little uncomfortable about it, and I also feel as if I am committing some symbolic offense against the baby.

When I see an article in the newspapers about AIDS, I read it now; it seems to matter more here than in Boston. I also read little notices about earthquakes all over the world. Did you know there was one this week in Indonesia?

After that you will think San Francisco has made me

morbid, and it has, a little—but also more spirited. When will you come out to visit me here, as you promised, so you can see the pink building I live in, and I can take you out to the Pacific Ocean at the end of the city? I want to apologize to you for something and to offer a sort of retraction. In our last phone call before I left Boston, I was ungracious enough to ask if you could try to come visit without Harvey. And, of course, the last time you and I saw each other in New Haven, I was shameless enough to actually break down and whine to you about how I wished you hadn't married him. I am also aware that I probably did not bother to be tactful enough to conceal from Harvey what I thought of the whole situation, even though he has never been anything but friendly to me. Anyway, I want to do more than apologize. I still think, I suppose, that he isn't good enough for you, whatever that means (I know I was rude enough to tell you exactly what I thought it meant last time), but I am not so naïve as to suppose that my own sentiments are free of Freudian complications. You, I know, do not think much of psychoanalysis as a critical method, but let it pass.

I started feeling different about you and Harvey when I saw how Christopher was reacting to me, to my moving in, the way he still reacts. He likes me, I think, and I have gone out of my way to woo him, but every now and then he becomes perversely cold to me, won't look at me when I try to talk to him. Once he actually bit my shoulder when I was holding him; he has tiny little teeth, surprisingly sharp. At first I thought he resented me for seeming to be replacing his mother, and I still think that may be part of it, even though I don't know whether he can really remember her. It's the photograph that started me thinking that what Christopher is really most concerned about is his father, and the fact that I've moved in with the two of them. I mean, if *I* look at the photograph and wonder how Huck and I would strike people, how does Christopher see us? Probably he's thinking: Who is this guy anyway, he's never even heard of "Small Hotel" or "Anyone Can Whistle," he's not nearly good enough to live with my father, he's completely unworthy to distract my father's attention from me even in the slightest.

I take it you've got the message. I look at Christopher, and see myself the way I imagine he sees me, that is, the way I see Harvey. And I see what an ass I've been, how unpleasant I've been to you. But what I want to say is this: come to San Francisco to visit me, and bring Harvey with you, if he wants to come. I promise to behave myself, and you can decide for yourself whether San Francisco has had an improving effect on my execrable character. I love you.

Adam

Dear Adam,

I suppose I am glad to hear from you, but your letter does leave me feeling—as you yourself seemed to anticipate—irritated and angry. The extended process of our deciding that our relationship was not good enough to keep going, then preparing to put an end to it, has left me spiritually haggard. I wish we could have had one giant explosion of a fight after which you or I just walked out forever in the middle of the night—instead of that long succession of pathetic squabblings and those endless, indecisive discussions about whether we should stay together. After all that, it's hard for me to think of you without some irritation, and I envy you being in a new place with new things and new people to distract you, so that if you choose to think about me, and even write to me, it's an act of self-indulgence.

I've decided to keep the apartment for myself alone—one bedroom is right for one person, and we were stupid to try to live in such a small apartment together. For the extra rent this fall I'll teach an extra discussion section in Klingenstein's big survey course on American literature. What a treat for me: getting to listen to fifteen more puffed-up-with-their-own-insights Harvard undergraduates explaining to each other what Emily Dickinson means—as if poetry actually means something. When will deconstructionist criticism finally make it possible for us to deconstruct the minds of our students?

Thanks to you (or thanks to us both) I do not have the concentration to think about my dissertation, so I have put Dreiser to one side. Instead I am working on Russian grammar, which is boring and mechanical. There is a vast literature on Dreiser in Russian; the Soviets love him. Most of what has been done there is pathetically stupid and ideological, but I think the fundamental meaninglessness of the criticism may help lead me into the fundamental inconsistencies of Dreiser himself. There, that's something for you to chuckle over in San Francisco: poor Suzanne, studying Russian so that she can read not Pushkin, no, not Tolstoy, oh no, not even Chekhov, heaven forbid, but reams and reams of bad Soviet Dreiser criticism. You're probably thinking that you'd rather talk about Emily Dickinson with college students or, better yet, with high school students.

As for you and your succubus Lucille, by assuring me

that you don't mean to be spiteful you succeed, I'm sure, in persuading yourself. But human spite, I think, is more devious than you are, and do not think that when I read about your ravishment I said to myself: Well, Suzanne, isn't it ducky about little Adam's adventures in San Francisco, learning to change baby's diapers and exploring the slavish side of his sexuality, but not both at once I hope, tee hee.

First of all, when I told you I was fucking Klingenstein, I told you in the context of a nasty fight (hoping, maybe, that you would finally walk out forever in the middle of the night), when we were both being abusive. Do not try to pretend that I offered it up to you as an intimate communication between friends, as you have now offered me Lucille. Neither did I detail for you the positions that he and I assumed—that I left to your erotic fantasy, such as it is. And incidentally I don't think my telling you was so exceptionally important for our finally deciding to separate—that was obviously coming anyway, sooner or later—and your fine protestations of manly jealousy were not even very convincing.

Second, I get the feeling that when you honor me with your intimate confidences because, you say, you have no one else to tell, what you really mean in the subtext is that you don't dare discuss such things with your marvelous mother. Once again, even on separate coasts, I feel as though I am being used to shield your Oedipal relationship from those forces that it might find too hot to handle. I have been thinking about this, though, and I'm not sure that it was fair of me to accuse you of choosing me as a convenient stand-in, when it could just as well have been I, knowing who your mother was, who chose you for the perverse satisfaction of standing in.

Which brings me to my third point: Do not suppose, just because I did not climb on top of you the day you first walked into my apartment to fix my phone, that you were not susceptible to manipulation, sexual and otherwise, even in your old "traditional love life." (Can I really suppose that you do not mean such phrases to be at least slightly offensive to me?) Suffice it to say that I think Lucille has a good eye for her prey.

And, finally, my last point (I am almost finished; are you relieved?)—I admit that although your true confessions did not delight me, they did satisfy an unwholesome and maybe even lingeringly affectionate curiosity about what you are up to in San Francisco. And so, if you like, and if you are willing to let me vent my irritation in abusive responses, you may continue to confide in me. Better all this by mail than across the kitchen, God knows.

What else is new? You forgot to inquire about my adventures with the eminent Professor Klingenstein. Yesterday, after I received your letter, I went to his office in Widener Library to discuss Dreiser, and, oh, very much to my surprise, we ended up going at it (not Dreiser) up on his desk. I was on bottom (you know how traditional I am!) with a volume of the collected works of Ralph Waldo Emerson propping up each of my buttocks. Does that titillate you? It certainly titillates Klingenstein. We do it in his office, not only because that is where Emerson is most accessible, but also because that is where he has told his wife he is working, and she just might call to check up on him. I have not told Klingenstein that you have moved to California, because I think it is more balanced if he thinks I am also cheating on someone (the imbalance of our academic relations is quite enough), and because I'm not eager to invite him back to the apartment. After he gave me and Emerson a good pounding, Klingenstein told me about the book he is writing on *Moby Dick*. It is to be a solid and (nowadays) old-fashioned structural analysis, rigorously insisting on the central binary opposition. You wouldn't appreciate it since you haven't read *Moby Dick,* but I think your mother might find it interesting. Odd, with you gone I have become very conscious of her as a purely academic figure again, the way I felt about her before I knew you. I love those early articles on "Bartleby" and "Benito Cereno"; they feel genuinely French, which is what structural criticism is supposed to be, and which good old Klingenstein, for all his binaries, will never be.

Adam, thank you for writing, enjoy your cable cars, and believe me if you can when I tell you that in spite of everything I still feel fond of you.

Suzanne

Dear Adam,

Thank you for your letter, and thank you especially for the photograph. I have it on my desk, and I keep looking over at it. May I tell you—I am slightly ashamed of this—that the sight of you with a baby makes me think of grandchildren. Until I got your letter with the photograph yesterday, I don't think I had ever thought about grandchildren, but now I feel as if I have been yearning for them always. But please, don't rush out and do anything impulsive; I can wait. You all three look so healthy and happy in this photograph, just as if California had some special power to transform and irradiate. But it is not California perhaps, only the camera, which acts like the mirror of Lacan to create an image of meaningful integration while inside the subjects there is only jet lag and inconsequent confusion. It is true that the three of you look like a family already, maybe from a world without women.

Of course I remember that Huck once had dinner with us, and was disappointed with my political indifference. He was right to scold me, I suppose, and I was even charmed then to be scolded, charmed that this boy truly cared about saving my poor soul and saving America. You also cared about politics then, but you either made an exception for me or you thought that I was hopeless. Only when I decided to get married, then you had to speak up to save my soul.

The other reason I have always remembered Huck is his name, or rather his nickname. If your life is devoted to nineteenth-century American literature, then you cannot help being interested in someone who chooses such a name (or is chosen by such a name) and wears it so well. Really, I think he has the true spirit of Huckleberry Finn, the essence of the American boy, and after he left Yale so suddenly I sometimes imagined that he was spending those years floating down the Mississippi River on a raft. But I recall that "Huck" is the name he uses instead of Henryk, and the last name is something Polish—something impossible to pronounce or remember.

I am very interested in names right now. If you consider literature as a closed interdependent system of works, then you see that inevitably the same names must keep recurring, and the patterns of recurrence will tell you something about the mechanics of intertextuality and the connections between the different works within the system. Also, the writer who names his characters exercises a special liberty (since objects and relations, generally, must be described according to conventional linguistic usage), and the marvelous arbitrariness of naming—it is a whole different kind of relationship between signifier and signified—must take the critic back to this question of other texts and implicit ways in which one text enters into or cuts itself off from another. Biblical names like yours are a good example.

Did you know that your father wanted to name you after Albert Einstein? It was, to a Jewish German physicist of his generation, the most heroic name. But I hated the name Albert (I don't know why), and I can't remember now how we decided to call you Adam instead. Do you ever find the biblical allusion oppressive, as if you must represent something too imposing? With Huck the allusion is one that he must have helped to choose, or at least been willing to accept, so he is perhaps partly a self-named character. (This can exist in literature artificially, for instance: "Call me Ishmael"— really, you must read *Moby Dick*!) Names like yours and Huck's (and Ishmael's too) have such strong allusive associations that they almost call attention to themselves as names, as if to say: we are the signifiers that the author has chosen. As if to proclaim their own arbitrary unnaturalness, the quality which Barthes so much prefers to the false illusion of realism.

You may object again that you and Huck (unlike Ishmael) are not the characters of an author, but here you are both in the letter on my desk (of which you are also the author). The name of the baby's mother also struck me. Miriam is the name of a character in Hawthorne's *The Marble Faun* (which I have just been rereading), a tragic character, and the story of Huck and Miriam and Christopher, even with so few details, seems to me deeply tragic. It is true just writing their three names together makes me feel nervous about looking over at the photograph. I will tell you that I like this friend Lucille who chooses to have no family name. Family names in literature pose a somewhat different critical problem, but I am afraid I will bore you if I go on.

I am not surprised to hear of Oswald Klingenstein's great idea about the opposition of whale and non-whale. Everyone knows he is writing a book on *Moby Dick,* and those who have read chapters have not been impressed with his insights. Oswald taught at Yale for a year, ten years ago, and that was when he had his great conversion to structuralist criticism (after structuralism was already dead in France, and practically dead at Yale), which he triumphantly took back to Harvard with him. I must say, however, that I do not think the work he has done since then is much worse than the work he was doing before. It is a pity that Suzanne is writing her dissertation with him. She is certainly more intelligent than he is. Do you think she knows that? I feel a little uncomfortable writing to you about her. I think it took me years to accept her place in your life, and now, when I am quite accustomed, she is not in your life anymore.

Shall I tell you something about Oswald Klingenstein? That year when he was at Yale (you were in college then), he and I had dinner one evening and had a long talk about Emerson. Too long. Let me confess: I think his scholarship is only mediocre, but I think he is an attractive man. To me he looks a little like Nathaniel Hawthorne. After dinner he invited me to his apartment in New Haven to continue our discussion (his wife worked in Boston and came to New Haven only on weekends), and, I admit, I was tempted to accept. But then I saw clearly that if I went home with him, sooner or later he would want to continue our discussion about Emerson. So I declined his invitation. And I have never regretted it.

Are you shocked to hear that I considered sleeping with him? I know I have never told you anything like this before. In fact, I have had several affairs (very few, really) during the last thirty years. Are you shocked now? Are there, as you say, "Freudian complications"? (You are right, I am not so interested in psychoanalysis, but I recognize that some of its theoretical formulations, like the Oedipus complex, correspond to certain structural patterns that emerge in literature and life.) Adam, I tell you about these few affairs now, not to shock you, not even to lecture you about psychoanalysis. I tell you because it is the best way for me to try to begin to talk frankly with you about Harvey. I accept your apology, of course, but I would prefer not to think that, as with politics years ago, here too you imagine that you are respectfully abandoning the cause of my salvation. I do not need to be saved. I tell you I have had some affairs because I want you to recognize that marrying Harvey is no leap into the abyss after thirty years of being a widow. This is something I could not tell you when you were being insulting about Harvey, but I can tell you now: I understand why you think he is not good enough for me; I understand why you consider him perhaps a comic character. However, I have lived alone for a long time, and, although I can take care of myself quite well, I decided that I want to spend the remaining years of my life with a companion.

I loved your father. I have had an affair with at least one man I am certain you would think was good enough for me, who many people would think is too good for me—but anyway he is married and he lives in Paris. I like Harvey, and he loves me, and I am remarkably happy living with him, even more than I expected. I am not interested in ophthalmology, but I think it is a respectable profession. It irritates me when Harvey uses French expressions in my presence, especially terms of affection, but, just by ignoring them, I have already almost completely eliminated them from his conversation. And he is quite a good cook (though not as good as I am). We take turns cooking for each other, and also I love having someone to go out to eat with. Adam, I almost love him, but I am not a very romantic woman, and I also think of this, a little, as a marriage of convenience. I want you not to have romantic ideas about me, but just to see that I know what I want to be happy, and to be glad that I can have what I want. I want you to accept Harvey, a little the way I accept him. That's all. Is it necessary for me to say that the person I love most in the world is you and has always been you? Give the baby a kiss from me.

With all my love,

Maman

P.S. Huck's full name finally came back to me: Henryk Malachowski. I couldn't believe I remembered it right, so I actually called the Yale admissions office, where someone checked

for me that Henryk Malachowski really did enter Yale in
1972. I love the transformation of signifiers from Henryk
Malachowski to Huck Finn.

P.P.S. You are right, I have never heard of the songs you
mentioned. But Harvey knows the song "Small Hotel," and
says it was once one of his favorites.

CHAPTER FIVE

PRIVATE EDUCATION

When Adam first sets eyes on the Stringfellow School, he almost cannot believe he has found the right place. It is a huge white Victorian mansion—there are bay windows and little balconies and odd turrets—set back from the street across a wide, freshly cut lawn. This is Pacific Heights, the wealthiest neighborhood in San Francisco, and Adam, though he has spent the last couple of weeks exploring, has not yet ventured into this part of town. He approaches the pillared porch by a circular path, obviously intended for horses and carriages, and there alongside the door an unostentatious plaque confirms that this is indeed the Stringfellow School, founded in 1909.

On this first day there are no students, only teachers submitting to orientation. The faculty room where everyone assembles is a Victorian parlor, with armchairs and sofas arranged in irregular arcs around the fireplace; there is piled wood but no fire. In front of the fireplace, facing the assembled furniture and faculty, is the most venerable armchair of all, with the highest back and the broadest arms. Adam, who remembers past orientations (never so comfortable) from his past jobs in Boston, can guess that this most venerable arm-chair will be occupied by a most venerable headmaster. And, before long, it is.

Jonah Stringfellow, grandson of the founder, is profoundly patriarchal in appearance; he gives the impression of being all beard, and his voice is deep, solemn, resonant with dignified authority. Thus it is a full five minutes into the opening remarks before Adam realizes that this voice is expressing a succession of incomplete thoughts in the most remarkably incoherent sentences. The headmaster, it seems, also teaches the advanced Latin class, and his speech is point-lessly, almost insanely, interrupted with Latin quotations from Cicero. Adam looks around at his new colleagues—there are maybe twenty-five—and thinks he can recognize the vet-erans by the perfectly serious masks with which they receive these resonant classical utterances; the few teachers with quizzical expressions, as if they are still struggling to extract some sense from the headmaster's remarks, must be new, like Adam.

Adam turns his eyes back to the venerable armchair, and tries to compose his face in the veteran manner. Jonah String-fellow is saying that the house was once his grandfather's, that the great San Francisco earthquake of 1906 destroyed the finest private high school in the city, and so the ancestral Stringfellow arranged for his sons to have lessons at home, then invited the sons of his friends, and that was the begin-ning of the Stringfellow School. The headmaster falls into a long Ciceronian declamation, and when he emerges from it he is prophesying the next great San Francisco earthquake, indeed heralding it, inspiring his faculty with a vision of the Stringfellow School's educational mission amidst the ruins of the city. This air of biblical prophecy, these apocalyptic utterances . . . Adam thinks of what his mother wrote to him about names, biblical names, names like Adam and Jonah, literary links from the text of the Bible to the text of—of what? His mind wanders further, from Jonah to the whale, and from whale to non-whale, and from there to Professor Oswald Klingenstein. Having wandered this far, Adam forces himself to refocus on the headmaster; he recomposes his face to match the professional attentiveness of one of his new colleagues across the parlor. But the young woman whose expression he is copying suddenly shifts her attention and catches his eye. Then she crosses her legs, as if to bring modestly to his attention an extraordinary pair of shoes. Doesn't Adam know her from somewhere?

After the opening session the faculty splits up into departmental clusters. In such a small school, this leaves Adam with Graham, a somewhat older man who teaches the American literature courses and who seems to want to make Adam feel uncomfortable and unwelcome, and Phyllis, a considerably older woman who teaches writing and of whom Adam is immediately fond. It is not until the afternoon, when everyone reassembles for coffee in the parlor (silver tea and coffee service, china cups and saucers) that Adam reencounters the young woman he thinks he recognizes from somewhere. And by this time he has remembered where.

"Yale," he says to her, approaching carefully with a cup and saucer in hand. "Class of seventy-six." He tries not to stare at her shoes.

"Yes," she says, "and what have you been doing all these years?" She is teasing him with her display of interest because the fact is that they barely knew each other at Yale, and right now Adam can't even remember her name. She has short dark curls that catch the light and dark pretty eyes. Earlier in the day, Adam had taken this face as a model of solemn composure, but now he can see how mistaken he was, or perhaps deceived. A pair of round-cut wire-rim glasses barely conceal an air of potent irreverence and irony.

"I've been living in Boston," says Adam. And then, giving his biography the twist that makes it just slightly less predictable, he says, "I spent a few years working for the phone company, climbing telephone poles, but mostly I've been an English teacher."

She is tickled. "I'd like to see you do that."

"Teach English?"

"Climb telephone poles."

"Tell me what you've been doing," says Adam.

"Oh, I've been in San Francisco for a while now," she says, "but before that I lived in Iran for a couple of years. I was married to an Iranian—but I left him just in time, and got out of Iran on practically the last flight before the Shah fell. The timing was actually a lucky coincidence." Her voice is smooth, almost demure, as if intended as an ironic counterpoint to the drama of her story.

If she has been amused by Adam's account of himself, he is rather overwhelmed by hers. "I'm Adam Berg," he says. "You might have forgotten my name."

"Amy Armstrong," she says. "More coffee?"

Adam declines. He remembers her name now that he has heard it. He has a vague memory of hearing her discussed among his friends as one of those much too serious Yale girls whom Yale boys swaggeringly dismissed. Too serious, too studious: that was how boys took revenge on girls who didn't notice them. Amy was, more or less, one of those girls; and Adam was, more or less, one of those boys. Now here they are years later, facing each other, each holding a cup and a saucer, in a room full of their adult colleagues.

"Is something wrong?" asks Amy, watching his face, then stepping back a step, as if to allow him a better view of those extraordinary shoes.

"Just thinking what a funny coincidence that we should find each other here."

"It's not really a coincidence," she says. "The headmaster went to Yale, class of 1850, and he is always richly satisfied, as he would say, to find a Yale man—that includes me—to teach at the Stringfellow School. He also has special connections to the Yale Admissions Office and tries to send our best students there—lucky them. The students are nice, you'll see. The headmaster, in case you were wondering, is a lunatic. But harmless. You might want to consider pretending to know a little Latin."

"How do you know I don't know any Latin?"

"Pardon. I guess I thought that knowing languages and climbing telephone poles would be too many talents for just one man." Very demure.

"I don't know a word of Latin," Adam admits. Then, as if to compensate, "I can manage in French, though. My mother's French."

"I can speak Farsi," says Amy, "but, believe me, it doesn't come in very handy."

"What do you teach?"

"Calculus and physics. I studied physics in college." Too serious, Adam recalls.

"My father was a physicist," says Adam. "But I don't know a thing about physics."

"My husband was a physicist," says Amy. "He was a graduate student at Yale when we were undergraduates."

She's pretty, thinks Adam, reluctant to think about the Iranian husband. What has become of him anyway? Instead he thinks about her shoes. Amy is wearing a forest-green woolen skirt, a white blouse with a red ribbon tie at the neck, very appropriate. And then there are the shoes. They are boots really, violently glossy, pointy black boots that button up the front to just above the ankle. The buttons are big rhinestones. Adam forces his eyes back up to the red ribbon at her neck, which now, for some reason, makes him think of Lucille—kneeling over him with scarlet lips forming a broad smile of sexual satisfaction. And from that image he focuses on Amy again, but higher still: pretty eyes, wire-rim glasses, his colleague.

"Are you all right?" She is watching his face, and he wonders what she can read there. Mentally he removes her glasses, not only to see her face, but to prevent her from seeing his.

"I'm fine." He is thinking: Ten years ago, when we were in college, she would not have been at all interested in me. And I wouldn't have been interested in her enough to care. But I'm not the same person I was ten years ago, and whatever is going on right now between the two of us is proof of that. He says, "Can I get you some more coffee?"

When Adam returns from his day of orientation at the String-fellow School, Huck and Christopher are not yet home, but Lucille is there—lying on her back on the love seat, her long legs bent over one of the upholstered sides, her unnaturally blond hair falling down across the rose-pink cushion. When Adam looks into the room she is humming to herself intently in a way that he now recognizes as her mode of constant rehearsal. She is always singing twenty Gershwin songs over and over in her head, rethinking the phrasing and rhythms.

He watches her with a certain, now almost habitual, amazement, as if he can't stop wondering what this strange creature is doing in his life. She is quite at home here, with her own keys to the pink building and apartment number three. Her building is right around the corner, a little lower down Russian Hill, but Adam has never been invited to her apartment.

Lucille hums her way to the end of a verse before in-dicating that she has noticed Adam. "Come over here, lover boy," she calls out. "Ravish me." She is teasing him, Adam knows; she is well aware of what it is he finds so disturbing and so exciting about their sexual encounters. Adam hasn't seen Lucille for the past several days; over the Labor Day weekend she was in Los Angeles—with a man, Adam can't help thinking, though she certainly hasn't told him anything.

"Today was my first day at my new job," he tells her, "at the Stringfellow School." He gestures at his own brown corduroy jacket, his tie: a field of dark blue silk with a pattern of tiny white diamonds.

"Ah yes, I'd forgotten. How were all those deliciously wealthy little kiddies?"

"No students today. It was orientation, just teachers, none of them wealthy, I'm sure."

"Any of them delicious?" She rises from her pose on the love seat, takes Adam's hand, and leads him to his room.

Still not much furniture: the mattress on the floor, now neatly covered with a bedspread, and the little wooden dresser. Adam has tentatively decided against getting a desk. Desks are for students (like himself ten years ago) or for scholars (like his mother, like Suzanne). The walls are surgical white, recently painted, and Adam has so far put up only one item for display. It is a map of the city, a large and detailed street map, fully unfolded and very carefully tacked to the wall. The effect is surprisingly crisp, aesthetically satisfying in an unusual way. Adam is pleased to think that the map sets this room apart from the other rooms he has lived in over the past years, and he has spent hours alternately examining the streets up close and admiring the wonderful arrangement of the city from across the room.

Lucille collapses on the bedspread, which has a black-and-white pattern of large jungle animals drawn with a sort of violent primitivism, the animals intricately aligned and entangled. Lucille stretches, very sexy, almost the full length of the mattress (she is taller than Adam). He knows that it is still not the moment for sex, that when it is time she will let him know. He sits at the foot of the bed.

Lucille reaches a hand to the floor next to the bed and

picks up two torn envelopes. "Postman's been around," she says, waving the envelopes, in a tone that suggests the postman makes personal deliveries to Adam's bedside.

"From my mother," says Adam, "and from the woman I used to live with in Boston." He is mesmerized by the sight of those particular letters in the clutches of those particular painted nails.

"What's the news from back East?" Lucille inquires. She sniffs at the letters, as if she can read them just like that.

Adam teases her. "I wrote to my mother about you, and she wrote back that she admires you for choosing not to have a surname. My mother is very interested in the literary properties of names."

"I'm flattered," says Lucille. "Does the woman you used to live with also admire me?"

She thinks you are a succubus, and that you have a good eye for your prey. Adam, of course, does not say that, but he remembers Suzanne's words exactly. And, because he is not sure just how much Lucille can read in his face, he leaves her question unanswered and changes the subject. "One of the teachers at the Stringfellow School," he says, "is someone who was in my class at Yale. Isn't that a funny coincidence? Actually, I hardly knew her in college."

"I think you should ask her out on a date," says Lucille, dropping the two letters where she found them.

Adam laughs. "Why should I do that?"

"For the sake of Yale," says Lucille. "I think it would be sweet." By now Adam isn't sure whether or not she is joking. She is toying with him in a way he does not quite understand.

"I doubt she'd be interested in going out with me," says Adam casually.

Lucille has finished teasing him now. She rises from among the jungle animals on his bedspread and crosses the room to her sequined black bag. "Look what I've brought you," she announces, and unrolls for him the glossy black-and-white poster for her Gershwin show. The title of the show is *High Hat,* and alongside these words is a stunning, immediately recognizable caricature of Lucille, black hat on white hair. Adam is dazed for a moment by this evidence of Lucille's celebrity. But then he decides what to do: he takes four tacks and carefully, evenly, sets the poster of Lucille alongside the map of San Francisco. They don't go together in any coherent aesthetic way—the dull pastels of the map, the glossy black and white of the poster—but Adam is pleased by the juxtaposition.

"Thank you," says Lucille, and she reaches for his tie; her fingers expertly undo the knot as if she knows all about men's ties. Because she wears them herself, Adam realizes. *Now,* he thinks—

But the front door opens in the hall, and they hear Huck call out hello. Hi, calls Adam, wondering what will happen next. It is Christopher's voice that calls back, Hi. Hello, Huck, says Lucille, full voice. Hi, Lucille, and then Adam hears Huck's steps moving toward the kitchen.

"He knows about you and me?" whispers Adam.

"Of course he knows," says Lucille. She does not deign to whisper, but neither is she projecting across the footlights. She begins to unbutton Adam's shirt, while he still wears his jacket.

"You told him?" Adam whispers.

"Of course I told him. He's my best friend." She un-
buckles his belt and unzips his pants, the khakis of a prep-
school English teacher.

"What did he say?" Adam whispers.

Her hands reach behind him, and he feels her nails on
his buttocks. "He told me to remember," says Lucille, "that
you're his friend, and that you're an innocent." And then she
pulls him down into the jungle.

The minute Adam steps into the room, he knows that this
class—an honors course on the English novel—is going to
be his favorite. The classroom is one of the corner turret
rooms, hexagonal, with windows on four of the six sides.
There are no desks, just a half-dozen comfortable chairs set
in a circle (or perhaps a hexagon); there will be only five
students and Adam. The first day of classes is rapidly con-
firming what Adam began to suspect at orientation: that he
is very lucky to be teaching at the Stringfellow School. He
almost envies his students who are getting all this, instead
of what he himself got at his public high school back in
New Haven.

The five students arrive: a bright and arrogant girl
named Alexandra (who makes Adam try to imagine Suzanne
as a high school student); a tall, cheerful, athletic boy named
Gary; Chinese twins, Wendy Ming and Mandy Ming; and
finally, last to arrive, an oddly intense boy whose presence
enables Adam to check off the last name on his class list,
Conrad Winterfeldt.

Adam crosses his legs, sits back in his chair, and looks

around at this class. The twins (are they identical?) sit up straight, heads cocked to the side (one to the right, one to the left), waiting for Adam to begin teaching. Gary, on the other hand, does not hesitate to recline, his long legs stretched out toward Adam. Alexandra leans forward on the edge of her chair, waiting for Adam to say something she can challenge. And Conrad has crossed his legs just as Adam has (and the moment after Adam did); the curious expression with which he watches Adam has nothing in common with the dutiful attention of Wendy and Mandy Ming. He seems to be daring Adam to speak.

Adam introduces himself, tells them he is new at the Stringfellow School, tells them how lucky he thinks they are to have such an interesting room and such a small class; then he passes out the syllabus of ten English novels for the year. They can decide together on two others to add, depending on what the class is interested in. Any questions so far? Alexandra immediately wants to know, please, could they substitute some other Jane Austen novel for *Pride and Prejudice*, she's read that before; and could one of the additional two novels be French or Russian so they can make comparisons between different literatures? One Ming wants to know if Emily Brontë and Charlotte Brontë were twins. No, Alexandra has answered her before Adam can speak. Conrad just stares at Adam until Adam feels compelled to address him: Conrad, do you have anything to say? Conrad glances down at the syllabus, as if he's just realized it's there. If anyone else is interested, he says, he'd like to read *The Picture of Dorian Gray*. At which Alexandra speaks up to say that *she* would like to read *Mrs. Dalloway*.

Adam is very much enjoying this class—the talk and energy and even the hint of tensions below the surface, all bodes well for class discussions. Why don't you tell me something about yourselves, Adam suggests, so I can get to know you; who wants to go first? Alexandra wants to go first, and she begins to launch into her autobiography; too late Adam sees that these kids already know each other's autobiographies. He interrupts her (after all, they can write an essay about their personal histories for him tonight) and asks what everyone else wants to know about Alexandra. The twins ask immediately and almost in unison: Where are you applying? Adam should have thought of that; these are high school seniors, and they are naturally obsessed with college applications.

Alexandra wants to go to Harvard or Yale. The twins tell everyone that the headmaster has told their grandfather he thinks he can get them both into Yale (it is apparently unthinkable that they be separated), but their grandfather doesn't want them to go so far away, and so they will be aiming for Stanford; Wendy and Mandy tell the story as if it does not concern them, only their grandfather. Gary, everyone agrees, is such an exceptional first baseman that he will have eager offers of admission and athletic scholarships from every school he applies to. He wants to go to Stanford, but his father went to Berkeley and is sentimental that way. Mr. Berg, says Mandy (Mandy is the one with the jade earrings; Wendy's are coral), where did you go to college? Yale (they all nod approvingly), and you can call me Adam (the twins giggle). Adam, says Alexandra immediately, do you think you get a better education at Harvard or Yale? I don't know,

Adam replies, unable to choose between fantasies of Alexandra interrupting his mother's lectures at Yale and Alexandra driving Suzanne out of her mind in the discussion section of Professor Klingenstein's American literature survey. Where are you applying, Conrad? asks the coral twin (what if she and her sister trade earrings tomorrow?), but Conrad replies, I really don't want to talk about it. Oh, come on, Conrad, says Alexandra with irritation, and Adam guesses that she has been saying this to Conrad for a long time.

Conrad, you haven't said anything at all about yourself, says Adam. And there is a moment's silence while Conrad does not reply. He has straight blond hair, carefully combed, and very pale eyes, icy gray; odd, pointed features, the expression neither kind nor happy; a stiffly ironed white shirt, contrasting with Gary's bright red Stanford sweatshirt. Conrad Winterfeldt, says Adam, tell me about your name; it's very dramatic. My family is from Germany, says Conrad, as if he is being forced to speak (which, Adam recognizes, he is), from Prussia, but my great-great-grandfather came to San Francisco in the nineteenth century. He adds, bizarrely: So we aren't Nazis. Oh, come on, Conrad, says Alexandra; nobody said you were a Nazi. Actually my father was from Germany, says Adam quickly, trying to smooth over this strange eruption, and he certainly wasn't a Nazi; he was a German Jew. My family is not Jewish, says Conrad, as if that too is a point on which he is sensitive. Mine is, says Alexandra, challengingly.

What does your father do, Mr. Berg? says Mandy, who recognizes the need for a change of subject but cannot bring herself to call him Adam. My father's been dead for many

years, says Adam, but he was a physicist; he taught at Yale
after he left Germany. The physics and calculus teacher here
went to Yale, says Wendy; everyone likes her, and she wears
the best shoes. We were in the same class at Yale, says
Adam—which information the twins receive with a solemn
nod, as if Adam had just announced that he and Amy were
soon to be married. How long have you lived in San Francisco? asks Gary. Just moved here two weeks ago, says Adam.
What do you think? asks Gary. It's the most fabulous city I've
ever seen, says Adam—which brings applause from everyone
but Conrad, who seems condescendingly amused.

Where do you live? asks Alexandra. Hyde Street on
Russian Hill, Adam replies. What building? ask the twins,
again almost in unison, an odd question. Not the pink building? Really? Our grandfather owns that building! Actually he
owns lots of buildings on Russian Hill, but that one is the
twins' special favorite. Their grandfather painted it pink for
their parents to live in when they got married twenty years
ago, and he's kept it pink ever since, even though their
parents have long since moved to Pacific Heights, and the
pink house has been turned into rented apartments. I know
that building, mutters Conrad, half to himself, half to Adam.
Great building, says Adam, half to Conrad, half to the twins.
My compliments to your grandfather.

At the end of the class Adam assigns the first five chapters of *Pride and Prejudice* (Alexandra overruled), and re-
quests a page of written autobiography from each student. He
is not entirely surprised when it turns out that Conrad stays
behind after class, and he is curious about what the boy will
want to say. But as Adam shuffles his papers together into his

briefcase, he sees, stepping up to the threshold of the class-room, an unmistakable pair of shoes. "Are you free next period?" Amy says. "I stopped by to see if you wanted to get a cup of coffee in the faculty parlor."

"I am free, but I just want to talk to a student for a few minutes. Can I meet you there?"

Before Amy can agree, Conrad is out of his seat, saying, "I really don't have anything to say, excuse me."

"Are you sure, Conrad?" says Adam, stepping toward him, and accidentally letting a small piece of paper slip from the stack he is shuffling. Immediately Conrad kneels to pick it up; he looks at it hard for a moment, then passes it to Adam, and walks past Amy out of the room.

"Conrad is an odd kid," says Amy. And then, "What's that, a photograph?" She draws near to see what it is that Conrad knelt to recover: a copy of the photograph Lucille took of Huck and Adam and Christopher. Adam hadn't realized that he was still carrying it around. What did Conrad think of it?

"That's Huck," says Adam to Amy. "He was in our freshman class at Yale. Huck Malachowski." She looks at the picture carefully, but doesn't recognize him. "He didn't grad-uate with us," says Adam, but doesn't explain further.

"Is he your—"

"He's my roommate," says Adam, much too quickly, and Amy looks at him sharply.

"I was going to ask," she says slowly, "if he is your baby." She places her finger just below Christopher's chin. "He's beautiful." She pauses deliberately. "I mean the baby."

"He's Huck's baby," says Adam, still uncomfortable. "His name is Christopher. I think he's beautiful too, the baby."

They go off together to get coffee in the parlor, but, remembering that sharp look, and maybe also remembering Lucille the day before, Adam ends up asking Amy if she'd like to go out for a drink after school. She declines; actually, she has to meet a friend. But she promises him they'll do it some other time soon. And he knows they will.

CHAPTER SIX

GOLDEN GATE

On the bus Christopher is difficult, won't sit still, keeps trying to wriggle down into the aisle, and he screams when they pull him back onto the seat; his face collapses instantly into infant contortions of outrage and misery. Both Huck and Adam try everything they can think of to distract him, and finally Huck succeeds by offering his head and hair for Christopher to pull on, then groaning with his own adult contortions of exaggerated pain. Christopher enjoys that. Adam watches with interest as Huck submits to having his hair pulled down hard over his forehead, his nose grabbed and twisted in a fist, his mouth invaded by Christopher's aggressive fingers; Huck shields himself only when there is a sudden lunge for his eyes. Adam pays no attention to where they are going, doesn't even look out the bus window, and so, after twenty minutes, when they come to the end of the line and get out, he looks uncertainly at Huck, as if to ask . . . where? And Huck gestures with the palm of his hand, look up, and the second Adam does so, there it is towering over him; he missed it only because he is actually standing so close.

He has seen the Golden Gate every day from the corner on Hyde Street, looking down Russian Hill, then over Pacific Heights and beyond to the distant Presidio, to the point where the bridge begins. His first day in San Francisco Adam felt as if he could almost reach out and touch the bridge from his corner, but since then, as the view has become more familiar, the bridge has come to seem more and more distant and inaccessible. Anyway, this morning Huck proposed a Saturday excursion with Christopher, and so now, for the first time, Adam stands at the foundation of the bridge.

They climb up an iron staircase that takes them to the level of the bridge itself. The fancy stroller has been left at home today, and Christopher rides in a backpack carrier on Huck. Christopher seems perfectly happy now that they are off the bus, and he smiles down at Adam from his superior perch, his head stretched to one side so that he can see over Huck's shoulder. Up on the bridge there is wind over the water, and more wind from the cars that are whizzing past across the bridge. Christopher's silky hair is blowing, his silver-blue eyes excited; as if to balance himself he holds a shock of Huck's hair clutched in his fist, but now he doesn't pull. There are moments, and this is one of them, when the baby is so transcendently beautiful that Adam can't keep looking at him. He looks away, out to the ocean, then up at the graceful red frame of the bridge, back to San Francisco behind him; and each view in itself is tremendously beautiful, each makes Adam dizzily happy, but it is the baby who has somehow become the infinitesimal point of focus for winds and vistas that carry the eye to the most distant and most splendid horizons. I will never forget this moment, Adam vows, and then the moment is already passing.

While Adam was looking away from the baby, Huck has begun on the pedestrian's path that leads across the bridge, and now Adam runs to catch up. He lets his eyes rest, not on Christopher, but on Huck and Christopher together. The baby alone is dazzling, but father and son together are only superbly handsome, and Adam is no longer overwhelmed, only touched with a pang of envy.

The noise of the passing cars and the whistling of the wind make it impossible to talk without shouting as they walk. Halfway across, though, when the red span above has descended to its lowest point and is about to ascend again, Huck stops and leans on the railing to look down at the water. Adam stops beside him, and Huck lowers himself a few inches to bring his head to the level of Adam's, moves close so that their ears are actually touching; Christopher is riding just behind that point of contact, still holding a handful of Huck's hair. And now, with the bay before them and the ocean behind, Huck's shaven cheek almost against Adam's beard, they are close enough to speak to each other over the traffic noise.

"If you fell off the bridge right here," says Adam, "would the currents carry you under the bridge and out to sea, or would you float into the bay and wash ashore?" It is the question of a young child, Adam thinks.

"Don't know," says Huck. Then, "Sometimes I imagine myself riding under the bridge on a raft and paddling across the ocean."

A raft. Adam thinks of his mother's letter, of Huckleberry Finn and the Mississippi River. But he says, "With Christopher?"

Huck closes his eyes, as if to consult his own fantasy.

"No," he says finally, "when I imagine it, there's only me. It's something that I've imagined for a long time though, since before he was born, really since I first came to San Francisco and walked across the bridge." It is as if he is apologizing for leaving Christopher out of the fantasy. But what he does not say is: Oh, you know, Huck Finn. Almost as if he is unaware of his literary namesake.

"What did you do after you left college?" asks Adam, thinking: How is it that I have not asked him this already? What is it about him that makes it so hard to ask him about his life? Adam is conscious of the point at which their ears are touching, of the baby behind them, and the ocean behind the baby.

"I went home to Michigan," says Huck. He speaks to the water, speaks smoothly as if he has learned his lines, but without altering his usual conversational tone. There are no emotional shadings of expression. "I got a job, assisting a housepainter, and I paid my father two hundred fifty dollars a month for my room and board. That was my triumphant return from Yale."

"Paint any houses pink?" says Adam, and it is as though, now that Huck is finally talking about himself, Adam can't help trying to stop him. "Did I tell you there are these Chinese twins in my English-novels class whose grandfather—"

"You did tell me," says Huck, resolutely returning to his story. "When I came home from painting houses, I watched TV all evening long, and on Sunday I went to mass with my mother. That was really important to her, especially because of my brother. You know, my brother, you remember—"

Adam nods to say that he does remember, since obviously
he's expected to remember, but not until after he nods does
it come back to him that Huck's older brother was killed in
Vietnam while Huck was still in high school, a Catholic high
school. How could Adam have forgotten something like that?
Now he can even remember Huck confiding it to him, from
upper bunk to lower bunk, in dignified secrecy, with a warning that this was not to be desecrated by being mentioned to
that young Republican in the adjoining bedroom, Slimy Sam.
Adam had solemnly accepted the secret, and then, over the
years, forgotten it.

"At first I used to watch anything at all on TV," Huck
continues, "you know, *Get Smart* and *Star Trek*, and then I
started to become interested in the bugging at the Watergate,
and I followed the TV news, and eventually it was the only
thing I wanted to know about. That summer I quit my job so
I could watch the hearings all day long, and when my father—you know, he voted for Nixon—told me to stop watching that shit, I took the little bit of money I had left and
bought my own television, and I watched it in my room with
the door closed. I was completely obsessed with Watergate for
an entire year; I mean, it was genuinely sick how obsessed
I was—my mother even asked the parish priest to talk to me
about it. I told him that in church on Sunday I prayed that
Nixon would be destroyed, and he told me he did too, but
wasn't it time for me to think about leaving home and getting
on with my life? But I wasn't ready for that until the next
summer, that was seventy-four, when Nixon finally resigned.
My father came home from work that day, and I was in the
kitchen with my mother, and he came up to me and said,

'Wipe that shitty grin off your face.' And very early the next morning I left home, stuck out my thumb at the corner, and started hitchhiking to California."

One night when Huck was returning to the Yale campus through the streets of New Haven from Democratic party headquarters, he came upon a three-legged dog. The dog followed him home to the dorm, and, since keeping pets was absolutely strictly forbidden, Huck and Adam both immediately decided to give the dog a home. He looked like an Airedale and was, therefore, a rather large dog to be keeping in secret refuge, but at least he didn't bark or howl much. Huck named him Kingman, after the president of Yale, and sometimes amused himself by addressing to the dog earnest speeches thanking him for giving them the best undergraduate education in America. Huck and Adam stole food for Kingman from the Commons, let him romp around in his awkward three-legged way in the Old Campus (insisting, if asked, that they didn't know whom he belonged to), and made a bed for him in the corner of the living room of their suite. Slimy Sam, to their relief, did not object, and even showed a certain interest in the possibility that Kingman might indeed be a pure-bred Airedale and, despite his missing leg, could perhaps bring in some money as a stud. Adam and Huck discussed the possibility of renting out Slimy Sam as a stud for fathering the young Republicans of the twenty-first century.

Slimy Sam was, of course, too slimy to have a sex life. Huck also had no girlfriend, although he was certainly handsome enough for someone to fall in love with, like, for instance, the girl who did the photography project. Adam, one night, met a girl from Albertus Magnus College at a mixer, brought her back to the room with him, and lost his virginity on the lower bunk in fifteen minutes of desperate clumsiness, while Huck sat at his desk in the living room, Kingman across his lap, sorting index cards with the names of registered Democrats. For all the talk of stud service, that was probably the only act of sexual intercourse consummated in the suite during that whole fall semester; they were, after all, just three college freshmen and a crippled dog. Adam can remember neither the name nor the face of the girl to whom he so ignominiously lost his virginity, but he does remember very clearly (could it have been late that same night?) Huck pressing the dog to his chest and saying, "Sonofabitch, Adam, I love this animal like a brother."

It couldn't last, of course. Eventually they received a note from a dean, reminding them that it was forbidden to keep pets in the dormitory, suggesting that they make other arrangements immediately if they were not in compliance with this regulation. So they schemed. Huck knew a girl who was a sophomore at Calhoun, where Huck and Adam, supposedly, would also be living sophomore year, and he prevailed upon her to keep the dog, as a favor, just until Huck and Adam could take him back next September; Calhoun, Huck reasoned, would be less under the eyes of the deans than the freshman Old Campus. But there was no sophomore year for Huck, not even a spring semester of freshman year. And it was that spring, while Huck was painting houses and watching television in Michigan, that Kingman was hit by a car two blocks from campus and killed. Adam only heard about it a week after it happened, when he ran into the girl at Calhoun; she was very sorry but also, Adam guessed, a little relieved to be rid of the crippled dog. Huck probably still doesn't know, after all these years.

"Remember that dog at Yale?" says Adam, testing, standing on the bridge.

It only takes Huck a moment. "Kingman," he says. "Remember how old Slimy wanted to rent him out to lady Airedales? I wonder what ever happened to Kingman." Adam waits. "Probably," Huck continues, "he's still at Calhoun, passed on from student to student over the years. I'd like to think that he's still giving them all the best undergraduate education in America." Adam and Huck both laugh. "Let's go," says Huck, "let's make it to the other side of this bridge."

"What's on the other side?" asks Adam. The map on his wall ends where the bridge begins, and he has been half supposing that they would now walk back to the side they started from.

"Just Sausalito," says Huck, "boutiques and souvenir shops, and a ferry that takes you back to the city. Oh, and pelicans, I want Christopher to see the pelicans."

Adam too would like to see the pelicans, is eager for the adventure of crossing to the other side. "Let me take Christopher on my back now," he offers. "You've carried him all this way." He takes hold of the backpack carrier, and Huck slides out of it, then Huck takes hold and Adam slides his arms under the straps. Christopher watches the whole maneuver with fascination, as if the two men were engaging in some ritual that had nothing to do with him. As they set off walking,

and the red span above them begins to ascend to the second
red tower, Adam feels Christopher's tiny fist grasping a patch
of hair and holding tight.

When they are finally off the bridge, on land again, they
pause by the side of a highway, still two miles from Sausalito
according to a nearby road sign. They start out walking.
Adam is growing tired, though, and beginning to be deafened
by the noise of passing cars; he is also a little nervous about
walking along the edge of a highway with a baby on his back.
Christopher is tired too, and, apparently indifferent to the
noise of the highway, he has fallen asleep, completely relax-
ing on Adam's back in a way that makes him seem twice as
heavy. When Huck suggests that they hitchhike, Adam (who
has hardly ever hitchhiked) at first protests on behalf of the
baby. But Huck, who once hitched rides all the way from
Michigan to California in the aftermath of Nixon's resigna-
tion, thinks there is nothing to worry about. What could
happen to two grown men hitchhiking? The only danger,
Huck says, is that nothing will happen, no one will stop for
them: two men is not the best combination for hitchhiking.
But the baby, Huck hopes, will make them seem benign and
might attract someone's curiosity or sympathy. He holds out
his thumb and turns Adam sideways, so that his profile with
the sleeping baby is visible to drivers. Adam feels uncomfortable and exposed. Huck, on the other hand, is clearly enjoying himself, jerking his thumb out every so often with a sort
of thrusting sexual energy. Adam thinks: This is what he can
do instead of floating out to sea on a raft. And then: But aren't
we too old for this now?

Huck is talking to Adam, shouting at him really, though
incoherently; half a phrase is lost every five seconds as a car

goes by with a zip and a roar. Huck is explaining his theory that when you have a baby you can't help devoting your whole life to the baby anyway, and so you have to try to live as much as you can just the way you would if it were you alone. Adam has heard all this before from Lucille, and, peculiarly, Huck's principle had a more convincing air when she presented it than when Huck himself is explaining. A justification for selfishness, Lucille had said, and, witnessing Huck's excitement now as he stands at the side of the road with his thumb stuck out, Adam can see that she was right.

What actually disturbs Adam most about this reflection, however, is his increasing consciousness of the complicated confidential connections between Huck and himself, himself and Lucille, Lucille and Huck. How is Adam to know which confidences are legitimately within the bounds of triangular friendship, and which might cross those bounds and be seen as betrayal of friendship? Adam and Lucille are lovers, of course—or at least sexual partners—but Adam suspects that they will never really be friends, or, if ever, only in the future. As for Huck, Adam cannot help feeling that the weight of their friendship lies in the past and perhaps also in the future—while their present relation has a certain vague and weightless unreality. The connection between Huck and Lucille is most mysterious of all; for, if it is friendship, it must be terribly intense, and if it was ever romance, then it has somehow strangely failed to find its form. Adam wonders: Why did Huck tell Lucille that I was an innocent?

"Damn, nobody's stopping," says Huck. "Hey, Adam, squat down. Let me take the baby and see if that will make a difference." Adam squats by the side of the road and feels Huck lifting Christopher, still asleep, out of the backpack

carrier. "Awww, baby, baby, baby, baby," Huck sings softly.
Adam rises, feeling miraculously light, and sees that Christopher is sleeping on Huck's left shoulder, the side away from
the highway. Huck's right thumb is now moving with a different motion, swaying, as he rocks from side to side with the
baby. For a moment Adam, dizzy with his own lightness, sees
the scene as a sort of religious painting: young father with
sleeping infant, hitchhiking by the side of a California highway. It seems very strange and also terribly moving. Then
Adam shuts his eyes hard, opens them again, and he sees
Huck and Christopher as they are, familiar figures, his new
roommates. He also sees a little red car pulling off the road
just past them, and Huck turning toward it, exultant,
"Sonofabitch!"

"We're just going a few miles down the road to
Sausalito," says Huck. He is sitting next to the driver with
Christopher in his lap. Adam is in back, feeling like an
unnecessary extra in this adventure and wondering still if
they aren't too old for this—except for Christopher, of course,
who is certainly too young. Christopher, Adam observes, does
not look angelically peaceful in the manner of the proverbial
sleeping baby; there is an almost grim set to his features, a
tension in his breathing, as if sleeping is something that calls
for determination. Which, under these circumstances, perhaps it does.

"My baby," says Huck to the driver, "cute, huh?"

"Real cute," says the driver, not pleasantly Adam
thinks. Adam takes an immediate dislike to the driver. He is
probably about the same age as Huck and Adam, with a thick
black mustache and a tee shirt cut off to show a flat abdomen
covered with black hair. Adam is aware that almost no one

would think this man was ugly, the opposite in fact, but there is something disturbing about the way he leans into the steering wheel, something almost nasty about the expression with which he watches the road. "Where's your wife?" asks the driver. "What are you two guys fucking doing with a baby?"

"My wife's an astronaut," says Huck, unperturbed, so easily that it takes a second for Adam to realize what is going on. "She's in training now for a big space mission," Huck further explains. "So I'm spending a lot of time taking care of the baby."

"One of those lady astronauts, huh?" The driver is impressed. "Who takes care of the baby when she's in space and you're at work?"

"Day care," says Huck.

"Day care!" exclaims the driver with odd relish, laughing and removing a hairy hand from the wheel to pat his flat hairy stomach. "Did you read about those day-care places in Los Angeles where they were sexually abusing the kids and making porno movies? Did you read about that? Shit, I bet that happens a lot." This is a topic the driver obviously enjoys. He seems prepared to talk about it at length, and Adam is greatly relieved that they are already entering Sausalito and can make their escape. As they are getting out of the car, when Adam forces himself to look directly at the driver and thank him, he notices that one of the man's hands, holding the steering wheel, is artificial, a metal mechanical device.

Adam feels disturbed by the ride and the driver, as though he himself has been somehow abused. He is glad that Christopher was sleeping through the whole thing, and will carry away no impression whatsoever of the nasty black mustache, the odd posture, the mechanical claw. Huck, on the other hand, seems quite content with the adventure as they stroll into Sausalito. "You do meet some weirdos," he comments, cheerfully. Adam reflects that the world is a sinister place, and that, above all else, they have to watch over Christopher.

After the lonely windiness of the bridge and the awkward vulnerability of the highway, Sausalito feels like a return to civilization. It is, as Huck said, a rather limited little civilization of souvenir shops and boutiques, with an appropriate population of tourists and shop attendants, moving through their prescribed motions in the California sunshine.

Adam and Huck step into a shop called The Golden Gate and aimlessly inspect an extensive collection of bridge paraphernalia: tee shirts, coffee cups, brooches, baseball caps, calendars, even a big room-size rug displayed on the wall of the shop. A tour bus of senior citizens pulls up in front, and the shop is invaded by elderly Texans who swarm over the collection, making Texan exclamations over the many precious items. Somebody drops a Golden Gate martini shaker, which shatters on the floor, but the attendant rushes to pick up the pieces, smoothly assures the Texans that it is nothing at all, please just go right on shopping.

"Aileen, will you just look at that sweet little baby sleeping up on that boy's back in that contraption."

Christopher has attracted the attention of the Texans. Aileen, however, who must be eighty, doesn't like what she sees, and doesn't hesitate to say so. "Young man," she says, and Huck turns politely, "that's not healthy for that baby to be sleeping up there like that. He's going to get bad cramps."

"I don't think so, ma'am," says Huck. "I think he's comfortable."

"He's going to get bad cramps," repeats Aileen emphatically. And then, irritated at being contradicted, "Where's that baby's mother anyhow?"

"She's an astronaut," mutters Huck, but Adam can see that his heart isn't in the game.

"Well, how do you like that, one of those lady astronauts! She just runs off to have fun in outer space and leaves this useless good-for-nothing boy to take care of that poor sweet little baby, when he wouldn't even know how to take care of a chicken. Young man, that baby is going to have bad cramps." But the group is getting ready to depart, and Aileen and her friend are called over to the cash register to pay for their kerchiefs and key chains.

Huck says softly to Adam, "It's true, I wouldn't know how to take care of a chicken."

"You'd manage," says Adam, who has picked up a paperweight, one of those clear plastic bubbles containing a little red model of the bridge. He shakes it, and a flurry of white snow rises to fall again over the tiny red bridge. He shakes again, fascinated. "Huck, does it ever snow in San Francisco?"

"Never," says Huck, also staring at the paperweight.

"I'm going to buy this," says Adam.

After they leave the souvenir shop, they move on to an ice-cream place, where Christopher finally wakes up and takes a messy interest in Huck's ice cream.

"Lucille told me you told her I was an innocent," Adam begins, as lightly as he can; has he crossed any invisible boundaries? And implicitly: she told me she told you about her and me. "What did you mean?"

Huck is not uncomfortable, or even surprised, so apparently no confidences have yet been violated. "I guess I meant that you were new in San Francisco, and so you had to be innocent. I certainly was—before I came to San Francisco."

This is entirely disarming, and all Adam can reply is, "What about Christopher? He was born in San Francisco. Isn't *he* innocent?"

"Guess not. He'll never be innocent now, born in sin and forever after." What exactly is that supposed to mean? "And besides, he's all wet. My baby is wet, wet, wet!" Christopher is separated, protesting, from the ice cream and laid out on his back on the booth seat beside Huck, who changes him with the casual efficiency that Adam finds so admirable.

As Huck is bending over the baby, Adam becomes aware of someone several booths behind Huck who is watching them, smoking a cigarette. Adam recognizes the face when the watcher finally approaches, walking behind a somewhat older man whose open neck is covered with shining gold chains. The man with the gold chains passes by, and a second later, long thin fingers touch Huck's shoulder from behind. "Howdy." The voice of Oklahoma. His hat is in his hand.

Huck looks around, startled, from the freshly diapered Christopher. "Wayne. I was wondering what had happened to you."

"I'm doing fine," says Wayne; he reaches out his long fingers and strokes Christopher's beautiful hair, now sticky in spots with melted ice cream. Wayne's friend has apparently stopped at the door to wait for him, because Wayne nods in that direction that he is coming. "Bye now," he says, putting on his hat.

"Call me," Huck says, "call me soon." As Wayne walks away, Huck watches him leave, and Adam watches Huck.

While they are waiting by the water for the ferry that will carry them back to San Francisco, Adam finds himself suddenly and inexplicably grabbing Huck's arm, as if to steady himself. The next moment he is apologizing, saying he doesn't know what happened to him. As he then looks around, he notices that the small crowd gathered at the ferry stop is all stirred up. People are hurrying away from the water's edge; one man is actually running. Up on the main street customers are coming out of shops, and shop attendants are hovering in the doorways. There is at first dead silence, then a roar of talking punctuated by a distant scream.

"Sonofabitch, an earthquake," says Huck excitedly, "an earthquake—come here, baby." Without waiting for Adam to assist him, Huck swings the backpack with the baby quickly off his shoulders and around, catching it easily. He takes Christopher into his arms, up against his chest, just as Christopher begins to cry in delayed response.

"An earthquake?" Adam is dubious; he really didn't feel anything; he was thrown, it seemed, by nothing at all. "Just like that?"

"Sure it was," says Huck, "your first earthquake. Now you really live in San Francisco." Huck seems to feel it as a matter of personal largesse. The earthquake is a gift, a treat, that he bestows first upon Christopher, then upon Adam.

"It was just a little earthquake," Huck continues, a hint of disappointment in his voice. "Just a little baby earthquake," he tells Christopher, who has stopped crying and is looking around him at the excited crowd. "People are afraid that it might just be the beginning, or the warning for a really big earthquake. That's why everyone's running around."

Adam looks over the scene, half expecting to see a great crack in the earth running down the main street of Sausalito, or fire in the hills above the town. The only surprising thing he sees, though, is a form in the distance that he thinks he recognizes, a form that immediately disappears into the crowd. Adam is feeling rather proud of himself for having survived his first earthquake, a little disappointed that it passed so quickly. "Do you think there's still going to be a big one?" he asks, turning toward Huck.

"Nope," says Huck. "Hey, look at the pelicans. They wouldn't be out if there was really something cataclysmic coming on. Look, Christopher, look at them dive." There are three of them, just at the edge of the bay, diving for fish one at a time, taking turns. Christopher watches intently, laughs when they dive, and then suddenly cries, "Da!" and points out over the water, showing Huck and Adam, who have been too occupied with the pelicans to notice, that the big ferry boat is arriving.

The couple in front of them in line for the boat carry on an extended debate over whether it is safe to go out on the water if another earthquake is coming. At the last minute, just before they reach the boat, the man, who is certain that a tidal wave is imminent, prevails over the woman, and they pull out of line to wait for the next ferry in an hour. Adam follows Huck and Christopher on board. Huck has no hesitations; he'd be whistling, thinks Adam, if he only knew how.

They sit on a bench on the deck. As they cross the bay, the sun is already setting, red-orange, descending toward the ocean in the west. It is a flaming disk poised between the two towers of the red bridge that now stands between their boat and the ocean, plainly a gateway. As they approach San Francisco, the sun falls below the bridge, crossing the point where Huck and Adam and Christopher had stopped to look down at the water hours ago, in the early afternoon. "Apoo!" exclaims Christopher, hungrily, pointing at the red sun, and Huck, laughing, tells him it is not actually an apple.

"I thought I saw one of my students back there in Sausalito," says Adam, "right after the earthquake."

"One of the Chinese twins who owns our building?"

"No. A boy, a strange boy named Conrad Winterfeldt. I thought I saw him first in Sausalito, and then again getting on this boat. Do you think it's possible that he's following me?" Huck shrugs, indicating that he does not think being followed is so unlikely as to be out of the question. "He stays after class every day, as if he wants to talk to me, and then he never says anything. And during class he says things, but they're usually not connected to what everyone else is discussing. And he addresses himself directly to me, as if no one else were there. I gave the class an assignment to write a short autobiographical essay, and the next day Conrad told me that he couldn't do it because it was too personal a thing, and what right did I have to ask him for the story of his life?"

"What did you say?"

"That it was an assignment, that he had to do it, but he was welcome to withhold any information he considered too personal for me to know. To which he said, Well, what was the point of his writing it then?"

"It sounds like he has a crush on you."

"That's what Lucille said," says Adam. "But, you know, I'm not the type of person people have crushes on." When Adam said that to Lucille, who obviously was the type, she readily agreed, perhaps too readily.

Huck, who is also the type, reflects for a moment. "There's something about the way you seem here in California," he says. "Still out of context, maybe, or a little foreign, or even innocent." He grins. "And it adds something to the way you come off to other people. Anyway you're his teacher, right? Hell, anyone is allowed to have a crush on his teacher. That's what education is all about. You really think the kid is on this boat?" But there is no sign of Conrad for the rest of the trip, and Adam does not see him when they get off the ferry in San Francisco.

The big earthquake is waiting for them at home in the pink building on Hyde Street, in an envelope addressed to Huck, no return address. He unlocks the mailbox with a tiny key, then uses a larger one to open the front door of the building. He gives the keys to Christopher, who jangles them while Huck opens the envelope in the mirrored lobby. Huck reads the letter, and then passes it silently to Adam, standing on the stairs under the rose glass chandelier. One sheet of notepaper with a single sentence scrawled on it: "I want my child." And a signature in the same block letters that identify the painter of the raging green sea with the pink spot that hangs upstairs in the living room. Adam reaches for the envelope, which Huck is still holding, and braces himself for the postmark: San Francisco.

CHAPTER SEVEN

THE WOMEN
AND THE BOYS

When Tommy and Timmy discover that Adam has never even heard of *The Women,* naturally they invite him along to the Castro on Friday night, when they are going to see the movie for the ninth and seventh times, respectively—four times together, and five and three, respectively, before they met. This fresh revelation of Adam's innocence, and the consequent invitation, take place as the three of them are running along the wharf. Of the four friends in the pink building—Huck, Adam, Tommy, Timmy—three of them now regularly go running together while the fourth (they take turns) stays with Christopher. Adam feels good about the running—the whole arrangement reminds him a little of playing basketball with his housemates in Cambridge years ago—but he also feels good about the days when he stays behind with Christopher. He has begun to take lightly the moments when Tommy and Timmy seize upon some beloved cultural totem and then profess themselves scandalized that Adam is quite unfamiliar with it—like "Anyone Can Whistle" and

"Small Hotel," and like this movie, *The Women*. Huck, on the other hand, who recognizes all these references, never uses them with Adam, leaving Adam with a perversely unsatisfied sense that he and Huck remain locked into the friendship they formed their freshman year in college. Although Adam's cultural consciousness has tended to revolve rather narrowly around nineteenth-century English literature and eighteenth-century classical music, he is altogether ready to embrace whatever San Francisco values; he is certainly ready to go to the movies with Tommy and Timmy. He even invites Amy Armstrong to come along.

Lucille thinks of nothing but Gershwin these days. The opening of her show is only a week away; she is perpetually humming to herself, turning the palms of her hands to slightly different angles. For her, sex with Adam seems to have become a highly concentrated distraction from Gershwin, and Adam is pretty sure that she won't invite herself along to the movies when, uneasily, he mentions only that he is going with Tommy and Timmy. As for Huck, he is staying home with Christopher. He talks a great deal about Christopher's birthday lately, and his mood alternates between jubilation and sentimental sadness.

"My baby isn't going to be a baby anymore," he says, half to Adam, half to Christopher. Adam combs his hair in the bathroom mirror, waiting for Tommy and Timmy to stop down for him, and Christopher is being diapered. Adam puzzles over whether perhaps his appearance has changed since he has arrived in San Francisco. He hasn't had a haircut, so his hair is certainly a little longer and fuller—but he wonders whether it might also be lighter in color, just the slightest shade. And his beard, which he has kept trim, might also be

a little less dark than it used to be. But above all Adam
wonders whether his whole face may not have become a little
more weathered, more settled, more handsomely aged. He
almost recognizes himself as embarked upon a new period of
his life. He finds he can imagine his appearance ten years
from now, and the picture appeals to him. His gazing into the
mirror is interrupted by a knock on the door. Adam opens it
to see, not Tommy and Timmy, but Wayne wearing his cowboy hat. Howdy. His eyes have a bloodshot look, and Huck
says hello to him with some concern, certainly with no sign
that he has been expected. A minute later the knock is for
Adam, and the three boys go off, leaving three boys behind.

At the corner of Castro Street and Market there is also
no shortage of boys. Adam has visited this block before in his
exploration of San Francisco, but hesitantly, by day. He
knows it by reputation as the center of gay San Francisco. To
see it now on a Friday night is to see it really living up to that
reputation, and Adam feels not so much uncomfortable as
dazed. Everywhere boys, and men who look like boys, and
men who are with boys, and short haircuts and leather jackets
and shiny metal studs. And something in the air that is
sharply male and unmistakably sexual. For relief he focuses
on the Bank of America across the street.

Tommy and Timmy have joined the crowd waiting under
the marquee of the Castro Theatre to buy tickets. Adam
stands on the corner alone, people passing, sometimes seeming to circle him. He is watching for Amy, and it seems it will
not be hard to pick her out of the crowd. From behind him
Adam too is being watched, by men and boys who are drinking under Tiffany lamps and hanging plants in a bar with
glass walls. When Amy steps off a trolley at the corner, Adam

waves to her, maybe too demonstratively, notices her shoes, then very consciously greets her with a touch of his hand on her elbow, a gesture whose warmth goes beyond that of their past exchanges in the halls and parlor and yard of the String-fellow School. He himself is half in the scene, and half watching from behind imagined glass.

She is not actually the only woman on the corner. There are several women there, and more under the movie marquee, so it must be just Adam's self-consciousness that makes Amy seem to be the only woman on the block. Amy herself betrays no sign of unease; Adam is watching. She is not surprised by the hint of demonstrativeness in his greeting, not surprised at being at the center of gay San Francisco. Adam introduces her to Tommy and Timmy, who are wearing matching kelly-green sweaters that Tommy acquired as a tribute to Timmy's Irishness. Amy and Adam also seem to match in style; they both dress for a date the same way they dress to teach prep school. The one incongruous detail is, as usual, Amy's shoes, which this time are scarlet high heels with a shiny pink rosette just above the toe of each shoe. Adam allows himself to steal quick glances without staring openly; Tommy and Timmy are bolder. But Amy preserves a pleased air of not noticing. She is a sort of mermaid, thinks Adam; she is totally transformed from the ankles down.

"How many times have you seen *The Women?*" Tommy is asking Amy. "I've done nine, and Timmy's done only seven."

"Only seven," echoes Timmy.

"I've never seen it," says Amy frankly.

"Never!" exclaims Tommy.

"Yes, never," Timmy tells him. "That's what she said."

"Just like Adam," reflects Tommy. "Why, you're both virgins!"

"Virgins indeed," says Timmy.

"Do you really think so?" says Amy, speaking with perfectly composed mock seriousness, while turning her shoes pointedly toward Tommy and Timmy.

After a moment Tommy says, "Love your shoes," as if it is the answer to her question. Adam, who has until now regarded Amy's shoes as somehow beyond comment, watches with interest to see how she will respond.

"Love 'em," says Timmy.

Amy smiles distractedly, as if she isn't quite sure that they are referring to *her* shoes, as if she really cannot account for herself from the ankles down.

The Castro Theatre is an enormous old movie palace, full of reflecting glass and worn velvety upholstery. There is organ music playing as the crowd pours down the long aisles, and the seats are filling up so fast that finding four together means approaching very close to the big screen. Amy mentions to Adam that she thinks she saw one of his students in the back rows, and he does not even turn around to see because he is sure she is right and equally sure who it is.

Adam is sitting between Amy and Tommy, and, when the organist changes tunes and there is a ripple of applause, it is Tommy who signals Adam: now the movie is about to begin. As the applause subsides Adam is surprised to hear that there are people in the audience who are singing along, and the refrain is the name of the city, San Francisco. A song everyone knows—another cultural totem that is brand new to Adam. He looks at Tommy, perplexed, and Tommy whispers a quick, incoherent explanation (the old movie, Jeanette Mac-

Donald, always before every show here); Tommy is half singing along himself.

> *San Francisco, welcome your wandering one;*
> *I'm coming home, to go roaming, no more.*

Great excitement and anticipation, combined with some of the air of Castro Street outside. The lights are dimming; the high panels of reflecting glass become opaque, then invisible. And a huge palace full of boys—well, mostly boys—is ready for *The Women.*

There are bursts of applause from the audience as the credits announce the actresses, mostly names that Adam barely knows. There are wild cheers for the name of Joan Crawford, and Adam, although he knows the name, is not sure that he will actually recognize her on screen. ("Joan Crawford?" he whispers to Tommy, who whispers back, "I'll tap you on the knee.") From the opening lines, Adam is aware that he is present at a cult experience, amidst an audience that knows the movie by heart, has seen it ten times and will see it ten more times. This he finds alienating, as if San Francisco is still posing him cultural tests of initiation that he will never be able to get beyond. Must he be enthralled by scenes from a women's manicure palace, and must he adore this woman who is so irritating and whose husband is surely entitled to be unfaithful, and can one actually distinguish all these women from each other? Restless, Adam shifts his weight toward Amy, then toward Tommy, then toward Amy again.

He is impatient with the movie, and his mind begins to wander.

There has been another letter. Adam took it in from the mailbox, immediately recognized the handwriting of the address, checked the postmark without much hope, and left it in Huck's room. Nothing was ever said about it between the roommates. Then yesterday Lucille appeared with the news that she thought she had seen Miriam on the corner in front of her apartment building, but the woman was gone a minute later when Lucille came out to look. (What, wondered Adam, would Lucille have said had they come face to face? What would Adam himself say to Miriam?) Did you know she was in San Francisco? Lucille asked Huck, and he nodded. Why didn't you tell me? Lucille demanded angrily, and Huck shrugged. *You* knew, didn't you? said Lucille, suddenly turning on Adam, who nodded. Why didn't *you* tell me? But Adam too could only shrug. He could hardly protest that he didn't know whether Huck had already told her, or wanted him to tell her.

Whatever construction of channels has come into being among us three, thinks Adam, staring at the movie, is not going to be strong enough or sure enough to handle whatever is going to happen next. His own connection to Lucille is too new, and his connection to Huck is too old. Besides, when it comes to the crisis, it will be the connection between Huck and Lucille that matters most, and that remains mysterious to Adam. He doesn't know its history or structure—what elements of friendship or love or sex go into it, and how they combine—but he senses that there is a tremendous emotional exchange that has somehow missed all the prescribed channels and created something that Adam could not easily describe or define even if he knew more than he knows.

Lucille wanted Huck to call the police, which he refused to do. He had already, however, called Miriam's mother, who had always hated him; she blamed Miriam's pregnancy for her mental disorder (although Miriam was never sane), and so she blamed Huck (instead of herself). Miriam, she told Huck on the telephone before hanging up on him, was no longer in the hospital—and Huck had better fucking stay away from her and put his Polack dick up his own ass. Delightful woman, muttered Lucille; a woman who might bestow upon her daughter a consummate refinement of manner. She has nothing to do with her mother, Huck insisted, maybe more for Adam's sake than Lucille's. Miriam's mother is a woman who, since her husband left her twenty years ago, has done nothing but get drunk in a big beautiful house in Beverly Hills, get drunk and drive her daughter mad. Huck refused to discuss it any further. In fact he infuriated Lucille by turning to Adam and asking how he thought they should decorate the apartment for Christopher's birthday party.

Adam begins to get the point: there are only women in this movie. And it bothers him. What would his own life be like, he wonders, if there were only women in it? If there were no Huck, no Christopher, no Tommy or Timmy—only Adam and Lucille on Russian Hill—it is almost frightening. And at school only Amy Armstrong in the parlor, no patriarchal headmaster, only Alexandra and the Ming twins to discuss Jane Austen (Conrad has disappeared into a great crack in the earth). Adam would still be able to write to Suzanne and his mother; in fact, he must write to them soon, he owes each of them a letter. With only women in his life, thinks Adam, it would be too stylized, or too threatening, or too completely unbalanced. Adam feels a wave of affectionate sympathy for his own sex—the weaker sex, he suddenly thinks—without which, it seems, he would not feel at home in his own life. Even here, in the Castro Theatre, where the boys all around him seem part of an alien culture, he is somehow reassured by their maleness. Adam imagines penises, rows and rows of them, erect, looking attentively, hopefully, upward toward the big screen, watching the movie—in which there are no penises at all.

There is a jab at Adam's knee, as the screen shows a woman behind a perfume counter: Tommy's signal for Joan Crawford. Adam doesn't think he has seen her before; the largeness of the features, somewhere between beautiful and grotesque, makes him think of Lucille and of the alien nature of women. He hears the passionate breathing of ecstatic admiration in the audience around him, and he finds himself erect, a figure in his own fantasy, reaching up toward the screen. As the camera devotes itself to that female face, now beautiful, now grotesque, always alien, Adam hears himself breathing sharply along with the audience around him. He senses that Amy has turned toward him. Did she see Tommy signal him with a poke on the knee? Can she recognize in the dark what is inside his pants? He shifts his weight toward her, brings his arm around the back of her seat, and rests a hand on her shoulder.

"Jungle red!" exclaims Tommy, out in front of the theatre after the movie, holding out his nails before his eyes. They are closely cut and completely masculine, and although the movie was very much concerned with jungle-red nail polish, Adam is not quite sure what Tommy is suggesting. "Jungle red!"

"That could be jungle red," says Timmy, respectfully indicating Amy's shoes. Amy looks down at them as if she has never noticed them before.

"I think jungle red is more crimson," says Tommy, "something bloodier."

"Bloodier?" reflects Amy meditatively, as if she has just pictured a new pair of shoes.

"Lucille wears nail polish that might be jungle red," continues Tommy. "But we'll never know what jungle red really looks like, since the movie is eternally black-and-white."

"Eternally," says Timmy.

"Lucille's show is opening next week, isn't it, Adam?" Why does Tommy appeal to Adam for Lucille's particulars? Does he know that they are lovers?

"Lucille, the cabaret singer? Do you know her?" asks Amy.

"Do *you* know her?" says Adam, too quickly.

"I saw her Rodgers and Hart show last year," says Amy. Adam waits for a judgment but none is forthcoming. He forces himself not to ask: What did you think? Considering the circumstances, it would not quite be in good taste for him to ask Amy to express an opinion about Lucille.

"She's a friend of my roommate Huck," says Adam, offering a highly dishonest truth.

They are now on the corner of Castro and Market, before the bar with the window front. Adam is again intently conscious of boys, of maleness, of sex between men—something that he can barely imagine. There is a tapping on glass from behind them. Everyone on the corner turns around, but the boy in the bar is signaling to Timmy, who goes right up to the glass and mouths hello. The boy beckons, and Timmy turns back to the other three. "Someone I work with," he says. "Want to go in and have a drink?"

"They scoop ice cream together all day long," explains Tommy grouchily, "and talk about opera."

"All day long," says Timmy. "Do you want to get a drink?"

"Yes, as a matter of fact," says Tommy, who seems to think it quite enough that Timmy and his colleague should spend their days together without him. "What about you two?" He is talking to Adam and Amy. "Want to know what the men behind the ice-cream counters are saying about opening night at the opera?"

Adam looks at Amy questioningly, but her face says that she is leaving this up to him. "No thanks," he says, half regretting it. What, after all, does it feel like on the other side of the glass?

Adam hesitates on the corner, just long enough to see Tommy and Timmy appear on the other side, then hears himself saying, "Do you want to come home with me?" Quickly he adds, "Maybe you could meet my roommate, the one who was in our freshman class."

"I'd like that," says Amy.

"Want to walk part of the way?" says Adam. It is a beautiful night, just a little bit cool, and Adam is really in no hurry to get back to the apartment with Amy. They will go to bed together now, he suspects, and that pleases him—but he feels no urgency.

They set out down Market Street, the great diagonal that cuts across the city; Adam knows it well from the map on his wall. For the first few blocks they pass boys who are on their way up to Castro Street, but then Market becomes more deserted further down, and Adam takes Amy's hand as they walk. Is it possible that Conrad Winterfeldt is following in the dark behind them? Adam wonders. He does not turn to see.

Amy walks with tremendous poise on heels that, to Adam, look rather high. When they pass under a streetlight, she lifts her feet with particular spirit; the pink rosettes look almost alive. Soon they are overtaken by a trolley, which carries them quickly to another trolley, which takes them to Russian Hill.

Their conversation, crossing San Francisco, is comfortably innocuous, and Adam now has the feeling, as he lets Amy into the pink building, into the mirrored lobby, that he knows her less well than he did an hour ago. Ever since they left Castro Street, ever since Adam began to suspect that they would sleep with each other, he has felt that he is losing his sense of her, has even wondered if she is intentionally effacing herself. Or perhaps, rather, they are both effacing themselves, in anticipation of a sexual encounter that will call for ritual behavior rather than personality.

"Huck must have gone to sleep," says Adam, as they enter the dark apartment. It is after midnight. "That's Huck's door there, and that's the baby's room. And this one is mine."

The one decorated wall has developed, grown; Adam sees it as a sort of live aesthetic process, a natural aggregation of items around the central map of the city—and also an extension of himself projected upon the wall. There is the black-and-white poster featuring Lucille in caricature. And beside it is a companion caricature of the mayor of San Francisco, a gift from Huck to Adam, drawn by the same friend of Lucille's who did her poster. (In the artist's eye, the mayor is obviously no more mayoral, no less a cabaret act, than Lucille.) There is also, framed under glass, the photograph of Huck, Christopher, and Adam taken by Lucille that first evening. Just above is a framed photograph of Adam and his mother: Adam two years old, his mother a young woman of the 1950s, at Yale. At the edge of the map, where the city ends and the bridge begins, Adam has displayed an old black-and-white postcard of the Golden Gate. There is also, under glass, a neatly posted clipping from the San Francisco *Chronicle*, describing the small earthquake that occurred last weekend, when Adam and Huck and Christopher were in Sausalito. The newsprint looks already old against the background of the sharp-white wall.

Beginning with the moment that he leans over and kisses Amy, Adam thinks constantly of Lucille. He is not comparing Amy with Lucille, not that at all, but rather assessing himself as a lover of two different women. It is as surely he who first kisses Amy as it was Lucille who first kissed him. It is Adam who reaches his hand under Amy's sweater and slowly raises it above her breasts before she pulls it over her head, just as it was Lucille who unbuttoned his shirt and pressed her palms onto his chest. Adam who slips his hand under the waist of Amy's skirt from behind, reaches his finger between her buttocks, just as Lucille unzipped his pants and marked the inside of his thighs with her painted (jungle-red?) nails. Adam who brings Amy down onto the bedspread, fucks her looking down into her eyes, the wire-rim glasses removed, her face even less familiar to him now than before, fucking her with a rhythm that he himself is setting, and varying, faster and slower, as he likes. She likes it too; he sees that and feels ridiculously proud. He holds back his own orgasm, showing her and himself that he can, and when he comes he is unusually unshaken by it, as if to prove that even then he need not lose control.

All this is observed only by Amy's two shoes, which she has posted carefully beside the mattress. They have the air of live creatures, and the two rosettes could be strange pink eyes. Adam invites Amy to stay the night, offers her one of his tee shirts to sleep in, takes her in his arms and tells her she is beautiful, all with self-conscious delight in the conventional ritual of the occasion.

"I hope you don't mind my mentioning this," says Amy at last, softly and firmly, "but, you know, you really ought to have asked about birth control first. It would have been polite. It would have been sensible too—unless you're eager to find yourself living here with two babies." And, before Adam even knows whether he is going to protest or apologize, she continues, "Don't worry—I put in my diaphragm before I went out to meet you at the Castro. Anyway I don't think I'm very likely to get pregnant."

"I apologize," says Adam. And then, still holding her, "Why not very likely? What do you mean?"

"I tried to get pregnant for years in Iran," says Amy, now more sad than firm. "And I just never succeeded. Of course it could perfectly well have been my husband's fault, but he didn't think so, and his family certainly didn't think so. It was really the end of my grand career as a Persian wife."

"The end?"

"His family became very keen on his picking up a second wife, an Iranian wife, a Moslem, someone who would produce babies. It would have been legal there, no problem under Islamic law. And my husband, the bastard, with his Yale Ph.D. and all the trimmings of Western civilization, was willing to go along with the scheme. Anyway, while he was working on the plans for the second wife, I was working on my plans to leave him and get out of Iran. And here I am."

"Are you still married to him?" Adam asks. "I mean legally, technically. Or did you work out a divorce?"

"He was executed after the revolution for no particular reason," says Amy. "Which is certainly worse than he deserved. Technically—to answer your question—I'm a widow. But all that seems like a long time ago, and it's surprising how little it seems to matter in my life nowadays."

What Adam is thinking, as he falls asleep next to her, is that Amy has already lived through the weird drama of her life, and put it behind her. Probably nothing else that ever happens to her will have the character of strange adventure, and that is what accounts for her confidence and composure. Whereas for Adam life has been relatively smooth so far, and if adventure and tragedy lie in his future, he will just have to wait for the course of events to carry him to that point. If in the meantime he is occasionally restless, well, perhaps he should not yet be too eager to feel at rest.

In the middle of the night Adam is awakened by terrible screams, the like of which he has heard only once before. He is half surprised to find Amy beside him on his mattress, and he notices that she too is awake, alarmed. It's the baby, he reassures her, and then remembers what Huck said that other night, Adam's first in San Francisco, that Christopher might be disturbed by having a stranger in the apartment at night. Guiltily Adam gets out of bed, leaving Amy, the stranger, behind. Huck is standing naked in Christopher's room, holding the baby to his chest, just as he was that other night. I'm sorry, Adam starts to whisper, but Huck says, Adam, please, could you get the bottle of milk in the refrigerator and dilute it with some hot water for Christopher. Sure, of course. On the way to the kitchen, Adam passes the open door to Huck's room and registers (he is too sleepy for shock) that there is a body in Huck's bed and a hat on the floor. In the dark it is only the narrowness of the body's outline that stays with him, but that is enough for him to know that it is Wayne; and anyway, now that he has seen, he is not actually surprised— has he suspected this all along? He feels foolishly relieved, since it is not necessarily Amy's presence that is giving Christopher nightmares. But there is no time to think of any of this now. The water from the kitchen tap has finally warmed, and as quickly as he can Adam fills the half bottle of cold milk with hot water, shakes the bottle to mix the temperatures, and turns back to Christopher's room.

CHAPTER EIGHT

TABOO

Dear Maman,

Last night Huck and Lucille and I finally sat down together to make real plans for Christopher's birthday party, a week from next Sunday. It's going to be quite an affair: we came up with more than a hundred names for the guest list, including ten babies and a monkey. Earlier in the day Lucille had asked me if, as far as I knew, Huck had actually been making any preparations. I said I didn't think so, and she looked concerned and said, if someone's birthday is in October you have to have the party in October, you can't put it off until February, and what was going on? Lucille was right. Huck had slipped into a sort of casual paralysis in which he was probably going to just keep talking about the party as something that was about to happen, and then just stop talking about it when the birthday went right by.

Lucille said to Huck: This is really sick, it's not your party remember, it's Christopher's. Christopher was climbing around Huck, on Huck's bed, and Lucille and I were standing in the doorway. Christopher could hear his name and knew that we were talking about him, so when Huck looked dejected Christopher pulled himself up so that he was standing, leaning on Huck's shoulders, and he smiled at Huck very purposefully to cheer him up. Huck smiled back, and the next thing I knew we were all sitting on Huck's bed, and Huck was making a list for invitations.

This is the part you like, right? The emergence of a text within the text of my letter, right? Well, it's just a list of names (but, of course, names are just what you are interested in now), and the only ones you'd know are our three at the top. Huck Malachowski, Adam Berg, and Lucille. The other names on the list tend to fall into a couple of broad categories: the babies in Christopher's day-care group and their parents, people Huck works with in the mayor's office, and other friends and neighbors in San Francisco. Lucille is inviting some people connected to her new Gershwin show (the pianist, the producer), and I think I'm going to invite some people from the Stringfellow School, maybe a couple of teachers and definitely some students from my favorite class. I'll tell you the best name on the whole list: Huck is actually going to invite the mayor of San Francisco, and he thinks she will at least put in an appearance at the party. Because she likes him, and she was delighted with Christopher on the several occasions that they have met. Her presence, of course, will make Christopher's party a real San Francisco event.

Anyway, if the mayor is the guest of honor, the monkey will be second in importance. Lucille's producer is a woman who lives alone with her monkey, and they are both being invited, which should be fun for the ten babies, who will probably not be all that impressed by the presence of the mayor, however glamorous. And Lucille's accompanist also belongs to a three-man jazz group, and Lucille thinks they might be willing to come do the music for not too large a fee. As for the food, this is what Huck has decided: we live right on the other side of Russian Hill from Chinatown, so the morning of the party we'll just dash through the tunnel under the hill, and dash back with Chinese dumplings and spare ribs and dim sum things, and that will be the food. Can you believe we're doing all this for a party for a one-year-old? It's crazy, isn't it? I'm almost embarrassed at feeling so excited about it.

I'm glad you like the picture of me and Huck and Christopher, and you can see what an amazing baby he is (Christopher, I mean). I have a copy of that photograph up on the wall in my room here. And also one of you and me: the one where I'm a funny-looking two-year-old in a sailor suit with an expression of terrible perplexity, and you are looking very beautiful and are obviously trying to explain to me whatever it is that I am finding so confusing. Could you send me a photograph of you and me and Papa—or even just of me and Papa, since I have the other one of you and me?

I should tell you that all this excitement here is combined with intense anxiety: Miriam, Christopher's mother, is now somewhere in San Francisco, and she has been sending Huck letters demanding her child. It's not clear exactly what this means or what she intends to do, but she is certainly not sane (you can tell just from her handwriting) and should certainly not have been let out of the hospital in Los Angeles, and Lucille thinks that Miriam might be following her. Huck doesn't talk about this much, but I know it's on his mind, and I'm sure that's part of why he was paralyzed about getting on with the birthday party.

I only know Miriam, so far, from her painting and from

a couple of scrawled notes—a set of texts, right?—but I am becoming curious to know more about her, even though I suspect it would be better if our paths never crossed. I confess I have a sort of fantasy that I sometimes fall into, a fantasy of meeting her, coming upon her when she is crazed and frenzied and desperate—and, in my fantasy, I say something to her, just a few words to soothe her, and they turn out to be exactly the right words, and after that she gratefully and gracefully disappears from our lives and the crisis is past. I wonder what she is really like, and I also wonder, if I understood better just what she was, would I understand better what Huck is too? There are things about him that I do not understand at all, and although he is not someone who strikes you as a mysterious person—on the contrary—still, I am starting to find living with him to be a sort of mystery.

Thank you for writing to me about your past, and a little about your love affairs, and how you feel about Harvey. I was shocked at first (do you think I am very innocent?) but when I reread the letter I was moved by your heroism (that's a strong word, I know), the heroic way you face your life and know yourself. I thought even your confession of unromanticism was, ultimately, romantic, and, I guess, very French. I'm not like that, I don't think: not French, and not in a straightforward relation to my own life. My life sort of leads me on, and I follow a few steps behind, confused. I am ready to like Harvey, I think, especially if you have really gotten him to stop using French phrases, and also especially if he knows "Small Hotel." Will you come visit soon? I want to take you for a walk across the Golden Gate Bridge. I know it's too late (and probably too inconvenient anyway) for you to come to

Christopher's party, but think of him, and come see him soon.
And come see me. I love you,

Adam

P.S. I have been through an earthquake, just a little one.
What do you think of that for a postscript?

P.P.S. After what you told me about your near encounter with
Oswald Klingenstein, I suppose I should tell you that Suzanne is having an affair with him. Actually—in case you are
now wondering—this did not really have much to do with our
breaking up. Shall I also tell you that, according to Suzanne,
his sexual practices require as physical props the collected
works of Ralph Waldo Emerson? How's that for a post-
postscript?

Dear Suzanne,
    At first, I admit, I was angry about your letter and
offended by your various insights into my character and motivation. This probably comes as no surprise, and I wonder if
you'll be disappointed when I say that, after rereading your
letter and thinking about it for a while, I am no longer angry.
In fact, I feel like I got the letter I deserved, maybe even the
letter I was angling for. I suppose the magnificent way you
took me to pieces reminds me as much of why I loved you for
so long as of why I've also hated you sometimes. And I
recognize that some of the things you said about me are true.
After all our years together, I guess you ought to know.

So imagine me smiling at you to show that I've gotten your various jokes, which were, I understand, at my expense. I don't mind seeing myself harshly from someone else's point of view, I've decided, since a harsh caricature is better than no clear picture at all. Suddenly, since coming here—maybe it's my age—I've begun to feel the need for a clearer picture of myself.

I am enjoying teaching my high school students. Since I know you don't even like teaching college students, I'm certain you will interpret this enjoyment as a flaw in my character. I have a favorite class, a very small one on English novels, which meets in a turret room with comfortable chairs instead of desks. There are Chinese twins, a first baseman, a girl who reminds me a little of you, and a very troubled boy who seems to be following me around San Francisco. The troubled boy was, at first, extremely morose in class; and sometimes nasty, but that was when we were reading *Pride and Prejudice*, which he hated. Now that we are reading *Wuthering Heights* he has become much more amenable to discussion, and was very clever on Friday when he was explaining why he saw Heathcliff and the narrator as the two polar figures in the novel, not Heathcliff and Cathy. At which the girl who reminds me of you (her name is Alexandra) accused him of ignoring the whole female side of the book. And then the twins and the first baseman lined up according to sex, and there was a rather lively, sometimes naïve, discussion of the sexual politics in *Wuthering Heights*. There was almost nothing for me to do but sit back and listen. I am very fond of this group, and am inviting them to Huck's baby's birthday party on Sunday. The troubled boy, I think, may even have stopped following me, since I have not sighted him lately; he does still have to write for me an autobiographical essay, which he has been obstinately, provocatively refusing to write. Everyone I know here says that the boy must have a crush on me, but I am not the sort of person people have crushes on, am I?

Something very disturbing is also happening at the Stringfellow School. The man who teaches the American literature classes, who is maybe ten years older than me and has never been very nice to me, has started missing school occasionally, and I end up having to cover his classes. This week, after he missed two days, he came back and accused me of messing up his teaching notes (which I had never even looked at), and I told him I had only covered his classes anyway as a favor to him and to the school, and he didn't have to be such a bastard about it, and he told me I was a piece of pig shit (do you agree?), and I couldn't think of anything clever enough to reply, so that round was over. Later I was talking to Phyllis, the other English teacher here—actually, she teaches writing. For the last forty years she has been writing novels that don't get published, and she is extremely sweet, and she mothers me (you know how I need that) and sometimes brings little treats to add to my lunch (honestly), but she also mothers him, my enemy, Graham. Anyway, she told me, very confidentially, that Graham has AIDS and he's going to die, and that's why he behaves the way he does, and she said I really should continue to cover his classes for him when he has to check into the hospital for a few days, so he won't lose his job before he's ready to resign. Well, how did I feel? Like pig shit, I guess. Very peculiar: to know, in secret confidence from a third person, that someone you don't like is going to die soon. It makes me wonder, I guess, what it would be like to know that someone you liked, or even loved, was going to die like that.

Having told you about Lucille in my last letter, and having been properly dissected and denounced for it, I feel somehow obliged, for the sake of completeness, to tell you that I am now also having an affair with a woman who teaches at the Stringfellow School, someone who teaches physics and calculus—what do you think of that? What would you think if I added that her great idiosyncratic passion is for extremely dramatic shoes? I await your reply, trembling—do not spare me.

Neither Lucille nor Amy knows about the other one yet, which may sound sleazy and sneaky to you, but it is really not, because neither relationship has actually gone so far that the two of them couldn't have other lovers too whom I don't know about. Lucille, I'm sure, does. Also, still for the sake of completeness, and at the risk of provoking your merciless criticism, I must tell you that Amy is not at all like Lucille sexually. To use your word, she is not a succubus. In fact I find myself rather self-conscious about the difference between them, and I wonder what it means. You'll tell me, won't you?

Amy was in my class at Yale, and after graduation— when I moved to Cambridge and discovered the world, and eventually discovered you and true love—Amy married an Iranian physicist, moved to Teheran, adjusted to a whole new world, then let it all go when she left her husband. Would you be surprised to hear that she makes me feel a little bit un-worldly? The other thing that she makes me feel, however, is that I have somehow successfully become an appropriate adult lover. You see, I know that she would never have been interested in me back when we were both in college—her great college romance was an Iranian graduate student, the one she ended up marrying. But now, mysteriously, she and I are right for each other, and I strike her as a desirable partner. And I would even become vain enough to see myself that way were it not for the fact that I look into her eyes and suspect that, for all my appropriateness and desirability, she regards me with a certain measure of ironic amusement. So I try to see myself that way too. The truth is, I still don't know Amy all that well, and when I'm not with her I don't even think about her that much, yet I feel that somehow, potentially, we are very much involved with each other.

Right now, the person I really do think about all the time is not Amy, not even Lucille, but Huck. There is something I want to confide in you about Huck and why he is so much on my mind. When I wrote to my mother a few weeks ago, I sent her a picture of me and Huck and the baby, and I made some remark (idly, innocuously) about people seeing us together as a little family and thinking maybe that Huck and I were a couple. And now I've found out that Huck really is gay, or at any rate that he sleeps with men, or at least with one man—a boy really, a boy from Oklahoma—whom I saw in his bed in the middle of the night. I have not said anything to Huck about it; I don't know whether I'm entitled to say anything. Eventually, I suppose, I will mention it to Lucille, and she will mention it to Huck, and it will be circuitously, or rather triangularly, discussed, and I will understand better what is going on. But right now Lucille is frantically involved with final rehearsals for a Gershwin show she's performing, and she has no time for discussing such delicate subjects with an innocent like me. Although she did find a half hour last night to knock me over backward and have her way with me.

And she is also willing to take time to help plan Christopher's birthday party. Still, I will not ask her about Huck until after her show opens. I'm not even sure what I want to ask anyway.

You may feel free to destroy my character in your reply. You may also write to tell me which classics of American literature you and your distinguished professor have been profaning in his office. As you know, I do not particularly cherish the classics of American literature, or even the sanctity of literary scholarship.

With love,

Adam

Dear Mr. Berg,

I refuse to address you by your first name. I know you mean well in asking your students to do so. I know you want to encourage a friendlier, less formal, less authoritarian relationship with your students. Still, I think there is something inherently condescending in your gesture (inherently I say, no particular fault of yours), and something unavoidably false. Also I don't want to be just one of your students with whom you encourage friendly, informal, non-authoritarian relationships, and anyway I am attracted to formality, and even to authoritarianism. So, Mr. Berg, I will not call you Adam. Remember, you are almost fifteen years older than I am; you are maybe ten years younger than my mother.

I have also, as you have occasionally been good enough to remind me, refused to write for you an autobiographical essay. I told you I considered it a violation of my privacy, but that is not quite the full truth. In fact, I would be glad to permit you to violate my privacy, to do whatever you wish with my privacy, to carry it home with you and devour it, but I resent being violated in this particularly trivial way, and in the company of Mandy, Wendy, Gary, and Alexandra. At any rate I have by now violated your privacy so egregiously by spying on you (as you have, no doubt, noticed) that I almost feel obliged to permit you to violate mine however you wish, even trivially. I am therefore writing you this letter, which I hope you will consider to be my autobiographical essay, and I am mailing it to your home address. I have passed by your building enough times over the last few weeks to learn the street and number, but I have not bothered to find out your zip code. I leave that to you as an unviolated mystery.

Did my classmates begin their essays by telling you about their family backgrounds? I know that Alexandra's grandfather was a poor immigrant Jewish socialist in New York City, and for some reason she is very proud of that. I know that Mandy and Wendy's grandfather was a poor Chinese immigrant who now owns about as much of San Francisco as anyone. (I wish *I* owned the building you live in.) My grandfather was not a poor immigrant, since it was *his* grandfather who came to America, and then out West to San Francisco at the time of the Gold Rush. That makes my family one of the oldest and most illustrious in the city, even though we aren't nearly as rich as the Mings. Actually, my family was from the Prussian aristocracy, but they couldn't have been very distinguished aristocrats there, or they wouldn't have ended up in San Francisco, would they? So don't be intimidated by my social distinction. Very funny, I know. You can call me by my first name.

Do you remember at the first meeting of our class how I made a point of insisting that my family had been in San Francisco for generations and so, despite our German name, we weren't Nazis? You probably thought that was weird, or at any rate gratuitous; actually it was a lie. My father's family has been in San Francisco since the Gold Rush, but my mother's father was an S.S. officer in Nazi Germany. He killed himself in 1945 when Germany lost the war, a few months before my mother was born. My mother and father met in Berlin twenty years later, got married there, and have been living in San Francisco ever since. So we really are Nazis, or at least one of my grandfathers was. You are the only person I have ever told about this, but then I only found out about it myself two years ago, and since then you are the only person who has demanded an autobiographical essay. How am I doing? How are you doing? Does it bother you that my grandfather was an S.S. officer, and your grandfather was a German Jew? Do you think it's part of why I am reacting to you the way I am?

I found out about my grandfather when I was in Germany two years ago. The Stringfellow School can arrange for you to spend a few months studying in a foreign country, so I went to Germany, of course. I had never lived anywhere except San Francisco, my whole life. People like you who come here from somewhere else always fall in love with the city, but if you have lived here all your life you end up taking it for granted, even if you are deeply attached to it in your own way. Anyway, my mother has an older brother who lives in Berlin, and that's where I went, and I became friends with my cousin who is five years older than I am, and he told me about our common grandfather. He also took me all over Berlin, and wanted me to sleep with him, but I wouldn't. You see, I was in love (or something like that) with someone else at the time: My cousin took me across the Wall to East Berlin one day, and I fell in love with one of the East German soldiers who stood near the checkpoint. After that I used to cross over to East Berlin as often as I could just to get a look at him, but he never said a word to me. I used to watch him march away when he came off duty, goose-stepping just like a real Nazi. I guess you and he are the only real people I've ever been in love with, although, frankly, I think the way I felt about him was closer to romantic love than the way I feel about you. Naturally, it's important to me that my autobiography should be as frank as possible.

Real people, I say, because I also fall in love with characters in books. Like *Wuthering Heights.* There is only one character in *Wuthering Heights* whom anyone could fall in love with, regardless of what Alexandra says. And I don't think there are any characters in *Pride and Prejudice* anyone could fall in love with; they are all so light and shallow and easy to see through. My favorite work of literature is *Death in Venice.* I learned German three years ago by reading *Death in Venice* in German and in English at the same time. My mother never speaks German, ever, and my father barely knows how. When I was living in Berlin I went with my cousin to Venice for a week (but I still didn't sleep with him), and decided that that is where I would like to die too. San Francisco is fine, but ever since I realized definitely that I was homosexual, I have wanted to leave this city, because it is too easy to be homosexual here. Next year I will probably go to

Yale, which is what the headmaster has suggested, and I suppose it will make my parents happy (my Nazi parents). In the course of spying into your life I have learned that not only did you go to Yale but also your mother is a professor there. My curiosity about meeting your mother might even sustain me through the unbearable tediousness of filling out the application. Would you like to write me a letter of recommendation? Ha ha.

I have never had sex with anyone. Ever. I am a virgin. I do not masturbate because I do not like the idea of it. Sometimes I come in my sleep, and I actually like the idea of that, but it hasn't happened to me now in more than six months. I would like to sleep with you, but I do not know whether you ever sleep with anyone besides your lover. He is handsome, isn't he? I am fascinated by the diagonal lines that descend from his nose to the ends of his mouth. I also like his name (Polish, is it?), which I have seen next to the buzzer for your apartment. Since his eyes are the eyes of the baby, I suppose that he is the baby's father, not you. I wish that it was you; I like to imagine you with the baby. I imagine you in all sorts of innocent contexts because, since I do not want to masturbate, I cannot allow my thoughts to become too explicitly sexual. I love to see you in the streets of San Francisco. You look somehow wrong here, just subtly out of place; there is something East Coast about the naturalness of your beard (it doesn't frame your face; it *is* your face), and there is something always a little confused in your eyes. I sometimes think of your face as a Jewish face, though I know you are only half Jewish, and I'm sure you are no more religious than I am. Still, I like to think of you as a Jew, and then I am touched with sympathy for you, and then deepest sympathy for myself. It's all right if you don't want to sleep with me. Precise consummation is not as important to me as vague yearning. Is that an eloquent note on which to end my autobiographical essay?

Conrad Winterfeldt

P.S. I am sending you a copy of *Death in Venice,* in English, along with this letter.

P.P.S. Who is the woman I once saw following me when I was following you and your lover? She looked very unhappy.

Dear Adam,

Sleazy and sneaky? Just because you are carrying on wildly with both Lucinda and Mamie, and neither one knows about the other, while I, your former lover, am selected to know all about both? You, sleazy and sneaky? Adam, what a babe you are. Certainly I would not say that you are the sort of person one would have crushes on, but perhaps you are such a babe that it makes you irresistible, at any rate to high school students. Incidentally, don't mess around with your students, one way or another. It is pedagogically unsound, morally questionable, and probably illegal.

Besides, you aren't gay. You don't have enough charac-ter to be gay. Sorry. I get the feeling that your astounding discovery about your roommate is intended to lead you into some utterly hypocritical and affected confusion about your own sexual identity. Don't even bother wondering. Remember, you are the gallant lover of Lulu and Amelia. Remember (as if there were any danger of your forgetting!) that you and Huck were freshman roommates at Yale, possibly the least potentially gay connection in the whole kingdom of Ivy League sexuality. Do not think that any of your sexual hints or poses are going to make an impression on me of all people. Remember, I know you pretty well.

By the way, someone called here last week and asked for you (you are still listed in the Boston phone book, of course), and I said you didn't live here anymore, and he said he was your freshman roommate at Yale, and I said you were living in San Francisco with your freshman roommate and he said he was *also* your freshman roommate and could he have your phone number, and I said I didn't have it but gave him your address and said he could find the number, probably under Huck's last name whatever that might be. Did you have a third roommate in college? He sounds creepy. Do you suppose it was actually some lovestruck high school student who plans to send flowers?

Actually I thought you and I might have a chance to have an abusive reunion in California, because Klingenstein is going to the Melville conference at Berkeley next month and I had thought of going with him, but now his wifey, suspicious little thing, insists on going along herself to keep an eye on her great white whale. So, alas, I will be staying home in Boston with Dreiser. How I should have loved to see you! How I should have cherished the opportunity to meet Anaconda and Luellen! Klingenstein took me to Walden Pond after dark one evening last week, and for a chilly but passionate half hour we went at it in the woods in the imagined presence of Henry David Thoreau. I am sending you, with this letter, a copy of *Walden,* both for your moral and spiritual edification and to help you get a feel for this memorable scene. As ever,

Suzanne

Dear Adam,

This is just a short letter, because I am working so hard on a paper. The paper is on naming and names in *Billy Budd,* and I am working so hard on it because I have decided that I want to deliver it at the Melville conference in Berkeley next month. I hadn't been planning to attend (most people say such stupid things about Melville at these conferences), but it would give me such a good excuse, and the paid airfare, to visit you in California. At first I thought I could never finish the paper in time, since I am teaching two courses this fall, but I've become determined to manage somehow.

What fun to make a list of people to invite to Christopher's first birthday party! What an honor for Christopher if the mayor of San Francisco comes to his party! I have to admit that I don't know anything about the mayor of San Francisco, which I hope you will not mention to your friend Huck, who already disapproves of my political indifference. Harvey, however, has heard of this mayor and says that she is not only an important political figure but also a Jewess. Harvey is the kind of Jew who always knows (and tells) who is Jewish and who is not. I know this seems a little obsessed and maybe simpleminded, but I am almost charmed by it since the instinct is so profoundly structural, the polarization of the world into two clearly defined moieties. It is as if he had read

Lévi-Strauss, yes? But, of course, you have not read Lévi-Strauss yourself, so you cannot quite appreciate. It is also anthropologically interesting to me that I have once again, exogamously, married a Jewish man, as if I too am living according to some implicit sense of marital moieties.

You write to me that living with Huck becomes more and more mysterious, and I think it is always like this when you live with someone. Even Harvey, whom one would not call a mysterious man, begins to seem mysterious to me as I go on living with him and growing fonder of him. How can there be such a person? I ask myself. And this interpenetration of familiarity and mystery is also, I think, a dialectical issue of structural analysis, obviously applicable in so many ways to the analysis of literature. Harvey cannot come with me to California in November—there is an ophthalmologists' convention that week in Acapulco—so you will have me alone, as I'm sure you would prefer, and as I would prefer as well.

I do not like the idea of Suzanne as the lover of Oswald Klingenstein. I think it is wrong for teachers to have affairs with their students. From her point of view, I understand that he is attractive; and perhaps she has been struck, as I once was, by his resemblance to Nathaniel Hawthorne. I wonder if she suspects that she is writing her dissertation under the guidance of a man whose literary sensibility is fundamentally stupid, who is less intelligent than she is, and whether having an affair with him is her way of running away from that suspicion. From his point of view, I find the affair morally reprehensible. Or rather—forgive me for taking you back to structural anthropology—there are certain patterns of coupling that are taboo, and it is this concept of taboo that helps to define for any society a certain structural coherence.

Adam, I am sending you with this letter a photograph of you with your father. You were just a few months old, and we were visiting Princeton for a physics conference. The shape on the left is, I believe, Albert Einstein—I am such a bad photographer that I cut off everything but a little white hair and an ear at the edge of the photograph. Still, you and your father came out quite nicely. As well as the photograph, I am sending two other items in a separate package: a copy of *Moby Dick* for you, and a teddy bear for Christopher on his birthday.

With all my love,

Maman

CHAPTER NINE

I'VE GOT A CRUSH ON YOU

The lights go down and then out, there are ten seconds of perfect darkness and silence, and then a single spotlight on Lucille: her face and hair, her long neck, just a hint of broad shoulders below. Then applause, lots of applause from all the little tables, because, after all, Lucille is a star in San Francisco, and this is the opening of her new show. Adam is applauding too, just as if he didn't know her at all (does he?), just as if he were not her lover (is he?), as if the spotlighted face were the authentic original and the face that he has kissed (been kissed by) only a less vivid, even counterfeit version. The vividness now is not just the redder than usual lips, the blacker lashes, the whiter hair, but the absolute isolation of that one circle of light in the darkness of the crowded cabaret. She is not beautiful, not even pretty, thinks Adam, who, like everyone else, can't take his eyes away from her perfectly solemn, outrageously gaudy face. And then the applause stops, the unseen piano is heard, the lips begin to sing.

I've got a crush on you, Sweetie Pie.
All the day and nighttime hear me sigh.
I never had the least notion
That I could fall with so much emotion.

Slowly the spotlight expands to show all of Lucille, all of the stage, the piano, the accompanist, and the shadowy forms of the audience, including Adam.

Adam is sitting with Tommy and Timmy at one of the little tables that fill the cabaret hall. He sips at his drink, stares at Lucille, and remembers watching *The Women* at the Castro Theatre. Lucille is like that: as alien as the women in the movie, a woman who seems to have been dreamed up to be watched, not touched, by men. And Adam must remind himself that he has, in fact, touched her, held her in his arms, made love to her (been touched, been held, made love to). No one else in the hall, thinks Adam, could possibly suspect that he is the only one . . . the only one . . . well, maybe not the only one; he swallows the thought.

Adam has not invited Amy on this occasion. He is now tensely conscious of the fact that he has two lovers, conscious of it whenever one of them is present. When he had slept with Amy only once, even twice, it was both titillating and reassuring (and essentially false, he knew *that* even then) to think of a night with Amy as an infidelity to Lucille (who never expected fidelity and so could not be cheated on). Now that he and Amy have spent three or four nights together (really, the telling point is that he isn't quite sure unless he thinks back carefully, three or four), now that he has had sex with Lucille maybe ten times (again, he isn't sure), now he is unquestionably the lover of both of them and must try to understand what that signifies. For certain, it means that he cannot invite Amy to Lucille's show. Amy still doesn't know about Lucille; whether Lucille knows about Amy is a matter of her own intuition and of Huck's sense of discretion in his triangular friendship with Adam and Lucille. Soon enough Lucille and Amy will come face to face—at Christopher's birthday party on Sunday.

Impossible for anyone to face Lucille tonight, certainly not as a rival, even an unsuspecting rival. Adam watches Lucille moving, singing, absorbing the spotlight and reflecting it back at the audience. The company of Tommy and Timmy is oddly reassuring to Adam. If anyone could see the three of them around this little table in the audience (but no one can, the light is on Lucille and everyone is watching her), they would appear as three friends, San Francisco friends. And even if someone supposed that Adam was gay, surely there could be no explicitly sexual assumptions made about *three* people out together. And how would the observer (do I live in a world of imaginary observers? thinks Adam) interpret the empty chair at Adam's side, where Huck was sitting—with Christopher—until two minutes before the show began? How would Suzanne comment on this scene, if she were the hypothetical observer?

Tommy and Timmy and Adam are wearing tuxedo jackets and black bow ties, and they are not the only ones in formal or mock-formal dress. Tommy and Timmy have their own matching jackets—dry-cleaned for opening night at the opera just last week. It was they who insisted on taking Adam out to rent a tuxedo this morning from a little old man in a shop on Fillmore Street, a shop full of tuxedo accessories and tuxedo paraphernalia, all for rent. Adam was meticulously fitted and equipped with a full evening costume, and tonight Timmy tied his bow tie for him while Tommy fastened the cummerbund around his waist. Huck and Christopher looked on, laughing. Huck also has a tuxedo of his own, for mayoral occasions; Christopher is dressed tonight in a black silk pajama suit from Chinatown. Adam has rented his costume through the weekend with Christopher's birthday in mind. Formal tribute for Lucille, likewise for Christopher.

Huck's seat at the table is empty because Christopher cannot be relied upon to remain silent while Lucille is singing. Christopher is here because except for day care (where everyone has been alerted to the circumstances), Huck now keeps Christopher with him as much as possible. Adam, Lucille, Tommy, and Timmy are the only trusted babysitters, and they are all here tonight. Lately there have been more scrawls from Miriam, more evidence that she may be lurking, watching, waiting for a chance to seize her child. So Huck brought Christopher along, had a drink at the table before the show, and has gone out to play with Christopher in the lobby. Adam has offered to trade places with Huck at intermission. And at the end they will all be there to congratulate Lucille, to celebrate at the opening-night party after the show.

Lucille, who often wears men's tuxedo pants and tuxedo shirts, is wearing a black dress tonight. Black sequins to the floor, no waist, no sleeves, hanging from one shoulder only. Lucille's shoulders are broad and very white; her skin looks familiar to Adam, but somehow transformed by the spotlight. She moves, turns, very tall; the sequins catch the light. The shoes tap as she turns, another element of rhythm that makes the voice and movements not quite familiar to Adam. Her voice seems to have two registers: very deep, a little hoarse,

not quite beautiful, and very high, intense, not quite beautiful—and nothing in between. Adam responds to the voice
with romantic longing and sexual excitement—but as if for a
woman who will never even know his name.

> *My one and only,*
> *What am I gonna do if you turn me down,*
> *When I'm so crazy over you.*

Adam tries to imagine that she is singing to him, but he does
not succeed.

"Was she wonderful?" asks Huck, when Adam emerges into
the lobby along with a part of the audience at intermission.

"Absolutely wonderful," says Adam, aware that he is
saying nothing. "You'll see now."

"Are you sure you don't mind?"

"No, no, of course not. You have to see at least some of
the show." Adam is sorry to be missing the second half
(though he will be able to see it any time over the next two
months; Lucille will be performing four nights a week), but
Adam is also enjoying the sacrifice. Dividing the show and the
baby with Huck seems peculiarly intimate, and also seems to
imply a sort of equality in their relations to Lucille.

"Thanks," says Huck.

"Don't thank me," says Adam, insisting on this equality.

Christopher begins to whimper on Huck's shoulder, and
Huck reassures him, "Baby, baby, baby, baby." Then he
reassures Adam, "He'll be fine as soon as everyone goes back
in. He's just scared because he had the lobby all to himself

for the last hour, and he could crawl all over—Adam, he was almost walking, he can do it if he holds on to my hand! But then suddenly all these people came out and invaded his territory, and he decided he wanted me to hold him. Baby love, don't pull on dada's bow tie. Mine's one of those already-tied items, so he can't pull it undone; he can only choke me. Adam, you look extremely swell."

"You too, roommate." Adam meets Huck's eyes and feels dizzy. Does Huck know that Adam knows about Wayne? Does he remember—it was in the middle of the night, and it's easy to be confused about things that happen in the middle of the night. Adam breaks the meeting of eyes, looks around, and says, "Some lobby, huh?"

Cowardly evasion—but the lobby really is splendid. The old Hotel Durand has a sort of shabby grandeur—unpolished mirrors and chandeliers, dusty marble floors. It must once have been a palatial hotel, and now it is all the more sentimentally stirring for having fallen on hard times. It feels like the right place to be wearing a rented tuxedo.

"You'll have to let Christopher give you the full tour," says Huck. "Just put him down, and let him crawl around, and he'll find hidden corners with little pieces of precious old rubbish from the 1920s. Don't let him eat any of it. And if he wants to climb the staircase, stay behind him; the marble steps are slippery."

"Why don't you go in now," suggests Adam, "and have a drink with Tommy and Timmy before the show starts again? I'll take the baby." He holds out his hands toward Christopher, who leans away from his father's shoulder toward Adam, clearly content to change perches. Adam takes him, without awkwardness, conscious of a hidden inner stupefaction at how comfortable this is—for himself, for Christopher, for Huck.

"Why don't you go backstage," says Huck, "and tell Lucille she was wonderful? She'd probably like to hear that before she goes on again."

"You go," Adam automatically defers.

"But I didn't hear the first half," Huck says, laughing. "I was out here, remember." He is right, of course. Still, the situation is more complicated, thinks Adam, than simple logic would suggest: Huck sending Adam with Christopher to see Lucille. A structural problem for my mother, thinks Adam: try to imagine it without the emotional, psychological dimension, merely a structural choreography of positions and directions and relations. But Adam, unlike his mother, cannot think that way. "There's the stage door," says Huck, pointing at a door with the insignificant air of a broom closet. "Just go knock."

Adam does. The young man who answers leads him down a long narrow corridor with paint peeling from its walls, and points at another door. Adam knocks softly, too softly perhaps, since he gets no response. But, when he turns the doorknob and hesitantly pushes open the door, there is Lucille, standing before a full-length mirror. She is abstractedly tying a black bow tie, identical to the one that Adam is wearing. The dress of black sequins lies draped over the back of a chair, and Lucille now wears black pants and a white tuxedo shirt. Alongside hangs a black jacket that looks very much like Adam's and Huck's and Timmy's and Tommy's; on the table is the black high hat that gives the show its name.

Lucille pulls at the ends of the bow tie to make it straight and even, but she is so preoccupied (she is humming, naturally) that she does not see Adam and Christopher in the mirror. Only when Adam calls her name once, then a second time, does she actually look into the mirror and see them behind her. "My one and only, how elegant you look, how sweet of you to come visit," says Lucille, turning to approach and plant a kiss on Christopher's forehead. "And hello, Adam." He gets a rather incidental kiss on the cheek.

"You were wonderful," says Adam.

"I'm going to be even more wonderful now," says Lucille. She places the hat on her head, and Christopher immediately reaches toward it. It is beyond him, but he is a baby with a sense of strategy, and now leans away from Adam's shoulder with little noises of intent—da! da!—to indicate that he wants to be transferred to Lucille's shoulder, within reach of the hat.

Lucille laughs. "Keep him, Adam. He'll completely destroy my makeup, and he'll probably manage to undo my bow tie." She puts on her jacket, kisses Christopher again (but not Adam), and moves past them into the corridor. A voice calls out, "Ninety seconds," and Lucille disappears in the direction of the voice.

Adam looks around the little room: more peeling paint, a mirror, a dress on the back of a chair, a table covered with little pots of makeup and powdery brushes. There is no spiritual trace of Lucille left behind; she has taken everything with her to give to the waiting audience. Adam feels forlornly deprived. He approaches the mirror, sees himself looking unfamiliar, elegant, silly, handsome; Christopher sees his own elegant reflection in black silk and tries to touch it, but comes up against glass, bewildered. Does he know it's himself? wonders Adam. Or is it just someone in the mirror who looks very, very familiar. And what about my reflection?

As they head back down the narrow corridor to the lobby, Christopher, in a moment of inspiration, takes hold of the end of Adam's bow tie and pulls. It comes completely undone in an instant, which leaves Christopher delighted and Adam chagrined. He allows Christopher to go on holding the shiny black strip—a trophy—since after all, Adam doesn't have the faintest idea how to go about tying it back around his neck.

Dada? Christopher inquires, looking up from his trophy, in the now deserted lobby. Dada will be back soon, Adam informs him. Mama? inquires Christopher further, and Adam quickly looks around the lobby, frightened, but there is only a boy in uniform at the bell desk. Huck has explained to Adam that *mama* is a word Christopher learned at day care, where mama and dada are connected concepts for most of Christopher's peers. Christopher, Huck thinks, uses the word very innocently, really not sure what it is supposed to mean. But still it makes Adam uncomfortable. He looks around the lobby yet again.

Let me see you walk, he says to Christopher, and sets him down on his feet on the dusty marble. Adam keeps hold of one hand, says, Okay, let's go, and gives a gentle tug. No, says Christopher, cheerful but firm. He pulls his hand free of Adam's, drops down on all fours, and makes straight for the bell desk with Adam trailing him on two feet. Hi, calls Christopher, hi, hi, hi. Hi there, sweetie, says the bellboy, who, up close, is no boy at all, but a small, trim man, maybe ten years older than Adam. This illusion of youth, the deceptive perspective, even the boyish geniality of the bellboy, all this seems appropriate to the aged grandeur of the hotel lobby, and that grandeur now begins to seem illusory, corrupt, even slightly sinister. Adam thinks of *Death in Venice*, which he has just finished reading. He can almost imagine the Hotel Durand on the Lido. Age and youth, grandeur and corruption.

Up, up, up, calls Christopher, whose thoughts and vocabulary are less profound but more clearly and frankly articulated than Adam's. Up, up, up. He wants to be up on the bell desk. May I? asks Adam. No, you're too big, but you can lift *him* up, says the bellboy with a humorous smirk. Adam, who knows he ought to be politely amused, immediately dislikes this man and his sense of humor. But Christopher is insistent—up, up, up—and so Adam lifts him onto the desk, where there is, in fact, a rather rusty-looking bell. Christopher manages to ring it, and then again, and again and again—a rattling rusty sound that echoes back from across the lobby. Aren't you just the sweetest little boy, says the bellboy. He is, says Adam—a little sharply, unasked, as if it is important to make clear that he does not think the bellboy is speaking to him.

Hi! hi! Christopher has sighted new people in the lobby. There are two older gentlemen, considerably older than the bellboy, descending the marble staircase, carefully groomed, conservative jackets, ties, an air of very dignified intimacy. They have been lovers for many years, thinks Adam. Hi! hi! hi! calls Christopher, and one of them nods in his direction as they cross the lobby floor toward the main entrance and step out into the San Francisco night. Bye-bye, says Christopher, a little wistfully, not loud enough to carry. And then, emphatically, Up!

Since he is already up (on the bell desk), Adam expertly interprets *up* to mean *down* (Christopher does not know the word *down*), and places him on the floor. Ciao, sweetie, says the bellboy, but Christopher snubs him (to Adam's satisfaction) and sets off crawling toward the staircase, which the two gentlemen have brought to his attention. Up, up, he says to himself, mounting the first step, and Adam is right behind him, alert to catch him in case he should slip on the smooth marble. The staircase turns, Christopher maneuvers the turn and keeps heading up, and Adam is looking down so intently that it is not until Christopher calls out, hi, that Adam looks up and sees, sitting at the top of the staircase, Conrad.

"Hi," says Conrad, very definitely to Adam.

"Hi," says Adam, shaken. And then, more controlled, "I suppose I don't have to ask what brings you here."

"Did you get my letter?" says Conrad. "You didn't say anything about it at school, but I suppose you couldn't."

"Yes, and the book," says Adam. "Thank you very much." Then, at a loss, "Can I sit down?" Conrad nods. Adam sits beside him at the top of the stairs and takes Christopher into his lap. He hangs the untied bow tie around his neck, lets Christopher gleefully pull it off, then again. Christopher is laughing, in high spirits, ignoring Conrad, while Adam feels deeply uncomfortable, painfully conscious of the boy beside him. He is very aware of the difference in their ages: that Conrad is almost as close in age to Christopher as to Adam himself. Adam looks across Conrad and between the miniature Corinthian columns of the banister, down to the empty lobby, a clear view. "How long have you been sitting here?" Adam asks.

"Since the beginning," Conrad replies. "I was watching your lover with the baby."

"He's not my lover."

"There's something about watching him with the baby, you know, something beautiful, I guess; it makes me want to cry."

"Yes, I know what you mean." Adam remembers Huck and Christopher that day on the Golden Gate Bridge.

Conrad continues with a sort of determination not to remain silent, a resolve to talk to Adam at all costs. "He's much more relaxed with the baby than you are, I guess because it's his baby. But there's also more tension between them, the baby sort of yapping when he wants to do something, and always restless, wanting to do something else. Do you think tension between parents and children starts that young? I hate my father. I wish your lover was my father, and I was this baby."

"He's not my lover—but I know what you mean. I sometimes feel that too."

"Did you hate your father?"

"My father died when I was two years old."

"Oh, right, I knew that, I forgot."

"The baby's name is Christopher," says Adam. "And my friend's name is Huck. We really aren't lovers, you know."

"When you got my letter," says Conrad, "did you think

I was incredibly weird?" Adam looks over at Conrad directly, and the boy looks away. Conrad is rigidly tense: pointed chin, sharp nose, starched white shirt.

"It was a strange letter to get," says Adam. He is feeling the responsibility of his age, choosing his words carefully with the knowledge that they will matter to Conrad. Adam accepts with a certain puzzlement that the difference in their years means that he should be able to help the boy somehow and at the same time extricate himself. "I thought maybe you might have made yourself seem stranger in the letter than you actually are. You know, as if it were a sort of caricature of yourself."

Conrad breathes deeply. "I think that's right," he says. "I'm glad you can see that. I wouldn't want you to think that I was the way I seem in that letter, but I just couldn't write it any other way." He hastens to add, defensively, "Everything I wrote was true; there's nothing I would want to take back or deny. It's just that the tone . . ."

"The tone was too certain. When I was your age I couldn't have sounded that certain about anything to do with my emotions. Not that my emotions were very complicated, not nearly as complicated as yours seem to be." Adam looks at Conrad and remembers the uneasiness of adolescence. When exactly did it pass away? Or—it suddenly occurs to Adam—does one just gradually get used to the uneasiness so that it becomes an unremarked part of one's adult personality? Perhaps that's all there is to growing up—not overcoming the uncertainties of adolescence, but becoming accustomed to them and taking them for granted. But what would that mean for Conrad?

"I was posing in the letter." Conrad laughs. "Did you

know that Oscar Wilde was accused of posing as a sodomite? That's part of what the trials were all about."

"Posing as a sodomite," echoes Adam, reflectively. "I guess all people do to one extent or another."

"Pose as sodomites?"

"Pose."

Just then Christopher leans across Conrad, holds out the shiny black strip of bow tie between the miniature Corinthians of the banister, and drops it down to the floor of the lobby below. Bye-bye, says Christopher sweetly. Conrad stiffens even more as Christopher leans across his lap; uncertain, uncomfortable, but curious and maybe even moved. That's how I would have felt when I was seventeen, thinks Adam, but he can't pursue the thought any further, because he can't imagine himself, at seventeen, embarked upon the emotional complications that Conrad seems to have chosen. Chosen?

Adam pulls Christopher back from the banister to his own lap and proceeds bravely, awkwardly. "Could we be friends?" he says. Putting the question, trying not to sound either condescending or inane, he feels impossibly, ridiculously old.

Conrad doesn't look at him. "I don't really think so. I think about you all the time. I suppose that when we're sitting here like this you can't imagine what I mean, but it's true. It's not a pose." Adam is suddenly powerfully oppressed by a sense of what Conrad does mean; without thinking he squeezes the baby too tight in his arms, eliciting a squawk of protest. "Have you read *Death in Venice*?" Conrad asks.

"Yes, thank you."

"Do you think it's a story about love? or only about obsession?"

Adam considers the story, considers what is the right thing to say to Conrad. "A kind of love," he says.

"Yes," says Conrad thoughtfully, "there are a lot of different kinds, aren't there?"

Adam thinks about that, about Conrad, about *Death in Venice,* about his own life. "Yes," he says, "there are a lot of kinds."

Now Christopher is restless again, ready for action. He starts to descend the stairs backward, and Adam must get up to stand behind him, also descending backward, while Conrad remains seated at the top. "I'll try not to follow you anymore," says Conrad, watching Adam back away one step at a time. "I'm really sorry about all this." Then, half joking, half despairing, "Tell me what to do."

Adam hesitates, then speaks, trying for the same tone, not quite serious. "Masturbate," he says. They are a ways apart now so the word carries, just barely, through the lobby. The bellboy down below looks up. Adam says, "It's what I did when I was your age. What are you trying to prove?"

Conrad shrugs but does not reply. Then hesitantly, as if he has been gathering courage for this, "Mr. Berg, if you want to go inside and see the end of the show, I'll stay here and watch the baby for you. My parents let me stay out until midnight."

Adam is touched by this, and would like to accept, more for Conrad's sake than for Lucille. But he can't, of course. "No thank you," he calls, stepping backward and down, holding on to Christopher. "But thank you."

———•••———

The party after the show is at a house on the beach, north of the city. The house is as big as the Stringfellow mansion, but it is anything but Victorian; there are glass walls everywhere looking out on the ocean. The house apparently belongs to a man named Eliot, whom Adam has met at the door but has not seen since in the rooms crowded with guests. Eliot is maybe sixty, older than Adam's mother, very small, with a button nose and a silver crew-cut. Lucille was standing next to him at the door, also greeting the guests, and towering over him. She was still wearing her second-act costume, and Adam watched as she removed her high hat and placed it on Eliot's head; it almost equalized their difference in height. Adam guesses that they are lovers, whatever it means to be Lucille's lover.

Lots of people at the party have come straight from the show, but Adam has a feeling that there are others here as well, some very striking-looking men and women he's sure he would have noticed in the hotel lobby or cabaret lounge. Eliot (according to Huck) has put up a lot of the money for the show and is happy to celebrate Lucille's triumph as partly his own. Huck stands now on the other side of the room, holding Christopher, who looks around curiously from his perch on Huck's shoulder. Adam remembers what Conrad said about how moving it is to see Huck and Christopher together. Adam can see that Huck is talking to Christopher, and envies him his freedom to disengage himself from this rather intimidating party. Adam, without a baby on his shoulder, feels that he ought to be talking to someone.

There is a tray of drinks beside him. He picks one up

and drinks it quickly; it is very sweet. Then, instead of setting out across the room to Huck, or in search of Tommy or Timmy, he approaches a pleasant-looking young man a few steps away, also alone. Not one of the striking people, just pleasant, with an open face. Hi, I'm Adam. The open face smiles hi. Some party, says Adam—meaning nothing in particular. But the young man seems to interpret it as something quite specific, because the next thing he says is Cocaine? Um no, says Adam, no thank you. Feel like going out on the beach and fucking? says the pleasant young man. Not really, says Adam, no thank you—very polite. It's pretty cold out there, says the pleasant one, who only now seems ready to make conversation about the weather. Pretty cold, Adam agrees. Surely too cold for fucking on the beach, he thinks.

But he is wrong, as he discovers a little later when he steps outside through a sliding glass panel. Oh yes, he is quite wrong; there are couples everywhere in the dark. The surf sounds loud and looks violent, and Adam hopes that at least no one is swimming, but it would not really surprise him if there were someone out there. Even the pleasant-looking young man. Adam is drunk, definitely; he has had four of those sweet drinks, and whatever they were, he is drunk. He goes back inside, then upstairs, and looks into various rooms: people smoking and talking, kissing, looking stoned.

In one room there is Eliot, still wearing Lucille's high hat, but without Lucille. He catches Adam's eye and beckons, friendly, but Adam pulls out of that room and looks into another. Eventually he comes to a wing of the house that has not yet been invaded by the party. He walks into a room with a bed, a cane rocking chair, a glass wall over the violent ocean. He sits down in the chair, rocks, watches the ocean,

then with a last drunken effort pulls himself out of the chair
and collapses on the bed, in his tuxedo, asleep.

He finds himself waking, a few hours later, and there is
still only the light of the moon coming through the glass wall.
It is just enough light for him to make out, on the floor beside
the bed, two men fucking, or rather one fucking another.
Adam has never seen anything like it before. The men move
slowly, as if with an effort of concentration, as if they too are
on the edge of collapse. Perhaps it is their rhythm that puts
Adam back to sleep, because he remains faintly conscious of
that rhythm, slow and precariously concentrated, while he
sleeps.

When he wakes up next, the two men are gone, but he
is certain that he did not just imagine them there before. After
all, why would he dream of something like that? Now it must
be dawn; there is just the faintest light in the sky, very faint
because, of course, the sun is rising in the east, and the
window on the Pacific looks out to the west. On the East
Coast, the Atlantic coast, the sun rises out of the ocean. In
the west, however, Adam can see the sun set into the ocean
every evening, but it lights the dawn only from the other side
of the sky. Before he actually looks around, Adam is already
aware that he is not alone in the room. Then he focuses on
the cane rocking chair: a man in a tuxedo, Huck, with a baby
in black silk pajamas asleep in his arms, Christopher. It is the
most beautiful vision Adam has ever seen. Huck's bow tie is
perfectly intact. The two of them, father and child, are rocking just barely, and the rhythm, unlike the earlier rhythm of
Adam's sleep, is profoundly soothing. Huck is lighted only by
the faint dawn behind him, maybe slightly less faint than it
was a minute ago. And there is also the sound of the surf—

Adam can just hear it—calm now, no longer violent like last night. He raises his head up on his hand and looks down through the glass wall to the barely lit sea; the waves seem to be moving in and out with the same gentle rhythm as the rocking chair. On Christopher's face Adam can make out a sort of exquisite pout. And Huck's long lips also seem somehow purposefully formed in his sleep, as if he were dreaming of a kiss, or perhaps trying to whistle.

CHAPTER TEN

LEPROSY

Amy points out to Adam, with a hint of amusement, that his tie lies reversed, the seam facing out. She also comments, definitely amused, on the unharmonious matching of stripes. The shirt is blue and white, vertical; the tie is red and green, diagonal.

Shit, says Adam, pulling the tie loose, stuffing it in the pocket of his tweed jacket; he cannot bring himself to go find a mirror and retie it. Last night, in the lobby of the Hotel Durand, his reflection was everywhere, but mirrors are not a dominant note in the Stringfellow décor. Since Amy is now obviously waiting for an explanation, Adam explains: that he was at a party last night, that he slept there in a tuxedo, that he got a ride back to San Francisco this morning with only just enough time (well, not quite enough time, it seems) to change his clothes for school.

Adam actually likes this: presenting his life in a context of muted comedy, letting Amy take it in that spirit. Suzanne's laughter was too often a little angry; Lucille's is dismissive, sometimes to the point of annihilation. Adam's mother may laugh at him, but he knows she fundamentally takes him seriously—which he likes, from his mother. But Amy views him, he has decided, as he would like to view himself, with something between affection and humor.

And so he explains further: that the party was for Lucille, um, Huck's friend, to celebrate her opening night. (If Amy knew about Adam and Lucille, would she find *that* amusing?) Actually, Amy has seen the review of Lucille's show in the *Chronicle* this morning, a rave review: "San Francisco's Judy Garland."

"There was a picture of her," says Amy. "And she certainly doesn't look anything like Judy Garland." Amy is wearing a sober gray wool dress, down to the knee, and there her boots begin: purple suede, dark purple, the color of eggplant, and the suede brushed to the point where it almost glistens, almost looks alive.

Adam is unwholesomely intrigued by the possibility of discussing Lucille's appearance with Amy, but he checks himself. "I hope you're coming to Christopher's birthday party on Sunday."

"I'm looking forward to it," says Amy. Then, rather shyly, as if it is the sort of confidence that she would impart only to her lover, "I've bought new shoes for the occasion."

Adam nods solemnly. He has seen her every weekday for the last month, and he has never seen the same pair of shoes twice. He imagines that she has hundreds of pairs, but he can guess from her tone that adding to the collection is always a momentous (though not infrequent) event. He feels honored, on Christopher's behalf.

As Amy pours coffee and Adam wonders what sort of shoes she has chosen for the party, Jonah Stringfellow himself enters the faculty parlor and greets Adam with a phrase of Ciceronian Latin. Adam has, as Amy suggested, allowed it to be supposed that Latin is one of his accomplishments, and the patriarch has responded enthusiastically. This morning, however, the garbled effusions do come to a point (in English): Adam is being prevailed upon for a favor. Graham Doyle, it seems, has to leave school early today for a doctor's appointment; can Adam cover his last class again? Jonah Stringfellow knows he can always count on a Latin scholar in a pinch. It is the advanced class in American literature, and they are reading *Moby Dick;* can Adam handle that? Jonah Stringfellow tells Adam and Amy, very confidentially of course, that Graham Doyle has missed classes rather too often lately, too many doctor's appointments for a teacher at the Stringfellow School. *Mens sana in corpore sano,* right, Adam?

Adam's star, on the other hand, is rising. Jonah Stringfellow has talked with the father of one of Adam's students, Conrad Winterfeldt. Conrad says that Adam is an excellent teacher; Conrad seems exceptionally motivated by the class. He has even agreed to apply to Yale, after first irrationally resisting, and he says it is Adam's influence that has helped him decide. Conrad's father has told Jonah Stringfellow that Adam Berg is obviously a fine role model for the boy.

"A fine role model." Jonah Stringfellow relishes the words. "A Yale man and a classics scholar. Adam, my boy, remember that your students look up to you." Then, pointedly, "And remember to wear a tie." Adam's hand clutches the tie in his pocket, as he nods, yes sir. Amy admires her boots, with a suppressed smile. Jonah Stringfellow turns to leave with a parting word of inspiration: "When the earthquake comes, that's when we're going to need our Latin scholars."

"That's when we're going to need our lunatics," mutters Adam, taking out the tie, wondering if everyone will comment on the clashing stripes.

"Your Latin is going to come in very handy after the earthquake," says Amy solemnly. "Very handy indeed."

"Your stripes clash," says Alexandra bluntly. They are in the turret room after class; she and Conrad have both remained, three chairs occupied in the circle of six.

"I know," says Adam. "I got dressed too quickly this morning." Surely Adam owes his students no more of an explanation than this? He has been self-conscious about his stripes all morning, but especially during this last class, where everyone was dressed up for the morning meeting with the Stanford admissions representative. The girls in proper dresses (Alexandra's rather more adult than those of the Ming twins), the boys with ties against absolutely solid shirts (Gary's Oxford blue, Conrad's bleached white). Adam, mismatched, still dazed from the night before, is left with the familiar feeling that his students are not only wealthier than he is but also more civilized and presentable. "So how was the meeting with the Stanford admissions guy?"

"What an asshole that guy was," says Conrad.

"He spent practically the whole time talking to Gary about the Stanford baseball team," says Alexandra.

"What an asshole," repeats Conrad.

They are a pair, thinks Adam, struck by the harmony of their judgment, which seems, on the whole, rather more significant than their irreconcilable differences over *Pride and*

Prejudice and *Wuthering Heights*. Adam used to tell himself that it was this little honors class in the turret room that mattered to him most of all his classes, but in fact, he now admits, it is really these two students who matter most. He enjoys teaching his other students, his other classes, but when Alexandra or Conrad says something about English novels Adam is genuinely interested. Do they recognize themselves as a pair?

"So you aren't going to Stanford then?" says Adam, addressing them both.

"Definitely not. I belong in the Ivy League, don't I, Conrad?" This Alexandra says with spirit, with a precocious sense of the connection between flirtation and intellectual arrogance. Adam is impressed, and nods his enthusiastic agreement when Conrad fails to respond. "What about you, Conrad," she continues, "what are you going to do next year?"

"Conrad is applying to Yale, like you," Adam tells her casually, trying to link the two of them further, wondering if Conrad will resent the indiscretion. "Your father told the headmaster, Conrad, and the headmaster told me this morning. I was glad to hear that I had helped you decide to apply."

"I knew you'd apply." Alexandra is triumphant.

"Well, of course, I want to be just like Mr. Berg."

Alexandra laughs. "You'll grow a beard," she says, "I can't wait to see it." She finds this very funny, and it is true, Conrad is so boyish that it's hard to picture him with a beard.

"A beard and a baby," says Conrad. "When you see Mr. Berg with his baby, you can't help wanting to be just like him."

"He's not my baby," says Adam quickly. "He's my roommate's baby." He sees clearly that Conrad is repaying one indiscretion with another.

"Where did you see them?" asks Alexandra.

"Last night, downtown," says Conrad. Then, to Adam's relief, "We ran into each other by accident."

"You'll see the baby on Sunday," says Adam to Alexandra, closing the subject. "You are both coming to the birthday party, aren't you?"

"Definitely," says Alexandra.

"Probably," says Conrad.

"One thing, Adam," says Alexandra. "This letter of recommendation for Yale." She takes from her bag a form and a stamped, addressed envelope. "Would you do it for me? Especially since you went to Yale yourself, they'd pay special attention to your letter, wouldn't they? I've asked my physics teacher to write the other letter, you know, Amy Armstrong." She looks at Adam sharply, and Adam thinks, This is a sharp girl, who sees things that poor Conrad, for all his spying, simply cannot see.

"I'll be glad to write the letter," says Adam. "I'd be glad to do one for you too, Conrad, now that you've decided to apply."

"Thank you," says Conrad. Then, meaningfully, "I hesitated to ask."

"Who will do your other letter?" asks Alexandra.

"I'm going to ask Mr. Doyle," says Conrad. "I was in his American literature class last year, and he seemed to like me."

"Someone told me he's been sick this year," says Alexandra. "He used to be nasty to his students. Was he nice to you?"

"Nice enough," says Conrad. "I didn't know he was sick."

Adam wonders what everyone will say when everyone knows.

"God, those stripes." From Graham Doyle, Adam knows this is meant to be unpleasant, and for the first time today he really minds.

"I like them," says Adam, irritated. "The world would be a better place if we were all a little braver about mixing our verticals with our diagonals." Where did I ever come up with a line like that? thinks Adam, pleased with himself. And then he is deflated: Is this dying man really likely to be amused?

"Here's the lesson plan," says Graham, completely ignoring Adam's remark. "It's *Moby Dick*, I'm sure you read it back at Yale." Very sarcastic. They are standing in one of the dark-paneled halls of the mansion. Graham is well aware that there is a little Yale circle at the Stringfellow School, is bitter about his own perfectly respectable education at his home-state university in the Midwest. And bitter about dying, Adam supposes.

"Thanks," says Adam, and then adds, dismissively, feeling perhaps that he should be thanked, not thanking, "I don't really need your plan. Maybe you should hold on to it."

"How will you know what they've read for today, clever one?"

"I'll ask them."

"And then make up the class as you go along, clever one?"

"Yes."

Graham is furious now, really furious, practically hissing. "And my students will think you're simply wonderful. Don't your own students think you're just the cleverest little teacher? Do they all want to take you home and eat you up?"

What is the point of this particular brand of viciousness? wonders Adam. He considers turning and walking away, considers refusing to cover the class, even considers saying something to let on to Graham that he *knows*. But Adam does none of these things, because here is Conrad Winterfeldt coming up behind them.

Graham becomes aware that someone is approaching. He turns, sees the boy, and regains possession of himself. "Ah, Conrad," he greets him. Then aside, without looking at Adam, "One of my students from last year."

"Actually Conrad's in my class this year. We know each other."

Adam takes in the picture of Conrad alongside Graham, a physically healthy (however emotionally disturbed) teenager alongside a dying forty-year-old man. Conrad's face is completely smooth, hairless, and Graham's is not only older and coarser and broken by a bristly short mustache, but also just noticeably marked. By disease, thinks Adam. They are the same height and size, both shorter than Adam and much thinner, though Adam is certainly not overweight. That picture of the two of them, side by side, is undeniably disturbing.

Imagine it from Conrad's perspective: Graham Doyle and me, how does the boy see the two of us?

"I'm lucky to find you together," says Conrad, with an effort, and Adam thinks, No, this feels oppressively unlucky. "I wanted to give you both these forms for letters of recommendation."

Adam and Graham each accept the proffered form and envelope, silently, regarding each other. Conrad waits for them to say something, then gives up. "Thanks a lot," he says. "I really appreciate it." As if he were just any old high school senior, thinks Adam, and not the one who has been following me through the streets of San Francisco. In fact, Conrad is honestly seeking a normal tone when he says, "I'll see you on Sunday, Mr. Berg."

"On Sunday?" Graham is unpleasantly curious, but Conrad has already walked away.

"A birthday party," says Adam, "at my apartment." Graham has not been invited.

"Well, well, a birthday party," says Graham, as he thoughtfully watches Conrad disappearing down a winding wooden staircase.

Adam is running along the marina between Tommy and Timmy. They are in their brilliant colors, purple and green, orange and red. Huck and Lucille are back at the apartment with Christopher, making last-minute plans for the party tomorrow and trying to figure out how many people will actually be coming. The sun is already high over the bay, late morning, Saturday, and Adam finds himself in the middle of a thorny discussion that has apparently been going on since Lucille's party, the night before last. Timmy, it seems, was rather charmed by a friend of Eliot's, a rich older man, a great patron of the San Francisco Opera—so charmed that Tommy came upon the two of them kissing in a corner at the party. And so, beginning with some bad feeling about whether or not this was, as Timmy said, nothing at all, a whole extended debate has developed on the subject of fidelity. And with Adam between them, jogging along the marina, the debate seems on the verge of becoming a symposium.

Well, what about AIDS? This is Tommy, reproachful, and Adam thinks: Yes, what about that? He has had it on his mind since yesterday especially, since his encounter with Graham Doyle, and, well, really since he moved to San Francisco. Fidelity is something else Adam often thinks about, of course, (Adam, the lover of Lucille, the lover of Amy Armstrong), but he has never felt obliged to consider the subjects of AIDS and fidelity together.

What about AIDS? replies Timmy, mocking: You don't get AIDS from kissing. That's not absolutely certain, Tommy insists, and anyway it's not the point, as you know *perfectly* well. (As I know *perfectly* well.) Adam remembers the other two men at the party, on the floor. Fucking. That, he knows, is how you get AIDS.

The point, continues Tommy, is that fidelity, nowadays, is not just a romantic ideal, and the price of infidelity is more than just romantic disillusionment. Now Tommy holds the floor, since he is in somewhat better shape than Timmy or Adam, and the two of them are becoming short of breath as they run, till Timmy can do little more than pick up a word here and there from his lover's discourse and mimic it breathlessly between exhalations. Only Huck can hold his own in a conversation with Tommy right to the end of the run.

When Timmy and I first became lovers and decided to

be faithful to each other, Tommy is saying to Adam, we were completely sentimental about it. And especially Timmy, who may laugh at me, but his own ideas about romance are more than a little bit influenced by Puccini. Fuck you, Timmy pants. And Timmy, continues Tommy, was much keener about fidelity than I was. I mean, I had never been faithful to anyone before, and I accepted it in a spirit of anything-once, not in the spirit of Madame Butterfly. Fuck you, says Timmy, wheezing.

And have you been faithful to each other? Adam asks between strides and breaths. They are heading out into the bay on the long, curving pier.

We haven't done so badly, says Tommy. Which Adam interprets to mean no. But the point—Tommy is finishing what he started—the point is that three years ago I wouldn't really have cared that much if Timmy went to bed with one of his ice-cream buddies or with some old rich bitch he met at the opera. (Fuck you.) I would have just paid him back with someone else, and probably I'd have been glad to have the chance. But now I do care, and it has nothing to do with romance. You're not kidding, says Timmy. (Is that what he minds? wonders Adam.) When I go to Los Angeles next week, says Tommy, I don't want to have to worry about what my boyfriend is picking up from the sluts of San Francisco. (Fuck you.) Do you know why I'm going to Los Angeles next week, Adam?

Tommy's office administers the federal school-lunch program for the western United States. In a public school district in Los Angeles there is a nine-year-old hemophiliac boy who has AIDS from a blood transfusion. And there is furious controversy about whether he should be permitted to go on attending school. (Adam thinks of Graham Doyle at school.) And, incredibly (but this is Los Angeles, and nothing is too preposterous for credibility), there has been considerable attention paid to the purely symbolic issue of whether he should continue to be served a federally subsidized school lunch. And so Tommy is being sent down from the San Francisco administrative office to write a report.

They accelerate for the last hundred yards to the end of the pier, and then, panting, brake to a halt, as if they were about to go over the edge and into the water. Adam watches Tommy and Timmy instinctively find the same pose, hands on hips, then rotate themselves, almost in unison, purple and green, orange and red, looking out across the bay. All three of them then walk back along the curving pier, the bay to either side, past Asian fishermen, back toward the city.

"I won't sleep with anyone while Tommy is in Los Angeles," says Timmy to Adam, the convenient intermediary. Tommy receives this as a statement of solemn concession. "But," says Timmy, his breath recovered, "I hate the fact that we don't dare try to live as we would live if there wasn't this plague."

Adam thinks of Huck, trying to live with his child the way he would if there was no child. Adam thinks of Huck and Wayne.

"The idea of being faithful is sordid and spoiled," says Timmy, "if that's why we're doing it."

"It doesn't have to be the only reason," says Tommy softly.

"Thank you," says Timmy, sincerely. And then, with more bitterness, "But I hate having to think about it."

"I know, love," says Tommy, and reaches around Adam to touch his lover's shoulder. There is an exultant cry from up ahead where a boy (is he Vietnamese? Cambodian? surely he has come only recently from a very different world) pulls his line out of the bay with a silver fish shining at the end.

"She will put in an appearance," announces Huck triumphantly. He is kneeling on the floor, tying the knot on a red balloon. Lucille stands on a chair, taping several others, blue and green and yellow, to the ceiling. Adam is sitting alone on the love seat, his lips clinging to the tiny rolled rim of a half-inflated balloon, catching his breath before finishing this one off too. It is very late Saturday night. Christopher is asleep; Lucille has just returned from her performance (all sold out).

"We will all be honored," says Lucille. "Such a distinguished public figure, our mayor. I'll whisper to everyone that she's secretly Christopher's godmother."

"I'll whisper to everyone that *you* are his godmother," says Huck, gallantly. "You're as much of a local legend as she is."

"Right, the Judy Garland of San Francisco—God, they say the stupidest things."

"You know, don't you," Huck continues, warmly, seriously, "that if Christopher had a godmother it would be you."

Adam is thinking that what people will be whispering about is not the identity of Christopher's secret godmother—but his mother, of course. Won't people wonder? Won't people ask? Adam himself has Miriam very much on his mind.

When he returned from running this morning, he found Huck and Lucille looking gravely at a new letter, the same message, the same scrawl. What could she be like, Miriam? She must be aware that tomorrow is Christopher's birthday.

Huck is apparently thinking the same thing, because there he is, on his knees, obliviously letting air escape from the red balloon, saying: "*She* asked me about Christopher's mother, asked me what she *did*. Christ, and I said we were separated, which *she* didn't know. It's true, of course, we're sure separated—but I wonder if I should have said more. Even when I said it I knew it wasn't really enough, and I had a feeling that if she thought the situation was, well . . ."

"Weird." From Lucille, up on the chair.

Huck neither accepts nor rejects the word, but continues. "Well, then she wouldn't come. And you know, if it weren't *my* situation and *my* baby, as a member of her staff I might have advised her not to show up. Naturally it's good politics to appear at an innocent, informal social occasion, and it's a classic to be seen with a baby of the city, but if the situation . . ."

A baby of the city, thinks Adam, a baby of the city.

"Relax, sweetheart," says Lucille, "the situation can't possibly affect *her*. Besides, you have no control over yourself when your fantasies are so dramatically at stake."

Huck doesn't respond to that. "It's a baby's birthday party," he says. "She'll know just how to be. Sonofabitch, it's my baby's birthday party. Adam, Lucille, can you believe it?"

Adam and Lucille both look at Huck with the deepest affection. Huck smiles at them, seeming genuinely cheered. "Well, tomorrow's party is going to be the most innocent, the most beautiful party San Francisco has ever seen."

Then, pleading exhaustion, Huck says goodnight and goes to bed, leaving Adam and Lucille alone. Is he really tired, Adam wonders, or is he showing some sort of tact? Adam continues blowing up balloons; Lucille goes on taping them to the ceiling, then to the walls. There are dozens of them now—red, blue, green, yellow, pink—the room is transformed. Vanquished are the more sinister elements of the Hopper nighthawks and the mad seascape.

Adam remembers the night Huck left the two of them to do the dishes, when Lucille pointed at the big blue cookie jar and told Adam about Miriam—and made love to him in the end. He knows that they are not on the verge of sex right now. And he thinks: If she decides she is through with me, as a lover, will she tell me? Or will she just never bother to sleep with me again, so that after a while I'll get the message?

"Eliot, is he your lover?" Adam hears himself saying this aloud. It is not something he intended to ask, but now that it is out he waits curiously—not for her answer, yes or no, but to see how she will react to his raising the subject.

"I thought we weren't asking each other such questions, my dear. I'm sure I've never asked you anything like that."

Adam feels himself driven from the subject of Lucille and Eliot, wonders if he ever really cared to begin with, wonders if he will have to pay a price for having asked. But never mind, the subject is finished, and another is opened.

"Wayne," he says, "Huck's friend Wayne, he and Huck are lovers, did you know that?"

"Are they?" Her face is purposefully blank, either because she does not know or because she is waiting to find out exactly what Adam knows.

"I saw him in Huck's bed, in the middle of the night."
What Adam actually remembers clearly is the image of Huck,
naked, with the baby; the form of the person in Huck's bed
and the shape of the hat on the floor remain only as vague
impressions. But Adam has no doubts about what he saw and
who it was.

"I knew they *were* lovers," says Lucille finally. "I didn't
know they still are. Of course Huck wouldn't have gone out
of his way to tell me; he knows what I think." She comes
down from the chair, stands before Adam. Something about
Lucille's face has changed, as if she has only just now stepped
offstage. Her white-blond hair and bright red lipstick are
suddenly a clown's mask, and the woman Adam sees looks
worn and disturbed. He has never seen her this way before.
She cares about Huck, observes Adam, more than she will
ever care about me.

"And what you think is that he shouldn't sleep with
men?" he says.

"What I think is that he shouldn't sleep with that Okie."

"Are there other men?"

"There have been lots of other men. Huck is gay—you
can see that, can't you?"

"But—"

"But Christopher, but Miriam, right? That doesn't matter. Just as if you were to sleep with a man, or even fall in
love with a man, you would still be straight. People's lives are
complicated, that's all."

"Especially here?"

"Maybe."

Adam has begun to put the questions he has waited a
long time to put, and he is more confused than ever, but he

will keep asking now as long as she will keep answering. "Why shouldn't he sleep with Wayne?"

"Because the little cowboy is a basket case."

"What?"

Whispering furiously. "A basket case, an adolescent wreck, a psychiatric casualty zone, a dope fiend, a cheap whore. An unbalanced little gay boy from Oklahoma who ran away from home when he was fourteen to come to San Francisco—and the big city has completely destroyed him. He is the most pathetic creature anyone could ever hope to find, especially Huck."

"But why—"

"Don't you see, Adam, don't you see anything? Huck is in love with him, loves him *because* he's pathetic. Our Huck is a poor stupid goddamn fucking saint. If the boy were a leper, Huck would love him even more. Don't you see, Huck is just as much of a basket case as the Okie—or maybe he's just the basket. But he is sick, sick, sick. Don't you see?"

"I see. And Miriam, Christopher's mother, the same thing." Oh yes, Adam does see now, Huck, Huckleberry Finn, all-American boy, man, hero, his heart to the needy, the pathetic, the hopeless, the insane. The problem of motivation (Catholicism? idealism? psychopathology?) is obvious and irrelevant at the same time; this is a question of love. The only observations that matter are structural, purely structural, between the hero and the hopeless, the basket cases and the basket. Adam longs to turn the whole goddamn mess over to his mother and let her tell him how to see it, but his mother is very far away, and this is no text.

"He met Miriam at the Grant Street Crafts Fair," Lucille is saying. "She was there with a few of her paintings. She was living on the street then, fresh out of the cookie jar, but not for long of course. Huck took one look at the paintings, another look at the wreck who stood beside them, and he just knew, of course he did. And it didn't matter that he was gay. She's the only woman he's ever fallen in love with, one of the few women he's ever slept with, and sonofabitch, as he would say, the bitch got pregnant. And, Adam, he took her into this apartment and lived with her here—can you even begin to imagine what that was like? But after the baby was born, thank God, they had to put her away again, and now she's back out and writing these horrible letters, and eventually they'll lock her up again, and then she'll be let out again, and he'll never get away from her. Or from the Okie, I guess. He was here before Miriam, and then for a while after she left, and now, well, again. Can't you see, Adam, that Huck is absolutely set on destroying himself, and there's nothing we can do about it, nothing at all?"

"I see." He looks at the seascape over her shoulder, the pink spot in the raging painted green sea. Then he looks higher, and feels tears coming to his eyes at the sight of all those colored balloons.

CHAPTER ELEVEN

HAPPY BIRTHDAY, DEAR CHRISTOPHER

There is indeed a monkey. And in the center of the living room there are ten babies, each reaching for the monkey. Around them is a circle of watchful parents, and around that circle, spreading out from the living room into the kitchen and down the hallway, are the dozens of other party guests, all occasionally looking over at the monkey and the babies at the center. From the kitchen there is jazz, live, but not very loud, animating the lively clusters in the hallway and on the periphery, but having somewhat less effect on the intense conversations further in, less still on the half-preoccupied parents, and none at all on the babies, who are responding only to the rhythms of each other and the monkey as it moves among them.

Christopher is of course one of the ten babies, and it seems to Adam that for all the festivity of his new sweatshirt (purple with neon-pink lettering: SAN FRANCISCO), he is not obviously marked as the hero of the occasion. People who don't know Christopher well enough to recognize him (there are such guests, Huck's colleagues, Adam's students) might not even be able to pick him out as the birthday baby. Adam, who believes he could pick out Christopher's eyes and expressions among thousands of babies, nevertheless sees that each of the ten is wearing an air of confidence: this celebration is for me, the others are the guests. The only one who *really* stands out is the monkey, who wears a pointed blue birthday hat. The babies have all refused to wear hats, all ten babies, unanimously.

"Good dim sum," says one of the parents, approaching Adam. He recognizes her, Deborah, the corporate lawyer, mother of Sasha, whom he met his very first day in San Francisco.

"Chinatown's just on the other side of the hill," says Adam, his ears attuned to his own voice, to the way he talks about the city after two months. He, like Deborah, holds a small paper plate of Chinese dumplings. "That's Sasha there, isn't it?" He points to a beautiful baby standing up, almost ready to take a step.

"No, no," says Deborah. "That's Jason." Jason actually does take a step, toward the monkey. "There's Sasha, sitting. She can't really stand up by herself yet."

Adam feels slightly chagrined at having failed to identify Sasha, but Deborah doesn't seem to mind. Sasha is beautiful; she is wearing a frilly pink baby party dress, short enough to reveal pink rubber pants underneath. Jason is also beautiful, wearing striped blue-and-white seersucker overalls. But to Adam's eye neither Sasha nor Jason is as beautiful as Christopher, who, at this very moment, happens to look over at Adam and bestow on him a dazzling birthday smile. Adam thinks: the reason his eyes and expressions seem so immediately recognizable to me is because they are Huck's eyes and expressions.

Across from Adam and Deborah, on the other side of the babies, is Lucille, who is talking to a small, odd-looking, older woman, the producer, the mistress of the monkey. Lucille is wearing a tuxedo and a red rose in her hair. Over by the window Tommy and Timmy are talking to Wendy and Mandy, who lived in this building when they themselves were babies, and who will perhaps inherit it one day from their grandfather. Adam has come to cherish the Ming twins and his interesting position as their tenant and teacher. Beside them, Gary the baseball player is sitting on the love seat with, of all people, Lucille's friend Eliot. What can they possibly be talking about? Adam wonders. Gary thumps his hand into an imaginary mitt, and the question is answered: baseball, probably the Giants. Huck, who like Adam and Lucille, the hosts, is dressed in a tuxedo jacket, stands near the door to the hallway, greeting people. At the moment he is talking to Amy Armstrong, who has just come in and is wearing a white blouse and navy skirt—and sapphire-blue high heels embroidered with gold and silver beads that sparkle across the room. Amy seems to be making a point about something to Huck— about Yale? about Adam?—and Huck replies with charm and a smile; it doesn't matter *what* he is saying, as long as he can smile like that, smile like Christopher. Adam feels a pang of jealousy—but of whom? He wishes someone would interrupt them, and, as if on command, Alexandra appears, nods to her physics teacher, and holds out a hand to Huck. Conrad has not shown up, not yet.

From where Adam is standing, by the babies, he can't actually hear the knock at the door, but he sees Huck hear

it, sees him step away from Amy and Alexandra to welcome
the new guest. There is no special flurry as she comes in,
smiles, puts a hand on the shoulder of Huck's tuxedo by way
of greeting and congratulation, casts a quick appraising eye
on the crowd in the living room, her citizens, who have not
yet noticed her. She is stunning, thinks Adam, certain that
Huck is thinking the same thing. Have I chosen to find her
stunning, Adam wonders, as a sort of tribute to Huck? Or is
it just because I'm infatuated with the city? She follows
Huck's lead, two steps, to rejoin Amy and Alexandra. Amy
is obviously surprised, maybe amused, and she almost begins
to curtsy as she shakes the mayor's hand. Alexandra is completely self-possessed and shakes hands as if *she* were the
mayor.

"Isn't that—" says Deborah, beside Adam, who nods.
Then someone next to Deborah looks up, recognizes, taps
someone else.

But now I want to see the baby, Adam imagines that she
is saying, and Huck gestures toward the babies, who are
hidden, surrounded by tall adults. Two men have moved
quietly into the apartment; they stay a few paces behind her,
talking to each other, watching her. As she moves toward the
living room, they move too, her escorts, slightly sinister,
slightly comic. More heads are turning, and Adam notices
Lucille's almost studied unawareness of the stir. She will be
the last one in the room, Adam guesses, to show herself aware
of the mayoral presence. But the presence is now just before
Adam, all in tasteful and expensive tweed, beaming down at
the babies. Huck bends over Christopher (everyone is watching) and lifts him up into the arms of the mayor, just as Adam
feels the tickling pressure of little feet on his shoulder and

sees the odd little pink fingers of the monkey seizing the last Chinese dumpling from his plate.

One afternoon in October—October 1972—Huck gave a party. It was right after a big rally in New Haven (well, not so big perhaps) where Sargent Shriver, McGovern's running mate, had done his earnest best to inspire a crowd of Yale undergraduates and New Haven Democrats with the certainty that November would bring victory. Adam cheered along with everyone else. And then there was the party, which, since Huck was behind it, was held in their dorm suite. The living room was full of students, no local Democrats. Crammed in, they passed around joints, and someone held one up to the mouth of Richard Nixon: a poster on the wall with the slogan "Would You Buy a Used Car from This Man?" Much laughter at that, more marijuana all around. The poster had gone up right before the party and would come down right after; this, let it not be forgotten, was also the living room of Slimy Sam (would you buy a used car from him?) and so had to remain politically neutral. The colossal McGovern poster was always in the tiny bedroom where Huck and Adam slept.

Huck arrived late, the last one to show up at his own party. He had spoken with Shriver for a minute (he told Adam later), even invited him to the party; the invitation was declined, and just as well. What Adam most clearly remembers is Huck opening the door, walking in, smiling, handsome (silver-blue eyes, long lips, high forehead, blond hair almost to his shoulders, his face unlined), taking the joint that was immediately passed to him and, still smiling, ostentatiously rubbing it out on the already grimy dormitory wall, just below

Nixon's ridiculous chin. An ashmark remained. It was not that Huck didn't smoke, no—this was a gesture of propriety, an insistence that the party was a semi-official occasion, an inane gesture of political circumspection on behalf of a hopeless cause.

Now everyone has recognized the mayor. She kisses Christopher happy birthday—a kiss he accepts with utter indifference, eyes fixed on the monkey on Adam's shoulder. She coos over each of the other babies as well, not missing one: warm congratulatory smiles to all the voting parents gathered around. Then she retires to a corner, away from the kitchen and the music, beneath the ominous seascape, and a circle of guests gather to hear what their mayor will say; other circles go on eating dim sum and hovering over the babies. Adam is again watching the door when the next person enters (surely almost everyone must be here by now), and this guest he does not instantly recognize, although he should. It is someone Adam has had on his mind, someone he has seen only recently: a heavy man, dark-shadowed jowls, a piggish expression. He is introducing himself to Huck. Huck starts to laugh, exclaims, Sonofabitch, claps the man on the arm, not quite warmly, and Adam realizes that of course it is Slimy Sam. Huck has not seen him in years, but Adam saw him just a few months ago in Boston, and—now he remembers—Suzanne wrote that he had telephoned to ask about Adam.

Quickly Adam crosses the room, says hello. Huck is still laughing, and Adam feels profoundly relieved that Huck is not angry or disgusted, does not see this unbeloved figure from their past as a blight on the birthday party. Slimy Sam is explaining: He heard (from Suzanne) that Adam was living with Huck, but he couldn't remember Huck's last name (Polish, right?) and so, since he had the address (from Suzanne), he thought he'd just drop in and surprise them. And what's going on here anyway—whose party? Huck tells him, then actually invites him to stay, urges him to go into the kitchen and get some dumplings. Which Slimy Sam does: though not before asking, How much do you guys pay for a place like this?

Adam admires Huck for being so good-natured, suspects that Huck might even be feeling slightly sentimental about Slimy Sam. And it is not unendearing that Sam himself seems to be sentimental about their freshman year, seems to have forgotten that Huck and Adam would have nothing to do with him, that Huck more than once called him a fascist. And, besides, Adam can't help being grateful: It was Slimy Sam, after all, who told Adam that Huck was living in San Francisco. Now Slimy Sam has tracked them down for this reunion. It will be, Adam imagines, a funny story that Adam and Huck will long tell each other and Christopher about Christopher's first birthday party. What am I thinking? Adam stops himself. Will the three of us, Huck and Christopher and I, just go on and on like a family, from birthday party to birthday party?

Adam sees Amy crossing the room, sees where she is heading, and wishes he could intercept her, but he can't—and really why should he? She introduces herself to Lucille, says something. Adam's imagination fails him (what would Amy say?), but whatever it is, Lucille is not uninterested. The rose in Lucille's hair perfectly matches her vivid red lips. But Amy's face—dark curls, sharp eyes, round glasses—is by no means annihilated by Lucille's glamour. Adam imagines Amy drawing spiritual energy upward from the sapphire shoes with the gold and silver beads.

Instead of that conversation, what Adam hears, over the general buzz, is an interplay of saxophone and clarinet. The jazz rhythms are not exactly his taste, but he cannot help imagining the saxophone line as Lucille and the clarinet as Amy. Both women seem beyond his grasp, almost beyond his appreciation, and, however trivial their conversation, Adam suspects that he would not be able to fathom its notes and nuances. Finally, they look up (and everyone else looks up too), when Huck calls for attention. Attention to the great pile of wrapped presents that the Ming twins are building as they carry package after package from the door to the babies in the center of the room. This is Adam's signal to hurry to the kitchen before the lights are turned out in the living room. Quickly he strikes a match, lights the single candle in the center of the cake, then the one beside it for good luck, and enters the living room to place the cake on the table out of reach of the babies. Huck lifts Christopher up to see the lighted candles, the jazz trio begins the familiar tune, and everyone sings.

Christopher can't quite blow out the candles, and neither can he unwrap the presents. Rather he begins to tear the paper, but doesn't seem willing to concentrate long enough to remove the gifts. Huck and Lucille and Adam help, unwrapping one gift after another, holding each one up for the admiration of the guests. Christopher quickly loses interest in the succession of fancy baby garments: tie-dye from Berkeley, shiny silk from Chinatown, even a miniature black leather jacket. Only moderately more compelling is the menagerie of stuffed animals: not just koalas and bunnies, but a pink flamingo, an alligator (with remarkably realistic scales), a tiny rhinoceros, and a slender, exotic stuffed monkey, which, in a sudden swoop, to everyone's uproarious approval, is seized upon by the live monkey, then indignantly let fall. It is not at all clear what is from whom, and Adam isn't even absolutely sure which of the four unwrapped bunnies is the one he picked out.

It is Huck who unwraps a small box that contains nothing but a pair of old-fashioned brass keys on a heavy brass ring. That's all. When Huck reads the engraved inscription on the ring—"For Christopher, The Keys to the City"—the party hums with immediate and unanimous appreciation. Only one guest could have offered *that* as a gift. And not only is the roomful of voters deeply touched, but the political instinct is shown to be nothing less than genius, for Christopher immediately expresses a desperate interest in this present and this one alone. Could *she* have possibly known (as Adam knows) of the daily disputing between Huck and Christopher for possession of Huck's keys? In fact, now the other nine babies also want the keys to the city, and the scene of supernatural infant harmony, which everyone has been commenting on with wonder, is shattered by frantic cries and lunges for the keys. The monkey, too, joins the fray. No one is willing to be pacified with the flamingo or the alligator or any of the poor bunnies, and, in the end, peace and harmony are restored only when nine reluctant parents have turned over *their* keys—while Christopher triumphantly fingers the keys to the city.

Adam's birthdays, when he was a child, were certainly not celebrated with parties like this. They were celebrated strictly in the family, and a very small family at that. His first birthday, naturally, he does not remember, but he knows it was the only one his father lived to see. Adam's second birthday came two weeks after his father's death, and, Adam supposes, was not celebrated at all. But after that, for years and years, his birthdays were celebrated in the same small company of his mother and his mother's parents. His grandmother always prepared an open apple tart, warm from the oven, no birthday candles. Adam hasn't tasted pastry like it since she died, and on his birthday the taste usually comes back to him, leaving him sad with craving. There was also, for each birthday, a wool sweater, a gift from his grandmother, which she had knitted herself, and which Adam always tried on immediately even though his birthday was in July.

Adam's grandmother was a sharp woman, maybe sharper in appearance than her husband and her daughter, the two professors. She did not do a lot of baking or knitting, but for Adam's birthday she considered it a matter of ritual to do both. Adam's earliest memory, he thinks, comes from one of those birthdays, the third or the fourth, when his grandmother cut the tart with a big knife (a tremendous knife in Adam's memory) and warned him sharply, "Take good care of your little fingers." That is the phrase he remembers, unsure whether it was spoken in English, or spoken in French and then translated in memory. Adam, his mother says, understood and spoke French perfectly until he started school. And then he unlearned it completely.

Although Adam was often invited to the birthday parties of children he went to school with, his mother remained too cut off from the world to be aware of proper American ritual. Adam never thought to ask her to arrange a children's party for him. He liked spending his birthday with his mother, and she liked spending his birthday with her mother. Adam's grandfather was always somehow marginal, and Adam has wondered whether his father would have been too, had he lived to complete these gatherings. They continued through Adam's adolescence, and the last one took place the July before Adam started college. Then his grandmother died. Adam still has the very last of the sweaters, heavy and hazel brown, with three knitted cables running down the front; it fits, and he wears it from time to time. Since then, Adam has sometimes visited his mother on his birthday, sometimes not. Certainly there are no more tarts or sweaters, because Simone Berg, though she can cook and sew, can neither bake nor knit.

"That monkey is going to bite someone," says a fussy father. And, though the monkey's patron insists that the monkey never bites anyone, in fact it is looking a little wilder ever since the disillusionment of finding its soulmate stuffed. The producer summons her pet to her own shoulder and allows it to eat cake off her plate. The babies are consoled by *their* cake, which they are rubbing into their hair and onto their clothing with such blissful intent that some parents are actually able to recover their keys. "That monkey is going to bite someone," mutters the same father, unmollified, a prophet of doom.

Adam and Lucille are cutting cake together, and have, as far as Adam can tell, a proper host-and-hostess air. It is not quick work, since there are ten cakes (including the one that Adam bore in so dramatically, candles lit, at the climactic moment). There are two chocolate cakes with fudge frosting, two cheesecakes with cherry topping, two carrot cakes with cream-cheese frosting, two banana-walnut cakes with buttercream frosting, and two unfrosted poppyseed cakes. They were all ordered from a bakery around the corner that specializes in the spirit of American home baking, and Adam, with Tommy and Timmy's help, picked them up this morning. These cakes do not at all resemble the tart that Adam associates with his own birthday. He is overwhelmed by the bounteousness of so *much* cake; he is also pleased at his position as dispenser of the bounty.

Huck appears and reports, "The mayor wants poppyseed." Adam cuts, Huck takes the plate, then asks Lucille, nervously, "Is that too big a portion?"

"She doesn't have to eat it all," says Lucille in a tone so mock maternal that Adam is taken aback when Huck fails to respond to the joke. He sets off with his poppyseed offering, and Lucille says to Adam, as they cut more cake onto more plates, "Such a big day for Huck."

"Well, it is," says Adam, defensively, aware of Lucille's irony without quite understanding the point.

"The baby, the mayor, everything triumphant, everything celebratory. And everything a little unreal—"

"Excuse me, you're Lucille, aren't you?" She is interrupted by someone who works with Huck, someone who has seen her show, wants to tell her how wonderful she is. Lucille graciously accepts all compliments, politely puts down her knife.

Adam continues cutting cake. There are still people gathering around to get some, or to get more. In the back of Adam's mind is what Lucille said last night about Huck. It all seemed tragically plausible then, but now, in the middle of a party, in a room full of cakes and balloons and babies, it is difficult to believe that Huck is a man who is courting self-destruction. That, Adam supposes, was the point of Lucille's irony. As if to tell him that he is right, a balloon overhead suddenly pops for no reason at all. Hardly anyone seems to notice, except for the father who takes the explosion as his cue to repeat his warning, "That monkey is going to bite someone."

"Don't you work for Weede, Weede, Vandenberg, and Silverstein?" says Slimy Sam to Deborah. "Weren't you working on the Western Utilities case?"

"Yes," says Deborah, one eye on Sasha, one eye on Slimy Sam. Adam can see that she remembers him, and that he did not make a very favorable impression.

"You're not Huck's wife, are you?" asks Slimy Sam, and Adam, overhearing, wonders how many other inquiries of that sort have been made this afternoon.

"No," says Deborah, with some irritation. "That's my daughter there, and that's Huck's baby right next to her." Sasha is leaning over Christopher's plate to attack his cake, her own ignored beside her.

"How much does it cost to take care of a baby?" Slimy

Sam inquires casually. "How much do you spend on her in an average month?"

To Adam's surprise, Deborah does not find the question slimy; in fact, she begins to elaborate a rough budget, as if thinking out loud. She mentions how much she spent on Sasha's fancy stroller, at which Slimy Sam cannot conceal his horror, at which Deborah cannot conceal her satisfaction.

"That guy," whispers Amy, who has come up behind Adam, "he was at Yale when we were. He's awful. He was one of the super-icky asshole pre-laws. What's he doing here?"

"He was my freshman roommate," whispers Adam. "Mine and Huck's. And he's sort of crashed the party, because he's in town on business."

"That monkey is going to bite someone," says the prophet. The monkey is back among the babies, to their delight.

"Do you really think he will?" Slimy Sam asks Deborah.

Adam looks around the room and sees Tommy and Timmy with Huck in the circle around the mayor. He sees that Lucille, having abandoned the cake station, is talking with Eliot; she reaches out her hand in an intimate gesture and touches the hairline of his silver crew-cut. Adam sees Conrad, finally, the last guest. He has entered while Adam wasn't looking, and now he's conferring with Alexandra, Gary, and the Ming twins—the whole class. Adam is relieved that Conrad has come, hopes that this signals a benign turning point in their odd relations. Alexandra appears to be directing Conrad's attention to the fact that the mayor is present; Conrad seems reluctant to be impressed.

"I introduced myself to Lucille," says Amy to Adam. "I told her how much I liked her Rodgers and Hart show."

"What did she say?"

"She said I should see her Gershwin show."

"Did she say anything about me?" Adam can't help asking, though he also can't look her in the eye as he asks. He looks down instead, down at those sapphire high heels.

"Why would she say anything about you?" says Amy.

And then, conveniently, the monkey bites someone. Or so it seems at the first notes of pandemonium, because over the shrieks of the child the prophet is exclaiming, "That monkey bit someone, I told you that monkey would bite someone." In fact, it soon becomes clear that the monkey is innocent and that the guilty biter is one of the babies. Sasha is the shrieking victim, and Deborah runs to pick her up; Slimy Sam is left hanging in the middle of a projected budget for child rearing. There is a great deal of adult concern, and several babies are crying, but it turns out that no blood was drawn (although there are marks), and Sasha is consoled with Christopher's cake. Deborah's panic subsides. The monkey is vindicated. And, as the commotion dies away, the jazz music seems even jazzier than before, as if all that fuss has somehow helped the party along, provided a little false excitement to heighten everyone's high spirits.

When Adam looks around the room again, he discovers that Conrad was not the last guest: someone new has arrived. She is a small and very thin young woman, neatly dressed, with beautiful gaunt features and long curly black hair loose around her shoulders. She is watching Christopher intently, and though Adam has never seen her before, he instinctively looks over to where Huck is standing near the mayor. Huck has already seen the new guest and is watching her as intently as she is watching Christopher. She begins to move toward the babies, hair swaying, her form even thinner in motion than at rest. Adam tries to catch Lucille's eye, but fails; she is deep in conversation with Eliot and does not yet sense that something is wrong. The monkey scales the bookcase to the ceiling and pulls down three balloons. They float down among the babies, and Christopher claps his hands together, quite unaware that his mother is approaching.

CHAPTER TWELVE

ALL ALONE

Dear Maman,

Everything has changed here, everything has become frightening. I am alone in the apartment. Huck has gone to Michigan to stay with his parents; naturally he has taken Christopher with him. And it's not certain when they are going to come back, maybe in a week or two, maybe in a month or two. The apartment feels terribly, terribly lonely without them. I hadn't realized how much I counted on having Huck around. There's something very reassuring about him, the way he talks, just the way he is—do you remember? He's the perfect roommate. I think I knew that ten years ago, and now I feel a little bit the way I felt when he suddenly dropped out of college.

But the one I really miss, even more than Huck, is Christopher. I didn't appreciate how much of a presence he was in the apartment—his noises, his movements (crawling all over), his little destructive adventures in the kitchen; the things that Huck was always calling me to come see, like how he could almost reach the third bookshelf, or how he could almost walk. Really, when I think about it, even missing

Huck is mostly missing him with Christopher—I mean, the sound of Huck's voice talking silly to Christopher. Sometimes I go into Christopher's room, and there's the empty crib, and there's the pile of birthday presents that he never got to play with. Yesterday I took all the stuffed animals (including the teddy bear you sent) from the pile and put them in the crib, just so it wouldn't be empty. Huck's room I don't go into at all.

Remember, when I last wrote to you, we were planning Christopher's birthday party, and it was going to be a great event, and even the mayor was going to come? She did come. And it was a wonderful party, with lots of babies, and a monkey, and balloons, and music. I have trouble recalling all these things now, though, because later the whole party was completely shattered. It was just last Sunday, yet it seems a very long time ago. This is what happened: Christopher's mother appeared, Miriam—I've told you about her. She just walked in the door and into the middle of the party.

She was beautiful, with a lot of long black hair. I can't picture her face to myself now, but it wasn't what I had been expecting. I mean I had been expecting that she would look deranged—after what I'd heard, and after all those notes she'd sent Huck—but she didn't look like that at all. Just very concentrated, and serious, and almost unaware that there was a party going on around her. She was looking directly at Christopher, walking toward him. There were ten babies, but she knew exactly who he was. When I noticed her looking at Christopher, I could see that she loved him, or that it was something like love—a word that doesn't actually describe anything very precisely.

By the time she reached the circle of babies, Christopher

had become aware that this woman's gaze was fixed on him, and he was returning the stare, as if he were hypnotized, as if he realized that something very strange and solemn was happening. I was standing right there, and I realized too, and Huck was watching from across the room, but pretty much everyone else in the room was completely unaware, and the party just went right on. Music, cake, balloons, conversation. Certainly there was a lot of party noise, and when Christopher and Miriam were about three feet from each other, I think that I must have been the only one, except for her, who heard what Christopher said. You won't believe this. He looked up at her, and he said: Mama.

He couldn't have known. He hasn't seen her since right after he was born, almost a year ago. But I know that he knows there is such a thing as mama, because he knows the other babies in his day-care group have mamas. And sometimes Christopher tries out the word, as if he wants to see whether it means anything in his situation. And this time he hit the jackpot.

Maman, did I use to ask about Papa after he died, and, if I did, what did you tell me?

When Christopher said Mama, just like that, it seemed miraculous to me, and Miriam must have thought so too. I'll never tell anyone else that he said it, especially not Huck. I'm afraid that it would hurt him, or make him feel guilty, and I'm afraid that telling anyone else would somehow be a betrayal of Huck. But I'm sure that Christopher's saying it was what made everything else happen. I don't think that Miriam walked into that room knowing what she was going to do. I think she just knew it was Christopher's birthday, and she wanted to see him.

But when he said that, said Mama, she just naturally bent down over him and picked him up, and he smiled, being friendly. And then, very calmly, she turned and started to walk with him toward the door. I was watching and Huck was watching, and I think then we were both paralyzed, and the party just continued all around us. Until the monkey began to screech. It was the monkey who realized that something was really wrong and sounded the alarm. His screeching was the most shattering alarm I've ever heard. I was susceptible, of course, I was psychologically ready for an alarm to be sounded, but everyone else at the party responded to the noise that way too: people started looking around for what was the matter, and parents reached for their babies. Then somebody said, Earthquake, and people began to move toward the door frames, and so Miriam was blocked on the way to the door with Christopher. I saw Huck, at the mayor's side, finally find the power to rush toward them, and then I couldn't quite follow all three of them in the crowd.

Miriam must have been out the door though, by the time he reached her, because suddenly there were screams coming from the hall, her screams, and there must have been some kind of struggle going on—for the baby, obviously—because I heard someone yelling, Call the police, and I saw someone else in the kitchen actually pick up the phone and call. But, by the time two policemen got there, Miriam was gone, and Huck was holding Christopher, and the other guests were leaving because the party was definitely over.

Huck told the police that it was nothing, and one of the mayor's attendants took the two policemen aside and whispered something that sent them obediently away. The two attendants then left with the mayor between them, and what was clear immediately to me—Huck was probably holding too tightly to Christopher to notice—was that the mayor was not pleased by all the excitement, not pleased at all.

The next day Huck asked for some time off from work, because he wanted to take Christopher away from San Francisco, and then he started worrying about whether they would welcome him back again at City Hall. But the day after that he and Christopher were already flying home to his parents in Michigan.

Which leaves me alone in San Francisco. Not really alone, of course, because I have my job and my students and some friends. I go running with Tommy and Timmy pretty much every day. But still I feel very alone in the apartment without Huck and Christopher, maybe even a little bit the way Miriam feels not having them. That's silly, I guess, since I have no idea how she feels, or whether she feels anything at all about Huck, but she does want Christopher, that I know, and somehow I want him too. I sit in the living room and work on the oboe line for Mozart arrangements, even though I don't know anyone here who might play the other parts. Is this some sort of complex metaphor, something to do with solitude and independence? I have this terrible fear that something is going to happen while I'm alone in the apartment. Wouldn't it be awful to be caught alone at night by a big earthquake? Sorry to sound so stupid.

It's a relief to me to think that I'm going to see you here very soon. So finish your Melville paper. I love you,

Adam

Dear Huck,

I am taking good care of the apartment. Yesterday afternoon Lucille was here, and she absolutely insisted that we deal with the things that are still left from the party. We moved the furniture back the way it was before in the living room, put away the supply of birthday paper plates for next year's birthday, and ate a good part of a leftover carrot cake. Lucille also thought we should get rid of the remaining balloons, which were, it's true, looking saggy and unhealthy. (I probably would have just left them to shrivel up through the winter—not that there's going to be any winter here.) I can't bear the thought of popping balloons, so I covered my ears and stayed in the bathroom while Lucille coolly popped them one after another with the point of a kitchen knife. A mercy killing, truly, and then I came out and we gathered up the colored scraps.

While I was in the bathroom I wondered how you are getting along without the diapering table. I know *you* can diaper Christopher anywhere (I'll never forget the time you did it on the cable car, downhill, surrounded by tourists), but I've never diapered him without the diapering table, so for me it seems like an essential piece of equipment. I can tell you it's not getting much use here without Christopher. Something else I noticed the other day, in Christopher's room, is that you left his warm sweater here, the blue one with the ducks. Like I said, we are having no signs of winter here, but I would guess that in Michigan it is cold in November (it certainly is in Boston), and Christopher will probably be needing warm clothes. I hope that both of you can manage to adjust to really cold weather. But I also hope that you will both be back in San Francisco before it gets really cold in Michigan.

I wasn't actually planning to write to you (I guess because I was pretending you'd be back so soon it wouldn't matter), but Lucille told me she'd written you a letter, and that started me thinking more realistically about your being away. I don't know how you feel about living in San Francisco after what happened, and I don't know exactly how things stand with your job. I mean I don't know how long you're thinking of staying in Michigan, or how exactly you'll decide when it's time for you and Christopher to come back home.

I am feeling tense about my own job—it's because of that student I told you about, Conrad, the one who was following me. You said right away that he had a crush on me, which was true I guess, although crush doesn't seem like quite the right word—it doesn't take the whole thing seriously enough. That was my problem, you see, that *I* didn't take it seriously at first, partly because it was so peculiar, and partly because I had just moved out here and *everything* was a little peculiar; nothing seemed real enough to be taken all in earnest. It wasn't until I began thinking about Miriam, actually not until I finally *saw* Miriam and saw what happened at Christopher's party, that I realized how stupid I had been about Conrad, not taking more seriously what was obviously a serious mental imbalance. (I mean, it's not normal for people to follow other people through the streets, is it? not even in San Francisco?) It's hard, isn't it, to guess at the degree—I mean to anticipate just what an unbalanced person might actually *do*. I thought the worst was over with Conrad when he actually showed up at the party—I would have pointed him out to you, but there wasn't time for that, was there? But just the fact that he came, you know, through the front door as a guest, I saw as a sign that things were going to stop being so strange.

The other thing that I was too stupid to think about seriously was that all this with Conrad, if it were to explode somehow, could be very, very bad for me and my job. Then, after the party, I thought that the whole thing was almost under control, that he and I would be friends of some sort, and that that was the most anyone in the Stringfellow School would ever make of it.

Well, I was wrong. There is another teacher at the school who suspects that there is something not quite right between me and the boy. And this guy, Graham, doesn't like me at all—for no good reason. I've never done anything to him. Anyway, he had Conrad in one of his classes last year, and now, suddenly, he has invited Conrad to have dinner with him—and made a point of telling me. I even wonder whether he was watching me to see if I would be jealous.

What I also know (and Graham probably doesn't know I know) is that he has AIDS; of course I don't know absolutely for sure, but I've been told by a mutual colleague who probably knows from Graham himself. I suppose that the actual relations among the three of us—Graham, Conrad, and me—would be the same even if Graham didn't have AIDS, if he weren't dying. (I mean, he would still dislike me, and he would still be curious about me and Conrad.) So the fact that he's dying really ought to be left to one side as far as this goes. But I can't help it: I feel extremely uneasy and even alarmed when I think of this sick, dying man suddenly befriending this very unbalanced boy, and probably doing it on my account, because he doesn't like me. I worry about protecting myself, worry about what Conrad will tell Graham about me, what Graham will guess, whether I am somehow going to end up in trouble at this new job that I like so much. I suppose, if the truth were to come out—the fact that Conrad followed me around San Francisco and was in love with me—there'd be no real reason for the school to hold it against *me*. But they might anyway, right?

All these complications—it makes me wish I was still dealing with crossed telephone lines. A few years ago I would just climb up to the top of a pole, straighten out some wires, and all the connections would come clear. Now I run my mind over and over the tangles without ever seeing my way out of the mess.

I have to stop going on about this. I know there's something a little ugly about me worrying this way about myself in a situation where the other two people have so much more serious problems than I have.

Huck, someone came by here for you the other day, your friend Wayne. I told him you were out of town, and that I wasn't sure when you were coming back, and he looked disappointed. I felt bad about it afterward, because I was afraid that what I said might have sounded like I was being mysterious and putting him off. If he stops by again, I will explain more to him—though perhaps you should write me just how much you would want me to explain. Sorry to be awkward about this. I'm about to write something I wouldn't be able to say to your face, but would much rather not suppress any longer: that is, I know that Wayne is your lover. Not that it matters—I mean, not that it's any of my business—just that I feel that by not mentioning it, by keeping it strictly to myself, I am making a big deal out of it in a sort of prurient way. Maybe you already know that I know, since I told Lucille, and perhaps she has told you (perhaps it is in the letter she just wrote to you—that thought occurred to me and is part of why I am writing this now), but, frankly, I'm not comfortable with this secret line of communication anymore either. Obviously, if I know that Wayne is your lover, you know that Lucille is my lover. Or was my lover, I'm not sure anymore.

It was impossible for me to tell you about Lucille and myself at first, not just because I wasn't sure how close you and I were, but even more because I wasn't sure how close you and she were. I think I understood from the beginning that, however things stood, it was not a betrayal, because (I always understood this) Lucille would sooner kick me off a moving cable car than even think about behaving shabbily to you. So I figured *she* must know how things stood, and if she thought it was okay, then it was okay. Living in San Francisco a little longer helped me to see that the whole thing didn't matter as much as I thought it did anyway, and then, knowing about Wayne, knowing that you were gay, or bisexual, or whatever, made me feel how stupid it was to be so secretive about sex. If I am not being clear, it is because I am genuinely confused.

I say that Lucille *was* my lover, because there hasn't been anything like that between us for a little while now (since her show opened), and although she hasn't said anything about it to me (or I to her), I have the impression that we may be done with each other for the moment (that is, she may be done with me). The more I feel this, the more I feel involved with Amy. I told you she had this strange Middle

Eastern marriage, but I don't know if I told you that her husband was executed (after she left him) by the revolutionary Islamic government in Iran. It weighs on me, this becoming involved with a woman who once had a husband who was shot by a firing squad or burnt at the stake or whatever it is that happens to enemies of the revolution in Iran. I feel like I'm somehow occupying his space, and it makes me curious about how exactly he died, but I don't really want to know, so I haven't actually asked Amy. I am overwhelmed by the way that she has put her past behind her. Remember, at the party she was wearing a very proper navy-blue skirt and a pair of completely outrageous shoes that I'm not sure I can describe? Sometimes I think of her as a mermaid, and sometimes I think I'm in love with her, and sometimes I think she's too serious for me, and sometimes I think I'm too foolish for her. I like the feeling of getting involved, but I also have this uncomfortable feeling that Lucille is willing my affair with Amy, that Lucille is settling me down.

Huck, I hope you don't mind about my knowing about Wayne. I am not so innocent that I have to be absolutely protected from everything, and, after all, I do live in San Francisco now. Knowing that you are gay, that you sleep with men, well, I can't say it doesn't change the way I feel about you, because of course it does. But knowing more about you makes me feel closer to you, not further away. Even though right now you are pretty far away.

Listen, about Christopher's warm sweater. Every year for my birthday my grandmother used to knit me a wool sweater, really beautiful wool sweaters. My mother has them in New Haven, I'm sure, and since she's coming out here to a Melville conference in two weeks, I'll ask her to bring the smallest one for Christopher. And, if you're not back here yet, I'll send it to you in Michigan.

I'm looking forward to seeing my mother. How are you doing at home with your parents?

I think about you and Christopher a lot.

Your friend,

Adam

P.S. Slimy Sam came by *again* before he left town. He loves us. He doesn't seem to have noticed anything strange about the way the party ended. He made me a proposition—are you ready? Next time he comes to San Francisco he stays on the floor in our living room, then he gets the corporate client to pay a hypothetical hotel bill, and he gives us a cut of the reimbursement. What do you think—has our old roommate found his place in the corporate world? He meant it all quite seriously and in a friendly way. Tommy and Timmy were there, and they were flabbergasted; they were even more flabbergasted later when I told them he was like that already when he was eighteen. I told old Slimy that I thought not, but I promised I would relay the proposition to you so you could decide for yourself. I hope you are laughing.

Dear Adam,

Fuck, that was some letter from you. I don't usually write letters (they make me feel uncomfortable, you know, being on paper, instead of alive), but I would be a complete creep if I didn't try to write to you now. Especially since I don't know when I'm coming back to San Francisco, don't even know what I'm waiting for exactly. Either something is going to *happen,* and I'll be snapped back, or else something inside me is going to snap and then it'll feel okay to go home.

This here is home too, of course, Michigan—that's what's so weird about it. This house—fucking absolutely the same—it's wonderful and it's creepy. Exactly the way it was when I came home from college ten years ago. Pretty exactly the way it was when I was in second grade. There is this bowl of fruit on the coffee table in the living room, where my mother has arranged two apples, two oranges, and a banana, in exactly the same configuration, I mean *identical,* for the last twenty-five years. You'd swear they were plastic, but they are not plastic, believe me, I have touched them all (carefully, so they won't shift position). You see, the miracle is that she *changes* them every few nights so the fruit will be fresh (even though nobody ever eats it—that would be inconceivable—this stuff is for the household gods, right?), but she always arranges it just precisely *so.* I think she must change the banana more often than the two apples and the two oranges, because bananas go bad faster, and I have never seen the banana with anything like a brown spot. You know what else is a miracle: Christopher *understands;* he does not touch this bowl of fruit. If I kept five pieces of fruit in the San Francisco apartment down at his level, he would figure out things to do with them that would get us evicted from the building. But here my mother has mysteriously communicated to him that this fruit has been dedicated to eternity.

My mother is *crazy* about Christopher and spends hours with him, and I sit in the same room and watch them, feeling like I'm not necessary or not even there or something: like he's *me,* right, her baby. I usually feel good about watching

the two of them, but sometimes I feel spiteful or even jealous
and wish he would qualify some of his affection for her with
some of that troubled disapproval I still feel coming from her
to me. My father I hardly see, though he is here all the time.
He retired last year, and stays in his room all day with the
television on. My mother takes him his meals. He is very sick,
and there is a doctor who has visited him twice so far. I think
my father is dying, but no one has told me in so many words.
He regards me (and my baby) with an air of indifference, and
I'm glad that it's no worse than that. I am full of terrible
emotional sympathy, maybe love, for both my parents, but
neither is willing to accept that from me—understandably, I
guess—and now I am suffering over it.

My room is pretty much the same as it was too—our
room, I should say, since I shared it with my brother when
we were kids. My parents have put up a framed photograph
of him here, *in uniform,* smiling, ready to kill fucking gooks,
ready to get fucking killed. This photograph is hanging right
over his old baseball trophies, which my mother keeps exqui-
sitely dusted. There is still a shelf across one side of the room
that has nothing but Hardy Boys mysteries on it—these were
very important to my brother, and to me. They are up high,
so they remain inviolate, like the fruit downstairs, but I've let
Christopher mess around with the rest of the stuff. He's really
into Chris's sports stuff, like the baseballs, which he can
throw three or four feet from a sitting position. And he's
completely fascinated by Chris's first baseman's mitt, though
he doesn't have the faintest idea what to do with it. Mostly
he tries it out on his head. (I am thinking that maybe I'll take
this mitt back to San Francisco for him—or do my parents
want it? will they care?) I've also messed up the room by

moving my bed over alongside Chris's and putting Christopher in that one so he sleeps between me and the wall.

We're okay without the old diapering table—enjoy it! And my mother found some of my baby sweaters and jackets (which were my brother's first) for Christopher. I'm glad, though, that you are thinking of Christopher for one your grandmother made for you. Thank you, Adam.

My parents don't ask questions about how I happen to have this baby who doesn't come with a mother. I guess they assume that there is some evil awful story behind it (which there is), and my mother seems to take for granted that I will go to church with her every Sunday and pray, which I do. Though I do not confess and receive absolution. I take Christopher with me (which is okay; there are other babies), and when he gets restless and starts to shred the missal, I take him outside and pray there.

Adam, I am not actually sleeping with Wayne. I know you saw him in my bed (yes, Lucille did tell me, and she was furious with me, and she does not really believe what I am telling you now): he was sleeping there, that's all, no fucking, no sex, none. He goes to sleep with his head on my shoulder—and even that has happened just a handful of times this past year. But I can't refuse my shoulder to this poor boy I love, or used to love, who maybe loves me. I wish Miriam would take my shoulder, I swear I wish she would, but she never will.

I don't have sex with Wayne because I am scared about AIDS. Wayne does intravenous drugs, lots, and sleeps with men, lots. I have not slept with *anyone* for a year and a half. When Miriam became pregnant (God, I wish that hadn't happened, but, God, how can I wish such a thing when I look at Christopher), I realized I had to stop sleeping with men because I could get the virus and pass it on to her and the baby. But at the same time I felt I couldn't sleep with her anymore anyway (sex was not, for me, the most important thing about loving her) in case I already had the virus. She didn't understand and thought I was rejecting her, but I was doing it for her sake all along, really. I suppose that since I was resolutely determined not to sleep with her I could have gone on sleeping with men and risked only my own life, but instead I became completely celibate. Because I felt so guilty. You see, the worst possibility was that I already had the virus and had already given it to Miriam and it had already gotten to the fetus. Guilty, guilty, guilty. And, Adam, do you see: AIDS is there for years before it shows, which means it's possible that all that *did* happen, a chance that all three of us—me and Miriam and Christopher—are going to die soon, *and we just don't know it yet.* That is what I think about, Adam, when I cannot distract myself with the rest of my life. But I don't ever forget it, believe me.

Adam, I just reread what I've written so far, and am sort of surprised by the plausibility of my arguments, this carefully reasoned justification of my own celibacy. Do not let me deceive you, Adam. All this is false plausibility and false reasoning. Remember, San Francisco is full of people who have not given up sex because of AIDS, people who have maybe adapted their sex lives a little. I have renounced sex not because I am more rational than they are, or even because my situation demands stricter caution. It's because I simply don't like the idea of sex anymore, can't even bear to think about it. Because I feel deeply, wildly, utterly guilty. Maybe you have to be brought up Catholic to feel this way—I mean really Catholic. You, Adam, a secularized half-Catholic, will have to take my word for it—but, in any case, don't be taken in by my rationalizations.

Miriam hates me. I think she has hated me ever since she became pregnant. I won't trust her with Christopher unless I'm there. I can't. And she doesn't want to see him if I'm there too. With her record she can't make much of a legal case for him, and, besides, she abandoned him right after he was born. You know, if she wanted to live with me and with him, she'd be living there now, in the room you're living in, and I would take care of them both. But it's better for me to live with Christopher alone, and better yet to live with him and you.

Lucille despises Miriam and is angry at me for not hating her too. Lucille insists that Miriam has ruined *my* life, but I know it's the other way around. In most things you'd be better off taking your lead from Lucille, but I hope you'll see this the way I see it and feel something for Christopher's mother.

Regards to the pinkest building on Hyde Street.

With love,

Huck

P.S. I have unsealed the envelope to add that I have just had a long telephone call from the mayor's office in San Francisco and even a few words with the mayor. I can come back to work whenever I want (thank God), but I'm not needed right now, and they are allowing me to stay away until I feel comfortable about coming back. I will come back, Adam, I will. *She* still wants me, Adam—that feels so fucking good.

P.P.S. Forgot to put in my check for two-thirds of the November rent. Will you make the payment? Ask Tommy and Timmy for the address of old Ming. Or just give it to the girls in your class. Thanks.

Dear Maman,

I have not received a reply yet after my last letter to you. I know you are working hard on *Billy Budd*. I did get a letter from Huck yesterday, though.

Do you think I could come home to visit you for a while? I'm not happy here, and I'm scared too, of nothing in particular. What I want is to leave my job and leave this apartment and leave San Francisco.

If you can find the sweater your mother made for me on my first birthday, do you think I could give it to Christopher?

I love you,

Adam

CHAPTER THIRTEEN

ADAM'S PENIS

Adam is lying on his mattress on the floor, naked, face up, on top of the blanket. He is reading *Huckleberry Finn,* but it is not holding his interest, and he finds himself turning pages almost idly. Beside him, very close (it is not a double mattress), is Amy, also naked, face down, under the blanket. She has a set of physics papers at the head of the bed and is grading furiously, drawing diagrams in red marker and writing out red equations. It is early in the evening but already dark outside. They have eaten in Chinatown after school, walked over Russian Hill together holding hands, made love, and now the rest of the evening is still in front of them. On the top of Adam's small wooden dresser Amy has posted her shoes, a pair that features interwoven bands of polished black and white leather; at the foot of the dresser lie Adam's scuffed brown loafers.

There is time, thinks Adam, to get dressed, to put on their shoes, to go out and see the second half of Lucille's show yet again (he has seen the whole thing three times now), and he catches himself on the verge of suggesting it; Amy would almost certainly agree. Instead, without thinking, Adam reaches a hand down to his crotch and finds, to his surprise, that he is hard again. There is something peculiarly meaningless about being hard without even being aware of it. In a few seconds—to escape this sense of meaninglessness perhaps— he has dropped his book, pulled the blanket down, and turned Amy at the hips. He enters her immediately. She is still holding on to the red marker.

Something about the way this happens seems to excite him further, and he is moving with real energy now, his head pressed down over Amy's shoulder so that he isn't actually looking at her. Adam feels that he cannot stop, that he has to keep moving in and out, but at the same time the sexual pleasure that he feels seems not exactly there in his penis. The motion of his hips is strangely mechanical, and his pleasure is abstracted from that movement, exists in his fantasy— a fantasy in which he is very young, a college student, fucking Amy with the energy that comes from being nineteen and very fresh to all this, desperately thrilled to be doing it at all. Amy, too, is nineteen, he imagines, torn away from her papers to submit to his adolescent energy.

And then he feels the felt-tipped pressure on his shoulder, marking him with broad strokes down the upper arm. It takes Adam a few seconds to respond, to control the motion of his body, to stop moving and raise himself up on one elbow to look, not at Amy but at himself. His shoulder and upper arm are inscribed with the equation "$F = ma$," which he vaguely remembers from high school physics. Adam is shocked, and as he turns his eyes from the blood-red markings on his arm, as he focuses at last on Amy, he realizes that (again without his noticing) he has lost his erection and is no longer inside her.

She is looking up at him rather coolly. "Force is the product of mass and acceleration," she says. "Do you think it's relevant?" There is something definitively crushing about this explanation and question. Somehow the equation is intended as a check on his fantasy, a response to the way he turned her over and entered her. Is it also meant to comment, ironically, on the rhythm of his motions, even on his penis, which is now completely without force? What Adam doesn't know is whether she is serious, whether she is angry at him or merely amused. Then she laughs, and he knows. In his fantasy (as in his adolescent college days) he was cherishing her seriousness as the flaw that gave him a spiritual edge over her, but her laugh shows that in fact she has the edge of humor and irony over him. It is not even an unkind laugh, so he cannot really resent her for it either.

"Don't you know the equation?" she asks, cheerful now. "If your father was a physicist, this is something you should have learned at his knee."

"My father died when I was two," says Adam, pathetically, inviting her to take pity on him. He tries to imagine himself at his father's knee, but he cannot. "I don't know anything about physics." He rolls off to one side, still raised on an elbow, looking down at her. She remains lying on her back, where he turned her, still holding on to the red marker, as if to remind him that she can protect herself with the spells and incantations of her science. He pulls the blanket up to his waist, covering himself.

"There was a wonderful course in college," says Amy, "that you should have taken. It was one of those science courses for people who aren't scientists, physics for poets, you know, physics without any of the mathematical complications.

I took it my freshman year, and that's how I first got interested in physics. Actually, that's also how I met my husband—he was the teaching assistant in that course—so physics for poets was fateful for me in more ways than one."

"It's not just that physics is too complicated for me," says Adam. "Poetry is too. English prose fiction is about the most complicated thing I've ever felt comfortable with. I'm sure I wouldn't have been a very good candidate for physics for poets."

Amy laughs. "When I applied to college, I wrote that I wanted to study psychology. I can't imagine now what I was thinking of."

"Why is that so funny?" asks Adam. But really he knows.

She is frank. "It's a hopeless thing, psychology, trying to understand why people are the way they are. It's hopeless, meaningless, nothing at all. Not like that—" She touches the red equation on his arm. "That's real, that means something."

To Adam, of course, it means nothing, but he takes its meaning on faith. At the same time something inside him rebels against what Amy says about psychology. He is reminded of his mother, who believes that only structural patterns are real, and that character motivation is impossible to discuss. He knows that his mother would be immediately sympathetic to what Amy is saying, and he yields to them both, yet he is troubled by the fear that part of what they are dismissing is him. Am I falling in love with her? wonders Adam, meaning Amy. I love her, he thinks, sampling the phrase in his mind and liking it. In fact he almost says it aloud, but his memory of what happened just moments before, the mark on his arm, the felt-tip pen in her hand, embarrasses him and he remains silent. Then it crosses his mind that her husband, the Persian physicist, might have been cruel to her, perhaps sexually abusive in some exotic way that Adam cannot even imagine, and he feels a sudden wave of hatred for Amy's husband, even a momentary flash of righteous satisfaction that the man is dead. This hatred quickly gives way to a wave of tenderness toward Amy. Adam wants to make love to her, really, not just to resolve the meaninglessness of an erection by fucking her with false adolescent energy. But now he has no erection, and, besides, he is too embarrassed to begin again.

So instead, ridiculously, he asks, "Have you considered going to graduate school, getting a Ph.D., becoming a professor?" It is the same question by which Adam had always felt implicitly threatened when he was living with Suzanne.

"I'm not good enough," says Amy, disarming him. "But I still love teaching the basic stuff to smart high school students. And I earn enough of a salary to live on, with some money left over for shoes."

I love her, thinks Adam again, captivated by the way she brings together shoes and physics, the twin pillars of her life. He also loves her because she does not reciprocate by asking him why *he* doesn't go to graduate school. He still doesn't say aloud that he loves her. Even so, perhaps she is aware, because already she is relenting. She runs a hand down his shoulder where she has marked him with the equation, then reaches further, below the blanket, to his penis. He kisses her. But now, much as she strokes him, much as he wants to respond, much as he wants to make love to her, he simply can't get hard. His mind is too distracted, and, after a while, he stops kissing her, and she withdraws her hand. He says, "Amy, I've been thinking about quitting my job and leaving San Francisco."

He stops short of telling her why, and isn't quite sure he could even if he wanted to. She doesn't react with great disappointment; certainly she doesn't beg him to stay. However, soon after, she gets up and gets dressed, carefully slips on her black-and-white shoes, and, despite his invitations to stay the night, she kisses him goodbye, rather indifferently. He hears the front door close behind her. He will have to get up to lock it, but for the moment Adam lies on the mattress, incapable of moving, looking up at the little gallery of photographs and postcards he has constructed around the map of San Francisco on the wall. He wishes that Huck and the baby were here.

In the middle of the night Lucille appears at the foot of Adam's bed. (The door, he thinks, I forgot to lock the front door.) Lucille is wearing the tuxedo in which she performs the second half of her show. She takes off the costume, slowly, piece by piece, while Adam prays silently that she will hurry, because he is desperate for her. Finally she sits astride him and fucks him slowly, while he longs for her to move faster. She sees the equation marked on his shoulder (how can she see it in the dark?) and laughs (silently). He tries to explain to her what the symbols stand for, but she insists, no, they stand for something quite different. Adam, in the dark, can't make out Lucille's face hanging over him. (A succubus, he thinks, who comes in the night.) He reaches up and touches her breasts, which are almost as flat as his. The red of her lips is just barely fluorescent. Then Adam sees the flash of metal (gold) in her hand and knows that she is holding a tube of lipstick, somehow threatening him with it. Still astride him, still moving much too slowly, she presses the head of the lipstick hard against his nipple and marks it red. Then the other nipple. Then she connects the two marks with a horizontal red line across his chest. From the center of that line she now draws a line (slowly) down his chest, carefully vertical, ending at his navel. Blood red, thinks Adam. Laughing (still silently), Lucille continues to fuck him, thinking only of herself, seeming to come and come, over and over again, appropriating Adam's body as an instrument for her own savage satisfaction. And Adam, marked in blood, flat on his back, desperately wants to but simply cannot come.

It is a dream, of course. Adam has suspected it all along, but is certain only when he awakes in the middle of the night. He is alone, covered with sweat, and his erection is so strong that it hurts. He grasps it with his fist, as if to subdue it, but that only makes it stronger and more painful. So he reaches his other hand down to his balls and, urgently, to gain relief, he starts to masturbate. He closes his eyes tight and scrupulously prevents himself from thinking about anyone at all. He concentrates on the thought of his own penis in his own hands, and on making himself come so that it will stop hurting and he can go back to sleep. Finally he does come, into his palm. Adam relaxes his concentration, idly begins to rub the sticky semen into his abdomen around the navel. Then, though his eyes are still shut, his breathing becomes lighter and suddenly he becomes aware that there is someone else breathing in the room.

He opens his eyes and looks toward the door, where he can barely make out a dark silhouette, really just a shadow. He knows who it is, though. In fact, he realizes, he has been unconsciously expecting this visit for quite a while now. "Miriam," he says aloud, and waits to see if she will answer.

Adam remembers the sound of the door closing behind Amy, remembers thinking that he should get up and lock the door behind her. He thinks back to earlier in the evening: Did he actually provoke Amy into leaving him alone for the night? Did he intentionally neglect to lock the door? Adam is sure that there was no one in the room when he woke up from his dream about Lucille. Which means that this shadow must have slipped in while he was masturbating, must have watched him finish, seen as much as it was possible to see in the darkness. Somehow Adam is certain that Miriam's night vision is far superior to his own, and that she makes him out much more clearly from where she stands than he does her. He does not, however, pull the blanket over himself (though he has begun to shiver). He is afraid of seeming afraid, and if, after all, she has been watching him masturbate, then there is little point in being modest now. He feels profoundly exposed and vulnerable—but isn't she vulnerable too, more profoundly than he is?

"Where's Huck?" she says. "What has he done with my baby?"

She takes a step forward, and as she moves a glimmering of moonlight catches the object in her hand, a long kitchen knife that Adam recognizes from his own kitchen, Huck's kitchen. Is she going to kill him? Is she going to castrate him? Adam's shivering has now left him ice cold, but still he does not raise the blanket. More than ever he feels he must try not to seem afraid. But he is afraid.

"They've gone away," says Adam.

"Where?"

"I don't know." And then, as gently as he can, "Can I help you?"

"I don't need you to help me," she says. Then pleading, "I only want my baby—tell me where he is. I don't want Huck, you can have him. I only want my baby."

The voice is hypnotic, very sad, peculiarly musical—and with an edge that is, Adam knows, the edge of insanity. He cannot see her in the dark, but he remembers from the party that she is beautiful. He remembers the abundance of black curls, and those are a part of the silhouette. He remembers her unnatural thinness, and that too can be inferred from the shadow. But the delicacy of her face: that is only a memory in the darkness.

"This used to be my room," she says. "Did you know that?"

"I know."

"I used to sleep on that same mattress," she says, "when I didn't want to sleep with Huck. And then later when he didn't want to sleep with me. Except I kept the mattress in the other corner, and I painted over here, by the window, in the light."

"I like your painting, the one in the living room." Adam does not mention that sometimes it frightens him, the pink spot in the wild sea. He senses her bewilderment.

"I saw it there that day, the birthday. I'd forgotten that

I left him that one. I don't remember what I meant when I painted it. But Huck chose that one the day I met him, so I guess he should keep it. He understands what it means, maybe. You know, Huck is sick, sicker than I am. It makes me uncomfortable to think that my baby is living with that painting. When he comes away with me, I'll show him all the new paintings I've done for him. There are ten of them, a series, ten faces of ten children. I wouldn't sell any of them, even though I was offered a lot of money. I painted all the time at the sanatorium, and they arranged for some of my stuff to be sold at a gallery in Los Angeles. I let them display the ten paintings I did for my baby, but I wouldn't let them be sold. I have some money now. I can take care of him.''

"Christopher?"

"That's not his name. That's what Huck calls him."

"What do you call him?"

"When he's really mine, I'll give him his real name. You do understand, don't you? I have to have my baby. I think about him all the time. I want to teach him to paint. You and Huck don't need him the way I do. You and Huck can have each other."

"Huck and I are not lovers," says Adam.

"But you can still have each other."

"Huck and I are roommates," says Adam. "We're friends. And Huck loves the baby."

"You love Huck," says Miriam.

Whatever that means, thinks Adam.

"But Huck doesn't have any lovers anymore," continues Miriam.

"No."

"There was a time when he used to sleep with a different man every night," says Miriam, "but he doesn't sleep with anyone at all now. He thinks it's because of AIDS, but really it's because he always felt tortured with guilt about sex and never understood that sex was for pleasure. Huck was a poisonous lover. He used to take you in his arms and provide you with spiritual salvation. When he first came to San Francisco he used to save a different man every night, because there were so many people in need of spiritual redemption. He redeemed me, for a while—and I loved him for that, for a while. And the boy from Oklahoma—do you know him?"

Adam nods. He is still lying naked on the mattress, sticky with semen, his shoulder marked with an equation he doesn't understand. Miriam has been moving closer to him as she speaks, a closer but still undefined silhouette in the darkness. He can't make out the knife clearly, but he knows it's there.

"You're lucky you're not Huck's lover," says Miriam. "It's better for you to love him this way. It's better for everyone that he's given up sex. You can't offer your body up for other people's salvation. Better for him to hold on to his body and save himself. It hurt me badly when I became pregnant and he stopped sleeping with me—to protect me, of course. I hated him for that for a long time, but not anymore. I don't care about him now. It's better for him to be celibate. He can join a monastery, or he can live here with you, or he can become President of the United States if he wants to—but he doesn't need my baby. Where are they?"

"Gone away." Adam is thinking that the most important thing is to be loyal to Huck. Which means not just refusing to say where he's gone, but also refusing to be seduced into seeing him the way she sees him; for there is something hypnotically persuasive about her, especially in the strangeness of the night. He reminds himself of Huck and Christopher together on the Golden Gate Bridge, the moment Adam vowed never to forget. Even if he cannot now conjure up the full inspirational joy of watching the two of them, it is sufficiently inspirational just to remember the vow. It hardens his resolve to protect them from Miriam, even if it means bringing down her fury upon himself. How much does she hate him for living here with Huck and Christopher? And another question is nagging at him still: has he been expecting this all along, this encounter?

"I know they've gone away," says Miriam. "I checked their rooms before I came in here. I can see that they've been away for a while. What's your name?"

"Adam."

"My name is Miriam."

"Yes, I know."

"Adam, tell me where my baby is."

"I don't know."

"I won't give up," says Miriam. "Huck has got to come back sometime. I know he'll come back. He'll never be able to live anyplace but here in San Francisco. He'll bring my baby back with him, and when they come I'll be waiting for them." For a moment Adam wonders if she means to wait right here in this room, with Adam as her prisoner. "I'm happy to be here, too, after all that time in Los Angeles in the hospital. I still love San Francisco, but not the way Huck does. I won't spend the rest of my life here. I'm just going to wait until I find my baby, and then we'll disappear together. San Francisco has changed too much, Adam. I came

here when I was sixteen—I ran away from home. You should
have seen San Francisco then; it was a different world. But
now it's not so different anymore, I guess. The city is full of
people who look like you and Huck, and it's not important
to me anymore to spend my life here. I'm just waiting here
now for my baby."

She takes a step backward, away from Adam, as if she
has finished, as if she is actually about to leave the room,
leave the apartment, leave Adam whole and alive. Adam feels
a sudden rush of wild relief, but then a sudden rush of
something else that he doesn't understand at all. He finds
himself speaking to her, halting her retreat, saying things he
surely never intended to say.

"You abandoned him after he was born," says Adam.
"You abandoned him, and Huck took care of him. He's
Huck's baby now, not yours. He's Huck's baby, *his* baby, *his*
baby."

And Miriam, just as he must have suspected she would,
rushes at him in a silent fury, and the next thing he feels is
her body—a wool sweater, that is—against his body, naked.
He turns quickly to one side and feels the knife grazing the
side of his thigh. It is electrifying, not painful, and now Adam
begins to scream.

CHAPTER FOURTEEN

THE WOUNDED HERO

Adam is reclining on the rose-pink love seat in the living room. He is not actually in pain—the long cut on his thigh has been stitched and bandaged, and his limp is only barely noticeable when he walks—but he is being treated like a hero, wounded in war. Huck, glowing with happiness at being back home in San Francisco, is happy in devotion to Adam, who has undergone such a strange and sinister adventure on his behalf. Huck sits on the living-room floor, at Adam's feet, and in the armchair, on Adam's other side, with Christopher on her lap, is Adam's mother.

Huck looks just the way Adam has been picturing him: the same boyish handsomeness (of which Adam has become so fond), the same silver-blue eyes and long lips. But Adam's mother (whom Adam has not seen in three months) does not appear exactly as he remembers her: she is grander and more beautiful. Christopher has taken to her in an extraordinary way; he sits in her lap in a sort of imitation of her own stateliness, with none of the restless wriggling that Adam expects from him. Yesterday, Christopher joyfully welcomed himself home by taking all the books off the two shelves within his reach. But today he is content to strike a dignified pose in the lap of Simone Berg, occasionally looking up at his model as if to check that he is doing it right. Adam would like to take Christopher onto his own lap, at least for a little while, but Christopher is not especially interested, and both Huck and Adam's mother have agreed that Adam's lap is still too fragile.

When Adam screamed that night (it was only three nights ago, though it seems mythologically distant to Adam) the whole pink building must have heard him, including Tommy and Timmy, who came rushing down to his assistance, who called the police, who called an ambulance. The ambulance Adam recalls with some embarrassment now, since, as it turned out, he was far from mortally wounded. The doctor at the hospital examined the cut on his thigh, administered a half-dozen stitches with great speed and an expression of total boredom, and then turned him over to a nurse, who carefully applied a cloth bandage. The nurse was a cheering young man, who commiserated with Adam over his "boo-boo," promised the possibility of an alluring scar, and then turned him over to Tommy and Timmy, who called for a taxi home. The whole episode lasted about an hour and a half. Miriam, on the other hand, remains hospitalized. Adam has learned that she is, in fact, about to be transferred to a hospital in Los Angeles, near her mother, and is likely to remain in medical custody for quite a while. Adam knows this because he called the police the day before yesterday to see if he could visit her (he wants to apologize, though he isn't quite sure why), but he was told that she was under very heavy sedation.

As soon as Adam returned from the hospital he telephoned his mother in Connecticut and then Huck in Michigan. He told them both what had happened, and though he did not actually ask either of them to come, forty-eight hours later they both arrived. Adam's mother canceled this week's classes and can now stay through the Berkeley Melville conference; she has a room in a deluxe hotel on the top of neighboring Nob Hill. Huck and Christopher, of course, have simply come home. To have his mother on one side and Huck on the other leaves Adam feeling utterly complete, even though the two of them don't quite seem to fit together. Huck's young all-American ease (never mind what lurks beneath) contrasts oddly with the aging European formality of Simone Berg. They are, Adam thinks, too charismatic in too divergent ways. The bond between them is Adam, clearly, but, really much more striking, there is now the bond of Christopher as well. Christopher gives himself to each of them by turns, while Adam remains inert between them on the love seat. Adam notes the structural pattern, knowing that his mother has noted it too.

The pattern is disrupted by the entrance of Lucille, who embraces Huck, welcoming him back, then pats Adam affectionately on the head. Adam's mother holds out a hand to Lucille, and Adam quickly introduces them. When Lucille then bends over to welcome Christopher, she finds that he too has extended his hand to her, in obvious imitation. Everyone laughs, and Lucille kisses the little hand, leaving behind, Adam notices, a smudge of lipstick. Adam knows how to take his pat on the head, knows that Lucille is his friend now, has given him up as a lover. She spent a whole afternoon with him, making him tell her exactly what had happened between him and Miriam. She too took Adam as a hero; she changed his bandage for him, and made love to him one last time—she told him it was the last time. Believe me, it's better for you not to carry on and on with me, she said, and Adam believed her. I won't forget this, said Adam, at a loss. I'll bet you won't, said Lucille. During that last sexual encounter, Adam felt (and perhaps relished) a peculiarly sharp and tingling pain along the cut in his thigh.

"We must go," announces Simone Berg, rising from the armchair with Christopher. She has on a suit of dark red wool (she wears it for lectures, Adam knows), and her hair, a contrasting auburn red, is elegantly coiffed. Adam also rises, unsteady not from his wound but from so much reclining. He too is dressed up (despite his invalid status), wearing one of the corduroy jackets from his teaching wardrobe, feeling not quite worthy to escort his own mother.

The invitation came the day before yesterday. There had been a small notice in the *Chronicle* about one Adam Berg, resident of Russian Hill, being attacked by an unidentified assailant, sustaining mild injuries. When the phone rang it was Conrad, to say that his mother had seen the article, recognized the name, and wanted Adam to come to dinner if he felt well enough. Adam accepted. Then yesterday he called to say that his mother had arrived for a visit, could she come too? Adam was confident that his mother's presence would dissolve some of his uneasiness about meeting Conrad's parents. Adam has not yet managed to put aside his fears that he and Conrad will somehow be found out, even though there is nothing to find out.

The house is in Pacific Heights, not far from the Stringfellow School—and just around the corner from the residence of the mayor, Conrad's mother informs them, implying with a sort of cheerful prurience that she could tell more if she chose to. She has heard with great interest, from Conrad, that the mayor actually attended a party at Adam's apartment a few weeks ago. There is more prurience in her inquiries about the assailant who broke into Adam's apartment, and her curiosity leaves Adam feeling, all the more, that he has something to conceal. Conrad, Adam knows, is obsessed with the fact that his mother is the daughter of an S.S. officer, but, despite her German accent, Adam doesn't find her sinister. She seems, rather, almost engagingly monstrous. She is immense, a magnificently fat woman with great big baby-blue eyes. What is most curious about the appearance of Trudy Winterfeldt, thinks Adam, is that one can so easily discern within her hugeness the slender form of a pretty young blue-eyed girl. This sense of superimposition gives Adam a shock, even suggests to him the notion that this woman, grotesquely imprisoned in such an implausible form, is being punished for the evil of her ancestors. And yet her stylish cap of blond hair, the careful makeup around the lovely eyes, and an obviously expensive caftan of royal purple all combine to tell of a vanity that has not been extinguished. Furthermore, her happy, unstoppable train of conversation and an unmistakable satisfaction with herself and her home make it impossible for Adam to find her pathetic. She smokes a long cigarette, held between beautifully manicured nails, with an air of completely sensual luxuriance. As she speaks, she waves and gestures with the cigarette and with her nails. Often she thus draws attention to Conrad's father—himself a large man, although not on her scale—and she talks about him to her guests rather than letting him talk for himself. He seems rather proud of his wife and defers to her in a manner that is distinctly chivalrous. But there is also something grim about his presence, and perhaps that is why Conrad hates him. Adam, having grown up without a father, is not well attuned to the tensions between fathers and sons.

Adam feels slightly embarrassed on Conrad's behalf (to have such a mother) and then again slightly embarrassed on behalf of his own mother (to have such a hostess). But Simone Berg does not even seem to be registering the character of her hostess; what, after all, is character anyway? She sits perfectly still, wears a fixed polite smile, and, as far as Adam can tell, seems to be charting the perpetual choreography of Trudy Winterfeldt's waving hand and cigarette. Adam watches closely, trying to see whatever it is that his mother sees, trying to interpret the significance of the movements. He also allows himself to think that his own mother is very wonderful, but undeniably peculiar.

The last to arrive is a guest who received a last-minute invitation: Alexandra. When you called to say your mother was visiting, says Trudy to Adam, I thought I should make the numbers even, I knew you would all get along. Conrad remains silent, but nods to Alexandra; he refuses to meet Adam's eye. It occurs to Adam that expanding the party has made the situation easier for himself, but that Conrad probably preferred the originally intended foursome, in which Adam was so clearly his guest and partner. He looks very young to Adam tonight, and deeply sympathetic; in his pressed white shirt (as always) and sullen silence (as usual) he seems to be struggling to construct some sort of dignity for himself in the undignified circumstances of his family and his own odd adolescence. Adam resolves to do something to show Conrad he understands and sympathizes, then wonders whether this is a dangerous resolution. They all go in to dinner, roast beef and potatoes prepared by the Cambodian maid.

It is Alexandra, addressing Adam's mother as Professor Berg and asking her about studying English at Yale, who alerts Trudy to her guest's distinction. There then follow many compliments about Adam, addressed to his mother by both of Conrad's parents: what a good teacher Adam is, what a good influence he has been on Conrad, how satisfying it is that Conrad has agreed to apply to Yale. "My father was a professor at Yale," says Adam's mother, replying to a question that Alexandra has asked, "but I didn't go to college there, because at that time only boys were admitted. There were no girls at all until around the time that Adam went to college. So, you see, I was a graduate student at Yale; that was possible. But I went to college at Bryn Mawr."

Trudy Winterfeldt, it turns out, knows quite a number of ladies in San Francisco who went to Bryn Mawr. She offers several names to Adam's mother, who does not recognize them. Adam's mother is, of course, considerably older than Conrad's mother. But that does not discourage their hostess, who proceeds to tell a long and amusing story about the perpetual war between one of these alumnae and another, who fought over the same Princeton man twenty years ago; both of them married and divorced him over the course of a decade, and now both live in San Francisco, each determined to ruin the other in high society. Trudy Winterfeldt, Adam gathers, is in high society, whatever that may be. She is eager to take Simone Berg to the monthly meeting of the Bryn Mawr book club so that she can see the two heroines with her own eyes, but Adam's mother politely explains that she will not be staying in San Francisco long enough to have the pleasure.

Trudy Winterfeldt, who did not of course go to Bryn Mawr, who did not even go to the university in Germany, always attends the Bryn Mawr book club meetings. She attends because the saga of the two rivals is so interesting, and the book club is a central forum for their struggle to the death. In the course of following their adventures over the years, Conrad's mother has become—incidentally, she admits—rather formidably well read. Reading is so much fun, she declares. It must be so much fun to teach literature, she supposes, addressing both Adam and his mother.

"I've just been realizing that I don't honestly like to read," says Simone Berg. "I like to reread books I've already read—that, I think, is not the same as reading. When you reread the relation is between your consciousness and your memory. Reading new books puts you in a relation with literature directly, and that I think I have always found fatiguing and futile. I have a feeling that I am going to spend the rest of my life rereading and writing about the same hundred works." My mother, thinks Adam, is a very strange woman. It's not just that the whole idea is perverse; it's the way she brings it out so conversationally at this dinner table.

"I really can't accept that," says Alexandra brashly. "If you hadn't read those hundred books for the first time, you couldn't reread them now."

"I can accept it," says Conrad to Alexandra.

Conrad's mother looks on, beaming, a purple presence, at this exchange of views. But then she seems to feel that she has allowed them their say, and now it is time to take charge of the conversation once again. Lighting another cigarette, she launches into a behind-the-scenes account of the San Francisco opera, whose committees she adorns. It turns out that Pavarotti himself, after the gala opening night, paid some very gallant compliments to Trudy Winterfeldt. Adam is wishing that he had brought Timmy, who has heard grotesque legends of the ladies on these committees, but has never known one personally. Along the way, Conrad's mother graciously recognizes the services of Alexandra's mother, who serves on some of the same committees in a less important capacity. If there is anything carelessly condescending in these remarks, Alexandra certainly doesn't take offense, because, Adam notices, she does not bother to listen to anything Conrad's mother says. The Cambodian maid brings out her own homemade strawberry shortcake.

After dinner Trudy Winterfeldt suggests that Conrad show Alexandra the house—but Alexandra refuses to be treated like a child and protests that she has already seen the house. Obviously she is curious about Adam's mother and would like to hear what else she has to say. And so it happens that Adam, his heart going out to Conrad, who seemed to be suffering throughout dinner, expresses himself interested in seeing the house. The two of them become the little boys who go off and leave the adults (their parents, in fact, and Alexandra too) to talk about whatever adults talk about. Adam climbs the stairs slowly, conscious (without actually feeling any pain) of his wounded leg.

In Conrad's room the walls are bare, barer even than Adam's own walls, and there is a particular odor of cigarette smoke that suggests a recent maternal presence. There is, however, a window, a very high window—they are on the third floor—that looks down on the not so distant lights of the Golden Gate. "The bridge!" says Adam, genuinely excited, but of course Conrad has long ago grown accustomed to the view. He stands beside Adam, looking out the window impassively.

"Don't say anything about my family," says Conrad. "Just don't say anything, I don't want to think about it."

"You're going to go away, next year." Adam says this encouragingly.

"I understood exactly what your mother meant about reading new books being futile. I feel that way about my whole life."

"Well, everyone feels like that sometimes. Until this week I thought I was on the point of giving up my whole life in San Francisco and just running away."

"But now you'll stay here."

"Yes."

"And I'll run away."

"For you it won't be running away, Conrad. It will be moving on. You're a lot younger than I am." Adam is suddenly reminded that Conrad is or has been in love with him, and that this being alone together upstairs could be considered dangerous and compromising—but the secret of their connection doesn't seem very important just now. Whatever was wrong between them, whatever was wrong with the way Conrad was seeing him, Adam feels that it is about to pass, leaving them both behind, a little older, moving on. It will be better for both of them, Adam believes, but Conrad, naturally, will refuse to believe it, even if Adam insists.

"I want to ask you something, Conrad."

"Not about my family, not now." He stiffens.

"No, not about your family, about Graham Doyle. He told me he invited you to have dinner with him."

"So?" Conrad is angry at Adam for mentioning this, and Adam doesn't blame him. But he persists.

"Of course it isn't any of my business."

"God damn you, it *isn't* any of your business."

"Or is it?" says Adam.

"We did talk about you," Conrad admits, as if he is being compelled to confess. "He asked me about you."

"What did he ask? What did you say?"

"He wanted to know what was going on, and I told him that you and I were lovers," says Conrad, icy-gray eyes fixed on Adam.

Adam doesn't even wince. "You didn't say that. I don't believe you said that."

"Of course I didn't say that," says Conrad. Then angrily again, "I'll tell you what he said. He said he could tell that I had a crush on you, and, when I didn't deny it, he laughed and asked why I couldn't see that you couldn't possibly be gay."

"I'm not," says Adam.

"Hurray for you," says Conrad.

And this moment of reluctant agreement is for some reason so exhilarating and at the same time so treacherously liberating for Adam that he doesn't even know how to pull back, the next moment, when Conrad clasps his head between two hands and kisses him, very hard, lips against lips.

Conrad's lips feel very thin, too thin to express whatever it is that Conrad is trying to express so intensely in this one kiss; and Adam is not sure what he is returning with his own lips, though he is terribly conscious of his mustache and beard, maybe more than he has ever been before. This is the first time this has ever happened to me, thinks Adam, and probably the first time it has ever happened to him, and this one kiss just goes on and on, both mouths pressed tightly shut against each other, his mother downstairs, my mother downstairs, cars crossing the bridge somewhere out there. Taboo, thinks Adam, teacher and student, man and boy, taboo; but the word is hollow, and the kiss is real. Adam, for some reason, thinks of the faint red markings on his arm, which proclaim that force is the product of mass and acceleration, markings that Conrad will never see or know about. And then the force subsides, and the kiss seems to burn out all at once, and Conrad's head is on Adam's shoulder, Conrad's body is shaking, and Adam is looking out the window at the lights of the bridge.

When Adam has left his mother at her hotel and returned home, he finds Huck sitting in the living room, Christopher asleep in his arms. A record is playing, a record that Adam has not heard since the day after he arrived in San Francisco.

> *I can dance a tango, I can read Greek, easy.*
> *I can slay a dragon any old week, easy.*
> *What's hard is simple,*
> *What's natural comes hard.*
> *Maybe you could show me how to let go,*
> *Lower my guard,*
> *Learn to be free,*
> *Maybe if you whistle,*
> *Whistle for me.*

Adam purses his lips, as if to whistle, but his lips seem alien to him tonight, and he's not sure he *can* whistle just now. He purposefully relaxes his mouth and doesn't try. When the song ends, Huck looks up and sees him, then rises and lifts the needle from the record, and there is silence.

"Your mother is a diamond," says Huck. "I think she's fantastic, and she really does look a little like, well, *her.*" Adam thinks so too. "More elegant," Huck continues, "and not so marked by power—but there's some sort of natural command and the same dignity."

All very well, Adam is thinking, but what kind of dignity does that leave for you and me, for the boys who are somehow not quite men, for the men who are still somehow little boys? Is there some kind of natural command that is out there waiting for us to grow into it? "My mother is a strange woman," he says finally. "She's obsessed with the relations between things, but she herself seems caught in some kind of state of hopeless unrelatedness. She doesn't quite connect with the world around her." Not even with me, thinks Adam unhappily; she almost connects with me, but not quite.

"Yes, that's part of what's striking about her," says Huck. "I like it. Even with Christopher, she likes him, and he adores her, but when she holds him she doesn't become just a person with a baby, the way I do, completely. Instead there she is, and there's the baby, and somehow they aren't quite touching even though he's sitting in her lap." Huck bends over Christopher, sleeping, to stroke him. It is true, thinks Adam, they are like one animal, but Huck after all is Christopher's father. "After you two left, Christopher was inconsolable without your mother. Apparently he thinks she's mama now because he heard you call her that. I think maybe he misses my mother too, after those weeks in Michigan, although my mother is nothing like yours."

Yes, Adam is lucky to have such a mother, who loves him (who has come all the way to California to make sure he is all right), even if they don't quite connect. And whom he loves, well, admit it, in a way that seems to put into perspective (if not virtually overwhelm) all the different kinds of love he has felt for the other characters in his life. (Characters, not people—that is her mark, surely.) What Adam feels about his mother is something that goes too deep for him even to try to understand; it must be something like what Huck feels about the sleeping baby he is holding.

"Let's put him to bed," says Huck, rising with Christopher.

Adam follows him into Christopher's room, and watches him lay Christopher out in the crib and cover him with a blanket. Christopher wriggles around for a moment, sorting out his limbs into a comfortable position, then settles with his face turned toward them, fast asleep, faintly illuminated by the light from the hallway. The tiny features are drawn tensely together in a pout, totally concentrated, dreaming perhaps of something very important. Adam and Huck peer over the side of the crib, entranced, and Adam thinks of the times he came into this room when Huck and Christopher were in Michigan, and the crib was empty, and how desolate it seemed. Miriam also looked into that empty crib, thinks Adam, and what did she feel?

"How's your leg?" says Huck, whispering. In fact, neither music nor conversation will wake Christopher once he has fallen asleep, but this is a sort of shrine and the whispering a token of reverence.

"It's nothing. I have to change the bandage later."

"I'll help you."

Adam reaches into the crib and picks up one of the stuffed animals that lies in a heap at the foot. It is a teddy bear, perhaps the one Adam's mother sent—but in this light it is difficult to distinguish among teddy bears. Adam strokes the bear, as if it were alive.

"Thank you," whispers Huck finally, with a certain momentousness.

It is his tone that tells Adam what Huck is talking about, what subject is finally being broached, and he pauses before replying. "Don't thank me, there's nothing to thank me for."

"Yes there is, and I'll never forget it."

"I didn't do anything." Adam wants Huck to stop.

"You stayed here when I ran away, and you faced what I should have faced, and you could have been killed. You did that for me."

Christopher begins to move restlessly, makes an odd hooting noise, as if there is something disturbing in his dreams, then settles down again, still facing them, still asleep.

By the time he is quiet again, Adam has almost fully realized what it is that he has been trying not to realize. There is the faint noise of a door closing somewhere in the building, in someone else's apartment, and it brings back the sound of the door that he did not lock that other night, and suddenly there is no getting away from the truth of the matter.

Adam steps back from the crib, and Huck does too. Now they look at each other, not the baby. Adam whispers, "You know what you're thanking me for, don't you? I set a trap for her. I knew she would come eventually, and that night I just happened to forget to lock the door. So she came in. And then when she was about to leave, I baited her. I didn't know what I was doing at the time, but I see now, I was baiting her so she'd attack me. I wanted her to attack me so that they would have to put her away. And then you would be able to come home with Christopher, and we would live happily ever after. And here we are. Go ahead, thank me. I wasn't a hero, I was a shit."

Adam can see that Huck already knows all this, knew it on some level before Adam did, without knowing about the door, without knowing the details. "You don't have to think of it that way," says Huck, urgently, still whispering.

"I do have to think of it that way. I'm glad that I did it, I can't help being glad that I did it. I'm incredibly happy that you and Christopher have come home. But I can't pretend to myself that all this worked out so conveniently all by itself. It would be dishonest for me to go on letting you treat me like a hero, when there was nothing heroic about what I did. It was something bad, Huck, my intentions were bad intentions, but I did it for the sake of something good. Or at least I think I did."

"You did."

"I did it for you, Huck." It is an invitation to Huck to assume a part of the guilt.

"Yes, I understand, for me and for the baby." Huck's whisper is trembling now; it costs him a lot to accept what Adam has thrust upon him. But he takes it. And then he takes Adam's hand in solidarity. Adam reaches his other hand up to the side of Huck's face, pulls him closer, and kisses him.

This, thinks Adam, is what that other kiss was leading

up to; it was to prepare me for this. And this, in fact, is not just a kiss: it is kissing, it is making love. It is sex, thinks Adam, as the cut on his thigh becomes sharply painful. Adam and Huck are both fully clothed (Adam still in the corduroy jacket he wore to escort his mother to dinner), and the baby is sleeping a few feet away. Nevertheless, Adam is certain that they will end up fucking, somehow, in some other room—he can vaguely picture the scene; only vaguely because, after all, what does Adam know of such things? It is not exactly a picture that appeals to him, but he feels wildly compelled to bring it off, to push this through to the end. Adam takes his friend's tongue into his mouth, and thinks again that were it not for the kiss in Conrad's room, the violation of that taboo, he would never be able to do this now.

Has Adam known all along that everything was leading to this? Has he been, yet again, coldly, exploitatively, dishonestly premeditating? But to be honest now: he feels something for Huck, there's no doubt about that, but the reason they are about to make love is fundamentally because Adam must justify to himself the way he behaved, the entrapment of Miriam. If he behaved basely that night, but did it for someone he loved, someone who was his lover, well, wouldn't that go some way toward redeeming his baseness? And if he is not sure he really wants to sleep with Huck, then, damn, that can also be his penance. Yes, that's it: penance and redemption.

It is Huck who pulls away, shakes his head, holds Adam's shoulders at arm's length with a force that both pleads and commands. Huck, after all, has renounced sex—in his own private pursuit of penance and redemption. Adam feels both cheated and relieved; he knows, in his heart, that had they ended up fucking they would have neither become lovers nor remained friends. Huck bends his arms and pulls Adam close, Adam's head on Huck's shoulder, in perfect silence except for the breathing of the baby. Adam feels, with regret, the pain along his wound subsiding, but he finds consolation in the thought that he will be left with a scar.

CHAPTER FIFTEEN

ON THE
THRESHOLD

"Yes, it's like the end of the earth," says Simone Berg. "And look, Adam, that must be the evening star." They are at the ocean, at the edge of the city, on the same beach that Adam found his first day in San Francisco. And indeed there is the evening star, due west over the Pacific, clearly visible even though the sky is still light. The red sun is at the horizon, sinking into the ocean, directly before their eyes.

"Christopher," says Adam, "it's the evening star, you have to make a wish." Christopher, supported by Adam's arm, holding on to his shoulder, looks up at the sky and follows Adam's pointing finger. Does he see the star? And, if he sees it, what does he suppose that it is? He looks back solemnly at Adam, their faces three inches apart, then over at Adam's mother beside them, eyeing her with the same solemn expression. He seems to feel that this is a momentous occasion, the three of them here at the end of the world, and Adam too, looking into the silver-blue eyes of the baby, knows that the whole scene is making its mark on his own memory.

"We'll make wishes for him," says Adam's mother. "Wish something for him, Adam, and something for yourself."

Adam wishes, for himself and for Christopher, that there will be more moments like this one: some lucky combination of people in some golden setting, moments of beauty. The wish is one of structure and relations, and Adam knows his mother would appreciate it, but he also knows that when you wish on the evening star you keep your wish to yourself.

It is his mother's last day in San Francisco. She has delivered her paper at Berkeley, and tomorrow morning she will be teaching at Yale. Adam has seen her every day or evening for the last week, has taken her all over San Francisco, has introduced her to his friends. She has crossed the bridge with Adam and been properly impressed; a bridge is something that, for metaphorical reasons, she profoundly appreciates. She has eaten in Chinatown with Adam and Huck and Lucille and Christopher, and politely sampled the various dishes; Chinese food is something that she does not particularly appreciate. She has been to the Stringfellow School, has admired the façade, the parlor, the turret classroom, been introduced to the headmaster. Jonah Stringfellow was honored to welcome a visitor from Yale, and opportunely warned her of the apocalyptic earthquake just around the corner. She has met not only Huck and Lucille, Tommy and Timmy, Conrad and Alexandra; she has also met Amy Armstrong, been given to understand that Amy is the woman in Adam's life, has seemed to approve. In short, Adam has presented to her his new life and, seeing it through her eyes, is now ready to accept it as a life worth pursuing further. And he cannot help feeling that his position in this new life is greatly enhanced by having presented to it such an extraordinary mother.

This afternoon, Sunday, Christopher refused to be separated from her, and so Adam proposed to Huck that Christopher go along with him and his mother to see the ocean. Adam then rummaged through Christopher's drawers to find his sailor suit, brand new, a birthday present. Definitely Adam is getting a particular satisfaction from this excursion of three, Christopher between Adam and his mother—without Huck. And it is not so unlike the satisfaction that he has felt alone with Huck and Christopher. That is, it must be something in the numbers, in the formula: two adults and a baby.

Standing on the deserted, windy beach, here where the city ends and the ocean begins, Adam can imagine how utterly anonymous they must seem to anyone behind them, three creatures against the sea, two adults and a baby. Adam looks over his shoulder, but there is no one, only the cars passing on the highway that separates the beach from the city. He looks up and down the beach, half expecting to see the two men who were kissing in the sand that first time he was here. Were they some sort of portent back then? And have they now vanished because whatever they portended has come to pass? Adam remembers Conrad's lips and Huck's mouth, but the memory, though vivid, has become distant in a week, the memory of something past and unreal.

Christopher wriggles in Adam's arms, calls out, Up! up!—which must mean down. With the waves breaking ferociously twenty feet away, with the posted warnings of the fatal undertow, Adam resists; a baby on this beach, he instinctively feels, should be in somebody's arms. But Christopher is quite determined, and it is his instinct that wins out in the end. He stands between Adam and his mother, each of them holding tightly to one of his hands. And he leads them in a shuffling dance, a few steps forward, then a few backward. From behind, their outlines must be even more striking now, and even more anonymous as the sun dips below the horizon. The evening star shines brighter and brighter, more and more magical, and they shuffle forward and backward, as if responding to the currents of the sea.

Adam waits in the hotel lobby with Christopher, while his mother goes to find her luggage. The lobby is full of rich-looking people, checking in, checking out, waiting for each other, and Adam feels somehow not quite an adult. Christopher, naturally, is unwilling to sit quietly and wait; he is eager to explore. Adam lets him down off his lap and walks a few paces behind as Christopher in his sailor suit crawls around the lobby, stopping to stare impolitely at anyone who interests him. Adam himself wears a sheepish, apologetic smile. Christopher pulls himself up alongside a couch and, before Adam can even see what is happening, picks up a woman's black leather purse, opens the clasp, and starts taking out coins. Adam grabs the purse from Christopher, and immediately the woman turns to see her purse in Adam's hands; she is plainly dubious about his apologetic explanations. Then he takes Christopher by the hand and walks him around, attracting some attention but causing no major mischief. Very soon, thinks Adam, Christopher is going to be able to walk around by himself.

Across the lobby Adam sees his mother emerge from an elevator, followed by a porter with her luggage. She is certainly not expensively dressed by the standards of this lobby, but there is something about the way she carries herself that makes her—to Adam's eye—the one aristocrat in a crowd of clowns. In that crowd, of course, he includes himself. She is wearing a dress of gray wool with a high neck, a paisley scarf, a long black cardigan. She is as striking here in the crowded lobby as she was an hour ago on the deserted beach, as she will be much later tonight on the other side of the country when she is met at the airport by Harvey, her husband, another one of the clowns. Adam is no longer bitter about Harvey; if she is to be married at all, then she can hardly expect to find someone worthy of her. That is the difference between her and me, thinks Adam, for I have everything to gain in love and marriage. Suzanne took him in hand—as Lucille noticed immediately, the very first day—transformed him from an unfocused young man into a more coherent adult. Lucille too took him in hand, taught him a few things about the world and about himself, then put him down again. And now Adam will entrust himself to Amy, because, after all, he can only emerge the better for it.

Maman, he calls. She stops, looks around her with an air of royalty, sees him, and starts again. Mama, says Christopher, interested, but he is too low down to see her till she has come closer. Then he does see her, calls out again, Mama, and pulls his hand away from Adam's. He starts to take a step, but collapses immediately onto the red carpeting and crawls joyfully forward to meet her. She kneels, magnificently, and lifts him up; they are striking together. They sweep through the lobby and out into the air, Adam and the porter right behind them. A taxi is summoned.

The front of the hotel is at the very top of Nob Hill, and before them, in the valley, are the twinkling lights of downtown San Francisco. As Adam and his mother stand side by side, looking down into the valley of the city, Christopher in her arms, another one of those moments seems to seize them, something transcendent.

"The hills and the valleys," says Simone Berg, "that's what is most fundamental here, yes?"

"Yes," says Adam. Naturally the structural polarity appeals to her.

"And the ocean, of course. Thank you for taking me to the ocean today. I'll always remember that, the city and the ocean and the evening star."

"I will too."

"Thank you for showing me the city; it's beautiful."

As she says this Adam is suddenly sure that she has been aware all along of what he needed from her visit, of what it meant for him to show her the city. And he is grateful to her for knowing him that well after all, but also a little disappointed to be so easily read.

"Goodbye, little one," she says to Christopher. "When we next see each other you will be quite changed, yes?" She kisses Christopher on both cheeks and passes him to Adam. "He needs a sweater; it is too cool at night."

"Maman, do you remember, I asked if you would send

me the first sweater your mother made for me. I want it for
Christopher. You forgot to bring it with you, but will you send
it to me?"

She pulls the cardigan around her, smiles at him, and
looks very beautiful. "No, I won't."

"No?"

"No. I don't know how to knit sweaters, so those sweaters will be for your children."

"For my children?" He repeats her words as if he
doesn't quite understand them, though her meaning is clear
enough. The taxi pulls up; the porter stows the luggage, tells
the driver it is to be the airport. Adam's mother leans over
Christopher to kiss her son, on both cheeks, gets into the taxi,
and a moment later Adam is left alone with Christopher and
the valley of lights.

Adam, holding Christopher, plots his way home: he will descend the slope of Nob Hill, then cross the city along Polk
Street, and reascend when he reaches the foot of Russian Hill.
His own children? How is it that he could have been living
with Huck and Christopher for the last three months and
never even thought about the possibility of his own children?
Adam entertains the cliché reply—he has not found the right
woman yet. On the other hand, it's not as if you could say that
Huck found the right woman. No, if Adam has not given
thought to a baby of his own, it is some telling failure of
imagination. Has he allowed Christopher to become too exclu-
sively the baby in his life? Or is the baby in his life himself?
Adam is pierced with sadness at the thought of his mother's
taxi racing through the night to the airport, but it is also a

sort of relief to be on his own again, out of the shadow of her presence and charisma. And what if, in the end, she should turn out to be the person in the whole world he has loved most deeply, most truly? Well, there will still be many other kinds of love.

The California Street cable car passes them as they descend, and Christopher looks up with excitement to salute the rattling vehicle. Then it is past, and they are alone on the dark slope, passing other lone figures here and there, passing the façades of Victorian houses, passing an occasional telephone pole that ascends into the night sky, finally turning onto Polk Street, where the city is more alive.

Loud music pours out of a gay bar on the corner; the door is open to the street. Inside is no great crowd, but neither is the bar empty on this Sunday night. There is something congenial about the impression Adam gets as he passes, not quite like Castro Street. Odd that Adam's recent experiences have not made him feel that this gay world is any less alien. He remembers Suzanne's mocking; he remembers Lucille's certainty: that even if Adam were to sleep with men he would still not be gay.

This is not the first time that Adam has walked down Polk Street at night, on his way home to Russian Hill, but he has never walked this way at this hour with Christopher. People are everywhere, but Christopher is the only baby. Usually Adam feels almost invisible on this street, unnoticed by the mixed throng of gay men, teenage punks, and city derelicts. Tonight he feels eyes turning to follow him, as if the baby he holds is a mark of character, of distinction. Christopher is a natural presence (like Adam's mother), carries himself (while being carried) as if he is the natural focus of all eyes, even goes so far as to hail passersby. Hi! Hi! he calls sharply, then laughs wildly at his own boldness and the attention he attracts. It is, Adam knows, that last burst of near-hysterical energy that comes not long before bedtime. Across the street Adam sees Tommy and Timmy, walking together, holding hands. Adam tries to wave, but his independent efforts are invisible, and they turn in to a laundromat without noticing him.

Meanwhile, as Adam was signaling in vain, Christopher has flagged down a troop of ten foreign sailors. They are in uniform and are much taken with Christopher's sailor suit. They exclaim over him in their language, which is not quite Spanish; Filipino, Adam guesses, totally incomprehensible to him. Christopher points at his new friends and demands, Hat! hat! And one of the sailors cheerfully places his cap on Christopher, who grins spectacularly (a perfect imitation of Huck's grin), passes it back, and demands a different hat. Each of them in turn tries his cap on Christopher, while the nightlife of Polk Street passes around this uncharacteristic cluster on the sidewalk. (What are these sailors doing here anyway? wonders Adam. Are they about to descend upon the gay bars, or have they gotten lost?) One of them knows enough English to tell Adam he has a beautiful baby. Adam thanks him, without correcting the misimpression. The sailor further inquires about Christopher's name and reports it back to the full troop, who are greatly delighted—like Christopher Columbus, the spokesman explains to Adam, this baby will be a lucky sailor.

Finally, there is one more question (Adam's significance is as Christopher's factotum-interpreter): may they take a picture? Sure enough, one of them has a camera (it looks very

expensive) and, after some fidgeting with the dials and me-
ters, snaps a picture of Adam and Christopher with a great
flash that seems to light up the whole street for a second.
There is a cheer from the troop, and then they all gather
around Adam, except the one with the camera, who focuses
for a picture of them all. At the last minute he stops a teenage
girl with green hair and ten earrings, politely gestures his
request, and joins the group. She takes the picture, and even
comments emphatically—Cute!—though it's not clear
whether she means the baby, the sailors, or the combination.
When she has gone her way the sailors also prepare to take
leave of Christopher, and Adam thinks of one more thing. He
finds a scrap of paper in his pocket and, awkwardly, holding
on to Christopher, he scratches down his name and address.
They seem to understand: he would like a copy of the picture.
If they send it to him, he will put it up on the wall over his
bed.

When Adam turns off Polk Street to climb Russian Hill,
he leaves the lights and people behind. Christopher seems to
recognize the approach to home, and inquires, Dada? Yes,
Dada, Adam assures him.

As Adam goes up the front stairs of the pink building,
he is thinking back to the day he arrived, three months ago.
Then he was carrying two suitcases—and no baby. He buzzes
the doorbell for apartment number three, although he has the
key, just to let Huck know they are home. Inside the lobby
Adam passes the mirrored walls on either side; the image of
himself and the baby seems very strange, yet when he looks
away from the reflection Adam feels comfortable enough. The
dusty rose glass chandelier hangs too low over the staircase,
and with a swipe of his hand Christopher sets it tinkling

furiously. Adam has a musical line in his head—"I can dance a tango, I can read Greek, easy"—though he can do neither, not even Latin.

At the top of the stairs Huck is waiting inside the door, alerted by Adam's buzz. Adam and Huck stand facing each other across the threshold, Christopher in Adam's arms. Dada, he comments, but does not demand to be handed over. Adam is thinking still of that first day, when they stood here meeting each other for the first time after so many years, when Huck was holding the baby. Other moments also hover on the edge of Adam's consciousness: the three of them on the bridge between ocean and bay, Huck naked comforting Christopher in the middle of the night, Huck asleep in evening dress in the rocking chair with Christopher asleep in his lap, Huck and Adam looking down at Christopher in his crib last week. These are not moments that Adam can sort out right now. Up! Up! demands Christopher, and Adam sets him down. Then, as Adam and Huck look on, not registering at first the significance of what they are watching, Christopher takes four steps all by himself, from Adam to Huck, across the threshold.